BRoken EXIT

By

K.N. Palmer

Grosvenor House
Publishing Limited

All rights reserved
Copyright © K.N. Palmer, 2018

The right of K.N. Palmer to be identified as the author of this
work has been asserted in accordance with Section 78
of the Copyright, Designs and Patents Act 1988

The book cover picture is copyright to K.N. Palmer

This book is published by
Grosvenor House Publishing Ltd
Link House
140 The Broadway, Tolworth, Surrey, KT6 7HT.
www.grosvenorhousepublishing.co.uk

This book is sold subject to the conditions that it shall not, by way of
trade or otherwise, be lent, resold, hired out or otherwise circulated
without the author's or publisher's prior consent in any form of binding or
cover other than that in which it is published and
without a similar condition including this condition being imposed
on the subsequent purchaser.

This book is a work of fiction. Any resemblance to
people or events, past or present, is purely coincidental.

A CIP record for this book
is available from the British Library

ISBN 978-1-78623-320-2

"Use your fear... It can take you to the place where you store your courage."

Amelia Earhart

Chapter One

Lee

He'd missed the last bus home again and had to pay for another taxi. Lee Bevan was an idiot and he smacked his palm against his head to acknowledge his own poor time keeping. Money was a huge issue for him at the moment. Having to repeatedly pay for taxis after a night out, was rapidly eroding his minimal bank balance. Although Lee worked and earned a good salary by today's standards, his separation from his wife had cost him. Not just money though. It had cost him his reputation, his friends and nearly his son. At times like this, he yearned for the past. Wishing he could turn back the clock and make things right. As they used to be.

Lee realised too late, that what he used to have was the perfect life in his eyes. Most people craved what he had let go. He hadn't recognised it at the time. Too few people do, and he, Lee, had taken it all for granted, desperate for something more.

The taxi rank was just outside the railway station in Nottingham, so he didn't have far to walk. It was just over the road from the bus station where he had entered, three minutes too late for the bus he had needed. Lee was out of breath though as he had sprinted from the pub on the market square. It was his favourite pub in the centre of Nottingham and he had spent far too many nights there, exploring the myriad of rooms with their exposed wooden beams resonating with the sound of laughter and joyful conversations. Since his separation, he was always looking for some company. Someone to notice him, ask him to join them and maybe, just maybe, become something more exciting.

He bent down, pushing his damp palms onto his knees and exhaling. "Bugger!" he exclaimed to no-one but himself. He could feel sweat trickling down his neck as his heart pounded, feeling like it might burst out his chest.

"God, I'm unfit" he thought. "I must start running again."

His hair was stuck to his head as the rain had begun to fall a little more heavily and the night air lost its mugginess. Sweeping it back from his brow with his left hand, he caught sight of a group of young guys staggering across the busy main road, hands aloft and shouting obscenities at anyone that passed within fifty metres of them.

"A typical night out for the youth of today" he muttered under his breath. "Getting pissed and looking for trouble. Or girls."

Lee hated guys like them. He hated the self-confidence they strutted with. The safety they had in numbers.

Although he did not want to be one of those apes, he loved the idea of having the courage to talk to attractive women for no reason. Seeing where it might lead. Yes, Lee was shallow; he hadn't always been, but since losing the love of his life, his thoughts often turned to random, one night stands. Craving some human contact. Passionate embraces. Lee was a dreamer. However, he lacked the courage to act on any of his desires.

Alcohol did not feature in his life in the same way it did for others. Lee abstained. The audacity it gave others, had also affected him at a young age. Sadly, his forehead grew, the limbs stretched until his knuckles dragged on the ground, his brain unable to comprehend normality. Alcohol, transformed Lee into an ape as well. The alpha male ape, full of testosterone and anger. Brainless thugs who want to kick the crap out of others, for no reason other than you may have looked at them 'the wrong way'.

Lager fuelled paranoia. A desire to start fights with anyone, regardless of their size. This got him into big trouble when he was only nineteen years old. Of small stature at about five foot eight, he was skinny too. Having been turned away from a nightclub whilst at University for being too drunk, he thought it was a good idea to take a swing at the next unsuspecting guy who walked past. Unfortunately for Lee, it happened to be a huge bear of a man with tattoos on the side of his neck who had trained in martial arts. Not only did Lee fail to connect his punch with the bear, but the bear responded rapidly with ferocious, yet controlled, punches to the chest and face before Lee could regain his balance. He had fallen to the ground with such force that the air was sucked from his lungs. Whilst he had felt like his ribs had broken, his cheek split open like a peach on a chopping board, but the pain did not end there. The Bear followed up his initial response with his feet, landing a fairly heavy boot in his stomach, followed with another, right against the bridge of Lee's nose. It exploded across his face, with blood cascading down his front as Lee's head was thrown backwards and smashed against the ground. His body had gone limp as he passed out. The Bear, thankfully, left him alone and walked on.

One of Lee's University friends had called for an ambulance, but not the police. After being transferred to hospital in the centre of Bath, Lee had spent two nights being stitched up, scanned and monitored. After coming round with an IV line protruding from his arm, he could only see out of one eye and found his parents looking forlornly back at him with tears in their eyes. His mum was holding his hand tightly. Eight stitches in the back of his head and four in his cheek had pulled his skin tight together with the substantial bruising around his broken nose. This would later be repaired with reconstructive surgery to rebuild the bridge and straighten his displaced septum. The bandages around his head prevented him from moving too much, but he felt his lips quiver and tears well in his eyes as his parents shook their heads in disbelief.

Lee was unable to tell his parents what had happened. He blocked any memories from his mind. His father had demanded the police investigate the case and they had been determined to press charges against the scumbag that had inflicted such hideous wounds on their beloved, harmless son. What kind of animal could do such monstrous things?

"He should be detained at Her Majesties pleasure as soon as possible." his father had grunted at the young policeman.

The police soon discovered some CCTV footage from a store on the opposite side of the street where the attack took place. Once Lee saw that The Bear had initially acted in self-defence, he withdrew any ideas of prosecuting anyone. How could he take more humiliation by confronting The Bear in court and have the defence team prove that he had acted to protect himself? No way was he doing that. Courage failed him again and his parents relented with their desire to see his attacker punished.

It was a sobering moment in Lee's life and he promised his parents, but also himself, that he would never drink again. Quite frankly he could not take the humiliation, let alone the pain. He'd had his arse kicked. What had he been thinking? Never again did he want to lose control of his sensible self and end up in a mess like this.

As he walked across the road, the lights of the cars coming towards him were hurting his eyes as he adjusted to the dark surroundings. The rain was persistent now and he pulled his leather jacket more tightly around his middle, pushing his hands deep into his pockets. He could see the taxis moving into the right hand side of the station entrance and coming out of the left hand side, taking people back to their homes or hotel rooms after their busy day of living. Some of the taxis around the city were driverless, but they had been met with solid resistance from the Taxi Drivers Association, who believed they were eroding yet more jobs from society. Here at the train station, the agreement was it had to be a human operative at the wheel. At least there were cars around and thankfully, he could see as he walked through the entrance, the queue was quite short.

Approaching the back of the queue, behind a young couple holding hands and laughing, he could see three men, all with very short cropped hair getting out of the taxi just pulling into the station.

They shouted obscenities as they pulled themselves clear of the cream coloured car. Sticking their fingers in the air, they started swearing at the now frightened driver and angrily spitting out.

The third of the group, kicked out his tight jeans-clad leg, with a tan coloured workman-like boot, connecting with the door as the driver was trying to get out of his car. It knocked him back into his seat, but he instantly went to get out of the car again, desperately wanting to take the fair he was rightly owed. By now, the small group of people waiting for taxis had all turned round to see what was happening, the trio of thugs had an audience.

"What you lot looking at? Fucking want some do ya?" the front man barked at them. As one, they all turned back the way they had been looking in the queue, clearly no-one was looking to be a have-a-go-hero tonight.

"That's right! You bunch of pussies, don't get involved!" the third man sprayed his venom across the waiting public. The veins rose to the surface on the side of his neck with the exertion, as he made the onlookers feel incredibly uncomfortable. Lee was no different to the others. How he wished he could make them pay the taxi driver the fare they owed him. If only he could take them down, one by one, with some slick fighting skills that he did not possess. Lee felt guilt sweep over him, just like he was sure the others were feeling. He was no hero and yet again, courage eluded him. He held the back of his head, rubbing the scar he had. It reminded him, he did not want another spell in hospital.

The three knob heads ran off cackling, smacking each other on their backs, as they made their way into the station to get their train, amused at their own bravery and how they had been able to humiliate the taxi driver. It was a bonus to them that he was Asian. Always a fair fight three against one.

The taxi driver would, at a later point in the evening, contact the police and make a futile attempt to get them to do something to trace the aggressive, non-paying customers. Surely there would be CCTV of the station entrance which would capture their faces? They'd probably be known to the police and it was likely to show them which train they got on and then they could be picked up in Derby or wherever they were getting off? Wouldn't it? Make the bastards pay for the misery they put on others. Caught without anyone having to put their body, or life, on the line for someone else. That was why Lee hadn't interfered. At least that was what he told himself.

Sadly though, the police were unlikely to follow up this alcohol induced, racially motivated crime. Since the government had changed just over a year ago, it was fair to say that racial tolerance was no longer on the agenda. A far more nationalistic approach had been adopted since the English Independence Party had risen to power. Lee was still not sure how it had happened. How could such bigoted racists now be responsible for running the country? The country that had always been proud of its record on fairness to all. Whatever your sexual orientation, colour of your skin, gender, or where you were born, the law treated you equally. Now though, equality was out the window quicker than the proverbial shite off a shovel.

When Huw Edwards had declared the exit poll at the last general election in 2022 as being a majority government, with the English Independence Party, or the EIP as they had become known, taking the most seats, with over three hundred and fifty, he, Lee, had looked at the TV and laughed. Laughed, because he thought it was the most absurd outcome, but also likely to be the biggest gaff by the BBC in its prolonged history. Someone must have been on the lash when they should have been working. Instead of asking people who they had voted for, the exit poll teams for Gfk-NOP and Ipsos Mori must have thrown their notes in the bin and gone down the pub for a laugh.

Unbelievably, the outcome was even stronger than the prediction of the exit poll for the EIP, with three hundred and sixty-five MPs elected across England. They had immediately set about trying to reverse the policies of the last thirty years. The first move was planning the 'PROPER' exit from Europe. Immediate blocks on any further migration, whether it be from the European Union, or further afield. British jobs for British people was something that had the potential to resonate for Gordon Brown and the Labour party a number of years back in 2009, but it never really gained momentum for them. Maybe because it was Gordon Brown?

It started to resonate when Barnaby Aitken had taken it upon himself as the newly elected MP in Dover to update it and make it work for him and the EIP, on many different levels. Since the Scottish National Party had annihilated Labour, taking fifty-six seats from the available fifty-nine, in the general election of 2015, Nationalism had become a growing issue across the rest of the country. Barnaby Aitken had a meteoric rise in terms of politics over the last few years. From business man to MP in 2015, winning a landslide by-election for Dover, to leader of the EIP in 2018. Now, amazingly he had become the Prime Minister and was in charge of running the largest majority government since the halcyon days of Tony Blair and New Labour in the late 1990's.

As the taxi queue got shorter and shorter, Lee finally opened the door of the next waiting cab and climbed inside. The warmth coming from the cars heater hit him and he undid his jacket and opened the window slightly. "Radcliffe Road, West Bridgford please?" he said to the driver. As he looked up, he realised it was the same driver that had just been done out of his fare by the three thugs.

"Did you see what just happened to me?" asked the young Pakistani driver. He had a clean shaven face, anger in his eyes and, Lee could see that he was still shaking from his recent torment.

"No, No. What was that then mate? I only just arrived in the queue," lied Lee, unconvincingly. He noticed the plastic screen between the front and rear seats that prevented the driver from being directly attacked by any passengers and the doors had locked and were under the drivers control until presumably the passenger had paid his fare.

"I thought you were in front of me when I pulled in," muttered the driver looking in his mirror at the man in denial, occupying the back seat. "Those men? They refused to pay, threatened me with violence. I had to let them out the car as they started to mess it up. Threatened to break the windows and urinate on the seats.

Bastards," he continued, focussing his eyes back on the road. "That was thirty-five quid they did me out of. I should have known when they got in, gone straight to the police station. Mind you, for what help these days? The police won't do nothing," he continued to jabber away at Lee, whose mind was already starting to wander back to the bar in the pub.

"Since that bloody government was elected, nobody gives a shit about people like me. We're not welcome in this country anymore. But it's my country. I am British, through and through." It was like he was appealing to Lee for some reason. "I was born here, just like you. But the police don't care. If your skin ain't white, or you weren't born in the UK, you're worthless in their minds."

The rant from the man at the front continued, but Lee had stopped listening. Instead, he was checking the seat to see if it was wet. He sniffed the air. He couldn't detect any urine, but the smell of garam masala and garlic was very strong in the back and could have disguised just about anything.

The car turned a left and then a right as it headed towards Trent Bridge and past the home of Nottingham Forest. A once great team in the top flight of football who now meandered up and down the lower leagues, fighting over the meagre bread crumbs on offer to keep the bailiffs from the doors. How the mighty had fallen since the days of Cloughy.

As the car braked suddenly at the traffic lights and the windscreen wipers squeaked their way across the glass, Lee was jolted back into conversation.

"Yes, sorry that you feel like that. We're not all racists you know. One of my best friends is a paki ... stani."

Lee

He quickly corrected himself and looked out the window. 'One of my best friends' he thought to himself. 'How lame is that?' He pulled his phone from his pocket to avoid further conversation and checked his messages. Nothing. It was nearly midnight and he clearly was not popular on a Saturday night. His friends really had deserted him since Nicky had kicked him out of their house. Normally, he would have been getting text messages, e-mails and social media alerts all night. Now he was alone and he was going back to an empty flat.

As the taxi made its way up the Radcliffe Road, Lee asked the driver to pull over at a turning opposite a small row of shops. "Just here please. How much do I owe you pal?" "Twelve pounds forty please" replied the driver, pointing at the meter. Lee pulled out a ten pound note and had to scrabble around in his jeans pocket to find the remainder of the fare. He couldn't believe it, he literally just had enough money and handed over twelve pounds fifty six.

"Keep the change eh!" he said rather pathetically and the driver looked at him without amusement. "Sorry about that," mumbled Lee and opened the door as the lock was undone from the front of the car. He pushed it open and climbed back out into the wet night, crossing over towards the hairdressers and bike shop.

Just to the right of them was a narrow driveway leading to a small number of flats behind. He lived on the ground floor on the right hand side. The weeds were pushing through the block paving and the bricks crumbling at the front of the building. As he put the key in the door, he noticed water cascading over the guttering from the top of the building. People renting didn't give a shit about the properties they lived in. No one did any maintenance and it pissed him off. In his own home, before he moved out, he was constantly doing DIY. Keeping on top of the painting, clearing gutters, cutting the grass, whatever needed to be done to keep his home as his castle. Lee was proud of what he had achieved and the comfortable home he had built with his wife, Nicky.

He hung his coat up in the hall way and flicked the lights on. Another night of unsuccessful liaisons in town. Another night of searching had come to nothing. Perhaps he had to be honest with himself. People who hung round busy pubs on their own, smiling at strangers and gripping a diet coke so that their knuckles went white, tended to unnerve people of the female variety. He would go to bed alone and he would wake up alone and he was profoundly starting to regret his misdemeanours whilst he was with Nicky. Lee was definitely not enjoying life on his own and he was absolutely missing his son, Aidan. His punishment, in his eyes, given he hadn't actually 'done anything' was far too great. To deny him his wonderful home and twenty-four hour access to Aidan did not seem right to him.

To say Lee had not done anything, would of course, be far from the truth. Life at home had become a little hum drum as the responsibilities of work and being a parent took its toll on their marriage. As time progressed, the excitement that he had at becoming a father dissipated rather rapidly. Nicky constantly complained that she was tired and spent all her waking time fussing around Aidan. Of course, it's natural for a mother to do this with her offspring, but Lee started to feel neglected. Rejected even.

Lee

Whenever he tried to give her a kiss, pull her over to his side of the bed, nuzzle her neck and pull on her pyjama strings, she would push him away. The Ice-Maiden, as he had started to call her, was frosty at the best of times. The passion they had shared; the way she dug her nails into the cheeks of his arse; the positions they found themselves in; the noise they made, Oh! God! the noise they made. It set the room alight and they would often be going at it for hours at a time, sleeping well into the morning at the weekends to recover. But that was a distant memory.

She had become like Pluto to him. Far off and bloody cold!

When Aidan had turned four, Nicky had started to get involved with the pre-school he was attending. Even less time at home and even less time for Lee. Like many men, Lee turned to a life online to see what that had to offer. As Nicky went to bed early, exhausted, he often shut himself away with his laptop, to connect with people he didn't know and couldn't see. It excited him.

Having been fairly active on Facebook with over three hundred virtual 'friends', he knew there were plenty of sites that would offer 'discretion' for men, or women, who were desperate to meet someone. To indulge in some 'adult time' as he liked to refer to it. His favourite was 'Flirtbox', or as he liked to call it, 'Shagbook'! He had created himself a secret email address and been careful to keep it to just to his phone, which he never let out of his sight. After posting a brief overview of himself, which of course was hammed up beyond belief, he uploaded an image of his torso, taken from the side, holding his breath and pulling his stomach in. It looked like he was well on the way to developing a six-pack. Well-trimmed hair across his chest and running down towards his stomach. What woman could resist the twenty-six-year-old that he claimed to be? After having a couple of positive responses from some 'twenty somethings' who were 'Busty' and 'Looking for some no-strings, adult fun' he started to send some more intimate photos of himself. He'd even agreed to meet someone. When he had turned up at the agreed meeting spot, he got cold feet and didn't stop.

How could he do it to Nicky? Flirting on line was one thing, but actually meeting someone … to lead to … who knows what it might lead to? It would be like an avalanche cascading down hill. A small movement, setting off a chain reaction, gather momentum and power, losing control as it increased in size and speed. Obliterating all in its path. A trail of destruction left behind it.

He couldn't do that. His wife, the love of his life and mother to his wonderful son, was too precious to lose. They would have to rekindle the passion they had once shared so actively; somehow. Having scared himself, things ground to a halt before they really got going and he refrained from any further on-line activity.

Lee thought of himself as technically savvy, but he wasn't quite as good as he thought. Nicky had bought herself a new phone and asked him to set it up for her, making sure he linked their photos so that they could share precious moments with Aidan. Lee duly obliged, ensuring the photo stream was switched on. Without thinking, he linked her e-mail addresses to the new phone as well. This in itself would not have been a problem, but whilst inputting them, he forgot what he was doing and connected his own e-mail addresses out of habit. Brain fade?

Lee

When Nicky next picked up her phone, alongside her daily alerts from Fat Face and Louis Vuitton she was confronted by several images of lithe young women. Pointing their over large and plastic looking breasts at the camera, they were pushing them upwards and almost out of their scanty underwear. They were asking Lee if he wanted to 'smother them with cream' and when would they finally get to meet and indulge in their secret fantasy? As she scrolled down, she found a picture he had sent them of him in his underwear, a hard-on, clearly visible, beneath the underpants that SHE, Nicky had bought him! BASTARD. There could be no denying. He had been messing around.

Nicky stayed calm for at least two minutes. However, her blood pressure had been rising towards boiling point as she read through the communication chain. Reaching the end, she looked up over her phone and raged at Lee, "Who the fuck is Messy Melinda?"

She shoved the phone under his nose so he could see the image of Melinda.

Lee immediately felt the hairs on the back of his neck stand on end. His body twitched involuntarily as though someone had walked over his grave.

"Ummm. I can explain. It's ... it's ... it's not what it looks like ..." he started, his voice wobbling uncontrollably.

No matter what he tried to say, it was unconvincing and sounded trite. Nicky started to throw things at him across the room. The vase that they got for their wedding smashed into the wall, blue glass exploding into fine needle like splinters. Over ripe fruit from the bowl, squashed onto the flocked wallpaper and slipped slowly onto the wooden floor below. She scooped up his beloved nano-pad and with all the rage she could muster, launched it at his head. He ducked just in time, but it smacked sideways into the doorframe, bending with relative ease, the screen giving way to the sideways torque it was not designed to withhold. At that stage, Lee thought he'd best leave and let Nicky calm down. He'd collect his thoughts and formulate an answer that would placate her. Then they could begin on rediscovering that passion they had lost. She'd see sense. He'd make sure of that.

When he had returned to the house a few hours later, everything was quiet and the house was in darkness. Nicky was out, her car had gone and of course she had taken Aidan with her. He began to wipe the pear and plum from the walls and then carefully swept all of the glass splinters from the oak engineered board. A final sweep with the ever faithful wet wipe, to pick up the last of the unseen shards and he thought to himself, "What did we do before these came into our lives?".

He couldn't have Aidan getting those in his feet when he was running around playing with his flying cars. Bending to put the glass in the bin, he saw the letter on the kitchen work top and stopped in his tracks. With his fingers trembling, he picked it up and started reading. It was short and to the point.

"Lee, I trusted you. You betrayed me and Aidan. I can't talk to you and I don't want to see you right now. I have gone to Dad's for a while, to think things through. Get your things and leave before I return. Nicky"

Lee slumped onto the bar stool at the breakfast bar and started sobbing. What had he done? How stupid. How fucking stupid. Over the course of the next few days he tried unsuccessfully to ring Nicky. He tried his father-in-law. That hadn't gone well. He tried his best friends, Leslie and Dan, to see if he could stay with them for a few days whilst he and Nicky tried to work through some difficulties. Nicky had got to them first and they 'didn't think it was appropriate after what he had done to Nicky'. They weren't taking sides they'd said, as every relationship has its ups and downs, but clearly they were.

His friends deserted him in his hour of need. He had taken a few days off work whilst he tried to sort the mess out at home, but he told them that his wife's mother was ill and he needed to take some time to sort out childcare for Aidan. Lee worked in the Healthcare industry and his manager was very understanding as a working mother herself. In typical jealous man-mode, he was convinced she had slept her way to the top as she seemed to have no understanding of project management. To be fair though, when it came to people, she was very empathetic with them and said if he needed anything, then to just ask.

Lee decided that he should check into a hotel for a few days whilst he worked things out. A few days turned into ten and no progress had been made. He couldn't afford to keep paying for a hotel, so decided to try and rent on a short term basis. Nicky had sent him a text message telling him that she had sought legal advice. He was not to come to the house and that he could not see Aidan until she was ready for that interaction to happen. Lee wailed in disbelief, but he would comply if it gave him a chance of winning back the woman he loved and with it, access to his son.

Lee moved into the flat on Radcliffe Road and gradually over the next six months, Nicky started to speak to him. She never engaged in social chit-chat and did not want to know what was going on in his life. However, she had realised that Aidan needed some contact with his dad. She had allowed him to pick Aidan up on a Sunday morning at ten o'clock and have the day with him, returning by five promptly. It wasn't much, but it was the highlight of his lonely week.

Tomorrow was Sunday and even though his evening had not been very successful and he'd spent it alone again, he would still go to bed with a smile on his face.

Tomorrow, he got to see his wonderful boy, Aidan.

Chapter Two

Nicky

As Nicky tucked Aidan into his bed, she leant over him and kissed him gently on the forehead.

"My gorgeous little man," she purred at him. "Hope you had a nice day with Mummy?" she asked, but Aidan was too exhausted to talk and his eyes started to close as she read him his favourite story, 'The Lorax' by Dr Seuss. It was amazing how it had stood the test of time over the years, as it had been one of her favourites from her childhood. Published nearly fifty years ago, yet it seemed to become even more relevant, rather than less, as the world moved on. Her father had always made up funny voices when being the Lorax, describing the 'sawdusty sneeze', squeezing his mouth and nose together so he looked a bit like a rat. She had always felt awful at how the truffala trees were chopped down in increasing numbers, drawing parallels with the real world.

Deforestation had been happening with increasing speed and the level of pollution was escalating at an alarming rate. That was linked inextricably to declining numbers of protected species as well. It often made Nicky pause and wonder just what the world would be like for her gorgeous little man in years to come?

Being a nurse, Nicky was acutely aware of increasing levels of pollution. At the Queens Medical Centre, one of the prestigious teaching hospitals, where she worked in the Accident and Emergency department three days a week, they were seeing much higher levels of respiratory admissions than four to five years ago. Many were simple to get control of. Twenty minutes on the nebuliser, gently inhaling a fine mist of corticosteroid and a long acting beta agonist to open up the airways. Relax the smooth muscles in the lungs and reduce the level of inflammation. Send the patient home with some inhalers and hopefully they would retain good control of their asthma.

Others though, were much more complicated. Severe, brittle asthma, which did not respond to the nebuliser, requiring patients be admitted to hospital. They were also starting to see other types of respiratory problems which seemed to be triggered or exacerbated by high levels of pollution. Nicky couldn't believe the levels of tuberculosis they were encountering with increasing regularity. Sudden Acute Respiratory Syndrome (SARS) and East Asian Respiratory Syndrome (EASR) also starting to affect the department, stretching its resources to the brink.

Other than pollution, Nicky could summarize the cause in one word: Immigration. Massive influxes over the last twenty years, or more, changing the dynamics of the UK beyond recognition. Society was an eclectic mix of multiculturalism on every street and national institutions could not cope any longer with all the expectations that they had been burdened with.

Nicky, stroked Aidan's hair, took one last look and retreated slowly from his bedroom, turning off the light and pulling the door too. His night light kept the room

Nicky

bathed with a dull, warm glow. Nicky crept down the stairs and turned the TV on as she walked towards the kitchen to pour herself a well-deserved glass of wine. Life on her own was hard work and she needed a little treat at the weekend. After a day chasing Aidan round the adventure park in the warm sunshine, she too was worn out. She loved the way he ran away from her, looking behind him to make sure she was still chasing, laughing as he did. She loved seeing him try to do the same things as the bigger children. Climb up the pyramid to come down the twisty slide. Walk across the wobbly chain, or swing on the big rope that went from left to right with real gusto. The only thing she didn't like was doing it on her own.

Nicky never planned to be a single mum. In fact, she'd needed some convincing to have children in the first place, believing kids were a nightmare, that would probably all turn out to be criminals. Taking drugs and getting into trouble with the police.

It was Lee who'd made her see sense. Made her see that she hadn't turned out like that and neither had he, or countless other kids across the world. With the right guidance from their parents, instilling positive values, explaining what was right and wrong, what was nice and what was not, the majority of kids got it right. There would be mistakes along the way, sure, but it would all be worth it, to receive that love back from a creation you had brought into the world. Nicky's view changed gradually. On falling pregnant, she had been ecstatic about becoming a mum from the very first moment she knew. She was still excited about being a mother, but she longed to share the pressures as well as the excitement with someone else.

No; not someone else. Just Lee.

Slumping down on the sofa, taking a sip of her large, chilled Sauvignon-Blanc, she automatically picked up her mobile and checked her messages. Three from her dad, a handful of 'Extra discount codes' for her favourite online shops and the rota for work for the following week. Amongst them were two messages from Lee, 'just checking that it was OK to pick up Aidan tomorrow at ten as usual? Lee x' and 'Could she pack his waterproofs for him, as it looked like it was going to rain tomorrow? Lee x'. As ever, he managed to get in her head with the slightest communication. He pissed her off and melted her heart at the same time. How could he manage to do it every time? Asking her to pack waterproofs because it might rain for fucks sake! Nicky always packed appropriate clothing for her son. It was her job.

It was the single kiss he put at the end of every message after his name that melted her heart. Why did he have to do that? He betrayed her, yet here he was trying to worm his way back into her good books.

It made her think of not just all the times they kissed, but the very first time they kissed.

God! Her feet had left the ground, her body had trembled as she was left completely speechless. That had never happened before. It was at an Ed Sheeran gig that they had gone to, with two friends, who had been trying to pair them up for a while. An open air concert on a hot, sunny day and the atmosphere was amazing. Ed was near the start of his incredible career and he seemed completely humble, engaged with the audience and played for nearly two hours. They had been dancing together and all four of them were laughing and enjoying the company of close friends. When Ed played 'Kiss Me' from his album '+', Lee, had taken her hand in his and looked with such devotion straight into her eyes. He mouthed the words "Kiss Me" and leant towards her, not taking his eyes from hers. She had lifted her hands to cup his face and placed her lips gently against his, pushing tenderly, tilting her head to one side.

The kiss got more passionate and the music faded into the background as they were both completely caught in the moment. As she moved her head back to look at him again, a smile reaching right across her face, setting her hair alight with the fire that burned from her lips, she spotted Leslie, her best friend, out of the corner of her eye. Leslie and Dan were watching them, faces poised with pleasure. They both broke into applause at the same time. "Hooray!" shouted Leslie, "About time," exclaimed Dan and they started to laugh together uncontrollably.

How should she respond to him? Nicky decided to do it the same way that she always did. Since he tore her heart out. She put the phone down without typing anything and turned her attention to the TV. Bastard; how could he do that to her? It was over six months now since she had kicked him out, but it still felt very raw. A deep wound that wouldn't heal. No medication from a chilled bottle got close to fixing this one back together, or make the pain bearable.

Nicky flicked through the channels where a breaking news story caught her eye and she stopped to watch what was happening. After years of migration getting out of control, it seemed that the people of the UK had reached the end of the road. At least, the new(ish) government had reached the end of the road. The English Independence Party had already gone a long way to ripping the UK apart over the last twelve months, but now they had effectively declared real independence from the European Union.

The Prime Minister, Barnaby Aitken, leader of the English Independence Party, had broken off ongoing talks, over free movement of people, with the head of the European Union in the last few hours. He was declaring the borders of England closed!

Since the EU referendum in 2016, when the people of the UK voted to leave the European Union, the government had failed on a colossal scale to implement this. The famous Article 50, had eventually been triggered in March 2017. David Cameron's departure had left Theresa May in charge and it was not clear to anyone through the next few years, exactly what the UK government had been trying to achieve. Other than to try and keep all options open to them. Anything they had been clear on had been blocked by the 'Remoaners', or the House of Lords. In trying to negotiate continued access to the European Markets, it had come with the condition of free movement of people. For many in the UK, this was too much to bear and the sole reason many had voted 'out' in the first place.

For too long, the UK had become the 'chosen land' for many societies across the Union. Those who wanted better healthcare; better schooling; housing; welfare; opportunity and acceptance. But the UK, no not the UK, England, could take it no longer.

Why didn't 'they' stop in their own countries? Countries like Bulgaria and Romania had prospered under the EU. There had effectively been socialism on a colossal scale. A redistribution of wealth, from the richer more developed countries like the UK, Germany and France, to the poorer nations. But in all that time, there had been an exodus from those poorer nations. That was the only way to describe it. Their populations had been decreasing over recent years and those of the leading countries in the EU had increased exponentially. Five years earlier, the population of the UK was estimated to be around sixty-five million. Net migration stood at about three hundred thousand a year. Now, the population was knocking on the door of seventy-five million. Net migration in 2022 had been estimated at nearly one million people. Two million people in one year!! That was staggering. The UK had become obese and was bursting out of its tight fitting borders.

Population diabetes was taking hold, killing the country slowly. Painfully.

As of tomorrow, the PM had exclaimed that, "Eurotunnel, all sea ports and air connections to the European continent were being closed, until an important bill had been debated by parliament the following week. No longer could the Government of England stand idly by and watch the resources of this great nation be raped and pillaged by people who did not want to contribute to anything other than their own wellbeing." It was language reminiscent of that used by Donald Trump in his run up to the Presidency in the US in 2016, describing the way China had, "raped America of its resources". He had continued the rhetoric when he took office, with disastrous consequences on many counts.

This stance had been coming for a while and Nicky wasn't too surprised to hear this radical, and quite frankly, racist announcement.

With a nod of her head, almost in approval, Nicky changed channel to find something a little more entertaining. She had never been sure whether free movement across Europe was a good thing or not, but she knew it was starting to impact on her work, the upbringing of Aidan and her future. She wasn't against it wholesale, but she had found herself starting to agree with some of the policies that the EIP were adopting.

Daniel Craig flashed in front of her, being chased by someone in his Aston Martin as 007, James Bond. Yet another showing of the best of the Craig era Bonds in her mind. *'Skyfall'* had been awesome, but *'Spectre'* was her favourite by a country mile. She must have watched it at least a dozen times, still getting a buzz from the opening scene in Mexico City. They had yet to find someone who could engage in the same way that Daniel had. The next two castings had only lasted one film each, flopping at the box office. It was similar to the days of Timothy Dalton back in the eighties.

"Bring back Daniel in those tight black trunks please," yearned Nicky. She'd already forgotten the newsflash as her mind moved on to action men in fast cars, holding big guns.

As she lifted her glass to her lips again, her feet folded underneath her on the settee, her phone vibrated demanding her attention again. It was Leslie asking her what she was up to tomorrow, given that she wouldn't have Aidan about. Did she want to come over for a BBQ in the afternoon, provided the rain held off, otherwise it might be inside and cooked in the oven? Nicky always found it hard when Aidan wasn't around and she liked to keep herself occupied so the time went more quickly.

Nicky

Sounded like a plan. "Yes, sounds fab. Do you need anything?" she spoke clearly to her phone, using voice to text, allowing her to respond rapidly and leave her hands free to move her glass back to her mouth on finishing.

Leslie became Nicky's best friend after they met on their first day of training to become nurses in Birmingham. They reached for the stylus to sign their names on the enrolment at the same time. Nicky pulled her hand away, offering it to Leslie first. Leslie, smiled kindly, introduced herself and put her hand out to shake Nicky's. From that moment the two of them didn't really leave each other's side all the way through their training, enjoying each other's company and realising they shared very similar back grounds.

Both lost their mothers far too early in their lives and naturally had become very close to their fathers. Leslie's mum had committed suicide after years of suffering depression and harming herself with knives. Leslie had been six and she had not really known what it was like to have a mum at all. She was never there, in the present, looking after her in the way that other mothers had looked after their children. Depression had taken her away from the family years before her physical being had left this world.

For Nicky and her family, it was another kind of tragedy. It was not depression and her mother hadn't died as far as she was aware. Her mother, Jenny, had been a highflying executive in PR. Fast paced and increasing pressures on a sector that was known for its champagne lifestyle in the late eighties and early nineties. It took its toll on a lady who'd not been able to move with the times. Desperate to maintain the lifestyle after giving birth to her two children, she became increasingly erratic at work and at home. Eventually the pressure proved too much. It culminated in a complete nervous breakdown. After a week's respite at home, barely coming out of her bedroom, the rest of the family returned from an outing one day around Easter to find a note on the kitchen table. Jenny packed a single bag, took a few belongings with her, some money and her passport. She walked out on her husband, Mark, leaving him with two young children, Nicky and her younger brother Ben. They would miss her terribly. Mark stood firm and coped admirably under the circumstances. Although desperately sad and constantly trying to find Jenny, he bought the children up on his own, the best he could, becoming incredibly protective of them both.

The phone vibrated again. "Do you have NE SSGs and lots of wine? B Lvly 2 CU" came the response from Leslie. Nicky immediately got up to go and check in the freezer to see if she had any sausages. She picked her way through the drawers one by one, lifting the refrozen Chinese take away boxes she used for half eaten casseroles and Bolognese sauces. She still hadn't got used to cooking less and ended up freezing, or throwing away, more food than she imagined. The ice was thick on the top as though they had been in there for an eternity. At the bottom of the last drawer she found a plastic bag from the local butcher with half a dozen fat pork and cider apple sausages that she absolutely loved. "Yum" she purred to herself as she thought of them bubbling and spitting on the BBQ, laden with ketchup, in a small, soft white finger roll. She took them out and dropped them into the half sink in the utility room to defrost, writing a 'post it' note to remind her to take them the next day.

Nicky

There was no point in checking if she had wine. She always had wine. In fact, since Lee moved out, she'd made a point of having more than enough wine in the house. The wine rack was always full and that held sixteen bottles. Anyway, there was an emergency case of Sauvignon Blanc and a half case of prosecco in the garage, just in case there was something unexpected to celebrate. It was almost non-existent when he lived there. It was her way of sticking her two fingers up at him. "It's my house now and I'll do what I like in it, when I like to do it," she often found herself mumbling under her breath, holding her fingers aloft.

As she shuffled back into the lounge yawning, her phone went again. It was a text from her dad. "Hi sweetheart. Tell Aidan to brush his teeth and I love you both. Dad xxx" He always spelled things out in full, no abbreviations from him. She smiled and sent a kiss back to him, "Love you too Dad and he has brushed his teeth. All tucked up in bed now. xxx".

As she slumped back into the sofa, the cushions letting their breath out through the cloth to accommodate her weight, she started to wonder again about whether she'd been too hard on Lee? She thought she might have over reacted on the night she had uncovered those e-mails and photos, but he'd hurt her. Stuck a knife in her heart and pulled it out slowly, twisting as he did so. How could he have even contemplated shagging those women? Surely anybody that put themselves up on websites like that was desperate. Sluts, laden with venereal disease and God knows what else. He could have caught HIV or hepatitis. And then given it to her, without her even knowing. Until she fell ill. It didn't bear thinking about.

Selfish arsehole. She was definitely better off without him.

As the rain came down harder outside, she heard it overrun the gutter and drop onto the electricity box. She really ought to get someone to come and take a look at that. Clear the drain pipe and refit the broken bracket. She missed having a man about the house. Although she knew it was a stereotypical task in this day and age, it was the sort of thing that Lee would have done in the blink of an eye. He loved his house and took pride in maintaining it. Her eye caught the far wall with the stain on the wall paper that she still could not bring herself to try and remove. The stain from the fruit that had hit the wall the night she had discovered his dirty secrets. It bought a tear to her eye and she hugged the cushion for comfort. Her mind started to question her own sense of right and wrong. As she had many times before she started to blame herself.

"Maybe it was my fault?" she thought. Fighting back the tears, reaching out for her glass she said out loud to an empty room "I had neglected him. Aidan came between us and he was just feeling abandoned. Was it my fault?"

The room listened without responding, but Daniel continued on his quest to uncover who was behind Spectre. Nicky, wiped away the tears, tilting her head back, she took another large gulp from her glass. Bonds plane lost its wings and started to chase the bad guys down the ski slopes. "He was no 007, but he was all mine and I loved him," she whispered to the nearly empty glass. "I miss you Lee Bevan."

Nicky flicked the TV off, finished her drink and moved towards the stairs, hitting the lights as she closed

Nicky

the door. After putting the chain on the front door, she crept upstairs to the bathroom. It was early still, but she was worn out and there really was no reason to stay up just to watch a film she had seen many times before.

The bed felt so large just for her, but she still slept on the same side as she always had. On the opposite side of the bed, Lee's pyjamas were still under the pillow. She had not been able to throw them out and she still found herself reaching for them in mornings. She held them close to her face and inhaled. It was her fix as his musty smell took her back to places she missed and craved. Her head hit the pillow and very quickly Nicky drifted in to a deep, but troubled sleep.

A recurring dream of Aidan being taken haunted her nights and she was sure that it was because there was no man in her life to make her feel safe in the way that Lee used to. Tight in his arms at night. Spooning.

That was before they had started to turn their backs on each other, to sleep separately in the same bed.

Chapter Three

Barnaby

It had been a crazy twelve months for Barnaby Aitken. He could never have imagined in his wildest dreams that he would end up being the Prime Minister of England. He made a point of saying England, even though Scotland, Northern Ireland and Wales had yet to succeed in extracting themselves from the UK. He was the Prime Minister of England as far as he was concerned. The other countries could, "Fuck off and fend for themselves," quite frankly.

When he was younger, if anyone even suggested a life in politics, he would have laughed it off, "No way! Not for me thanks. I want a proper job." He'd been set on running his own business from a young age. He wasn't what you would call entrepreneurial by today's standards, but he'd run a successful, small business in his time. Based in Kent, often called the Garden of England, it was 'God's country' in Barnaby's eyes. He'd owned and run a factory that made lightbulbs, employing about forty people. It hadn't made him mega-rich, like the YouTubers of the last decade, but it had given him a great way of life. More importantly for him, he'd been his own boss.

With a passion for physics and mechanics when he was at school, Barnaby then attended university to study business. This gave him all the grounding he needed to set up and run his own enterprise. Manufacturing light bulbs, suppling the entertainment and domestic industry. Barnaby bought a failing company from a retiring man who'd not been able to keep up with competition in the mid-nineties. He poured over the books with a fine tooth comb, identifying a few areas where he could decrease costs, yet increase productivity. They would start to develop some new types of filament that emitted high levels of light, with very low power consumption.

He outsourced production to China for a short period of time, whilst he re-built the factory in Ashford. The modernisation he bought about, with some automated systems, had been expensive at the time, but enabled him to gradually bring the production of the incandescent lightbulb back into the UK. All at a much lower cost, than when he'd bought the business.

Barnaby was English through and through, believing wholeheartedly, that you should employee local people to keep a business successful. Put back into the community as much as you got from it. He was not into cheap labour for the sake of making oneself rich. That, he believed, would lead to short-term gains, but long-term failure.

A member of the Roundtable in his thirties, he ran the local circle and focussed members completely on fundraising for local charities whilst ensuring they had fun along the way. He treated people with respect and compassion. Barnaby was also passionate about the local environment and wildlife, campaigning against the Eurotunnel from its conception, as he thought it would destroy the beauty of the Kent Downs. A minor scuffle with the local constabulary in his twenties, resulted in his arrest and being charged with public disorder. The charge was later dropped though, due to a lack of evidence. His passion in all walks of life, eventually resulted in friends, employees and even the public along the way, coming to love and respect Barnaby Aitken.

Barnaby's foray into politics had come completely by accident as far as he was concerned. The European Union, a non-elected government in his mind, with really no legal jurisdiction over anyone, had been dictating what countries could and couldn't do, for far too long. Crazy rules about 'straight bananas' that came into law in 1995, had most people laughing at the madness that 'Governments' could, or should, concern themselves with such ridiculousness. How could a European Public body legislate over nature? Of course, there was more to this much maligned mandate. But in Barnaby's mind, if they could make such preposterous laws about such things, what on earth were they capable of where the frontiers of man were concerned?

He didn't have to wait too much longer before he discovered that European law would destroy all that he had worked to build. From 2007, the European Union decided they were going to phase out incandescent light bulbs, implementing new energy standards, otherwise known as the 'Energy Efficient Light Bulb'. Barnaby's company had been taken a little off guard. Although they had some of the most energy efficient filaments in their bulbs, they did not have the technology to produce the new bulbs that contained mercury. They had also been unsuccessful in gaining a license to handle the toxic liquid metal required, in constructing the new types of bulb.

It seemed however, that a competitor for the Ashford based lighting company, who had been failing to make a profit, had been thrown a proverbial life line by the European Union. 'Tolle Beleuchtung' was a similar sized lighting company based in Frankfurt. With nearly fifty employees, they'd been struggling in recent years. The owner had lost touch with the needs of its clients and pushed down the cost cutting front, whilst at the same time, fraternizing with powerful people in the European Government. Experimenting with new types of lights that they believed were more energy efficient, they were rumoured to have paid a lot of money to politicians. A campaign to highlight the need to move on from incandescent lighting in times where the world was being scrutinised for its energy consumption. Although no one would ever be able to prove it, they paid handsomely for reform of the lighting industry and it was about to reap some serious rewards.

Of course, what the politicians failed to understand was the wider environmental issue that these new types of light bulb gave rise to. There were several issues: Consumers don't like change forced upon them and initially the new bulbs were just bloody irritating to consumers, as they failed to give out bright light immediately. More importantly though, the recycling that was supposed to go alongside these new bulbs because of the mercury contained within them, never really happened. Most were either recycled along with normal glass, with the mercury contaminating all sorts of recycled materials, or worse, thrown into the main waste and making landfill even more toxic. The final, controversial straw was all about the 'lasts a life time' claim, where supposedly the light lasted for over a thousand hours. It was very quickly realised to be a load of bullshit, often emitting light for less time than the old bulbs they were to replace. Not only that, but they were ten times the price of the marvellous lightbulbs that Barnaby had previously supplied! What a fucking scam! Whilst supposedly using less energy to give out light, they required more energy to produce and with the heavy metal deposits leaching into landfill as nobody recycled them in the way they were supposed to, they were considered an environmental disaster shortly after their introduction by various environmental groups.

Quite frankly, the European Union dropped a ball.

That ball, sadly, cost Barnaby his business.

On a Saturday afternoon, when he would rather have been playing golf, or watching motorsport, he now found himself being briefed on the latest terror threat; immigration numbers; the last death throes of the NHS; overcrowded prisons; failing schools and so many other depressing things. He realised why previous Prime Ministers looked so haggard in such a short space of time after taking office. There was too much to fix. Not enough money in the savings plan. Everybody had bright ideas and was full of the answers when they were in opposition, but realised soon after taking office, that it was an impossible job.

Whatever move you made, words you used, actions you took, it was scrutinised by society on an unimaginable scale. Television, printed press, social media. Online, twenty four hours a day. Nothing was ever right, or good enough. You had to trust what you were doing was for the best and ignore the critics. Claim and counter claim. A fog of deceit that few could ever find their way out of. Real facts interwoven with 'Fake News', as the now ex-President Trump, had called it.

In Barnaby's eyes, May and her cronies had let the British people down on a major scale and he was not going to fall into the same trap. He had been given a mandate to get Britain, correction, England, out of this tangled web and put it back on the right path to greatness again.

After hearing from the most senior civil servant just this lunchtime on the latest annual figures for net migration to the UK, he had decided enough was enough and he had to act now. An immediate press conference was called and Barnaby Aitken took confidently to the podium.

Ten minutes and a few sharp questions from reporters later, Barnaby left with a spring in his step, but many shaking their heads in disbelief. Against the back drop of failing schools, a broken and exhausted NHS, but most importantly, an economy that was thriving outside of Europe, but stagnant when within it, immigration had reached unacceptable levels. The latest figures put the estimate for net migration at an unprecedented nine hundred and thirty thousand.

"It could go on no more," declared a defiant, ebullient Prime Minister. How were our schools supposed to cope with the ridiculous pressures on their demands? Not just having to cater for children with special needs, but having to accommodate those who could not speak English. Teachers were being asked to do far more than teach their chosen subject and had left the profession in their tens of thousands. Under the last Tory government, they had seen the need for qualified staff diminish in an effort to attract willing people to engage in the profession. Those that stepped forward very often did not speak English as a first language themselves.

GP's were unable to cope with the demand from those who were always ready to call on their doctor. It was free. Such a caring country.

"I sneeze, I cough. Why stay at home to self-medicate when I can see a doctor and it costs me nothing?" was the mentality of most.

Surgeries with touch screen registrations in over twenty languages. What other country in the world would accommodate such demands without charging for the service? Those who were really sick, veins filled with the sludge of cancer; pensioners bewildered with brains crammed with crossed wires; those jaundiced with liver disease; the unlucky ones cursed with HIV; all struggled to get access to the life giving care of the GP.

Of course, the only real answer was to privatise the NHS, but everyone knew that was the biggest political hand grenade, guaranteed to illicit the destruction of the party stupid enough to throw it into the commons for debate. A nation that spends a fortune on its pampered pets, the British public would rather see World War III, with all its nuclear warheads raining down around the globe, wiping out humanity, than have the indignity of having to put its hand in its pocket and pay for their own health. Millions did nothing to keep themselves healthy, a lack of physical activity and a diet rich in sugar and fat. Obesity had been a major public health and economic crisis for a while now.

Housing had been unaffordable for over a decade for the working masses. A matter of supply not keeping up with the stratospheric demand. The proliferation of multiple families living under one roof, had meant that laws were often flouted by landlords, determined to make as much as they could, whilst they could. Councils did not have the resource to check compliance of such properties, with the health and safety regulations meant to protect those in the dwellings. Rotation of young people in bedrooms, meant there were often twenty to thirty people living in accommodation designed for a maximum of four of five. How were the next generation of homegrown Brits supposed to be able to ever leave the family nest?

Britain was broken. Dilapidated beyond repair. But Barnaby needed to start somewhere.

On hearing the astronomical figure, approaching a million new migrants to the UK, Barnaby was forced to take action. He declared the UK, specifically England, closed to all immigrants with immediate effect. All sea ports would effectively be on lockdown, not allowing anyone into the country from the European Union, or from further afield.

Parliament was to discuss an emergency bill the following week on how to end this debacle. How it should once and for all sever its ties with the European Union and break the agreement regarding the free movement of people. Quite frankly, the economy of Europe had failed its communities. The UK however, was not responsible for supporting them.

Arriving back at his weekend retreat, Barnaby sank into a seat, raising his hands into the air. "Well there we go. I have started what should have been done years ago Maureen" he called out to his wife as she handed him a cup of tea.

Maureen, a demure and very supportive wife, said little. She always sided with Barnaby. He gave her a good life, treated her with respect and never hurt her. He rarely even raised his voice. For that, she was very grateful. Maureen had been the pillar of the family, raising their two girls almost single handedly, whilst Barnaby built his business in Kent. Always adorned in very elegant and stylish outfits, Maureen believed it was her duty to look her best, not just for herself, but also for her husband. She cooked her way to Barnaby's heart after meeting at University and they'd been inseparable since. She loved nothing more than Sunday lunch with her whole family around.

Maureen was playing the patient game with her daughters now, desperate for them to become mothers themselves, bestowing her the gift of a grandchild. Susan, now thirty, must surely be getting maternal by now? Married three years previously to Jack, a professional rugby player, but was tied up in her own career, giving the impression she would be a latecomer to parenting. The younger one, Lisa was twenty-seven and yet to meet anyone who interested her enough to really make a serious go of it. Maureen wasn't even sure if Lisa was inclined towards men, women, or something else. Having travelled a lot after leaving university, Lisa had really not seemed to settle down on a permanent basis, choosing instead to keep her options very widely open, on all accounts. She would work for short periods as a translator, a lucrative service in great need these days, then head off, travelling to South America and other exotic countries that caught her eye.

Maureen sat down next to Barnaby on the leather sofa, "Well" she paused, "It needed doing Barnaby. I always knew you would stick to your promises. We have to try and fix this wonderful country, its gone to rack and ruin."

Maureen spoke with the authority of a natural born citizen. She was however, an immigrant herself, coming to the UK in the late sixties as a small fair haired girl with her family from Australia.

It was something that they rarely talked about.

Chapter Four

Chaos

Sunday morning was wet and windy. It was the 24th September 2023 and it felt like autumn was already in full swing. Aidan woke just after seven and pulled himself clear of the tangled mess on his bed. Soft toys everywhere. He yawned and stretched, grabbing his favourite, Beano. Beano was a light brown monkey with a small tuft of grey hair on its head, that looked like it had been throttled continuously since birth, with that smell about it that said, 'Caution – owned by small child: contains sweat, tears and spittle!' A hot cycle on fast spin should bring some life and freshness back, whilst downgrading the Biohazard risk.

He padded out to the bathroom barefoot, past his mother's door, where he could hear her breathing gently in her sleep. After successfully hitting the pan through the loo seat, he flushed and headed downstairs. He pulled a yoghurt from the fridge and grabbed his kindle from the side, before making himself comfy on the sofa.

Thumbprint and he was in. Straight to his favourite YouTube channel where he kicked off the latest video. He'd have about an hour before mum would surface and wander down to get breakfast. He'd have to get as many videos in now as he was off out with dad later.

Aidan smiled to himself as he thought about his dad. Dad made him laugh, always spoiled him and they had real fun together. The only bad thing about dad picking him up was the frostiness between his parents. Although he was only six, Aidan could sense the tension between them. He could sense the barbs spring from his mother who turned into a porcupine whenever Lee opened his mouth. It made Aidan feel awkward. He'd always been taught that if he couldn't say anything nice to people, then he shouldn't say anything at all. That rule did not seem to apply to his parents for some reason. Venom often spat forth from his mother's lips, like a viper spraying its next meal with cold, deliberate death. He knew his dad had hurt her badly, but he was told to 'make up and move on' when he fell out with friends, so he was at a loss to understand why they couldn't. Adults seemed to be very complicated.

He didn't like it when they argued. He winced when they shouted and it made him mute for a while, at least until he was well away from the shouting, secure in his dad's car and being whirled off somewhere exciting. It was a while now since his dad had moved out the house. A memory that lingered long in Aidan's mind, bringing a tear to his small, brown eyes. Since then, the house had felt odd. Like a car that was trying to drive on three wheels instead of four. It was unbalanced, unable to gather speed and navigate its way round obstacles. His mother was stuck in second, not knowing how to move up a gear.

"Hey little guy! Good morning gorgeous," his mum said gently as she kissed the top of his head and messed with his mop of hair. Moving towards the kettle, her phone beeped, grabbing her attention.

Chaos

"You want pancakes for breakfast?" she enquired, reaching for the phone. It was Lee reminding her he'd be there for ten and was taking Aidan into Nottingham as there were some celebrations going on for the UK City of Culture.

Nicky glanced at the time. She had slept well and for once felt quite refreshed. "Oh my God! Its nine thirty Aidan – why didn't you wake me honey? Your dad will be here soon. No time for pancakes, get dressed quickly and I'll do you some toast. C'mon turn that off and get upstairs" she pulled the kindle from his hands as he glanced up at her for the first time.

"Mum, I was watching that," he grumbled at her, half-heartedly.

Aidan scampered upstairs singing to himself as he went and was back downstairs three minutes later ready for a day out with his dad, he retrieved his kindle to resume his devotion of silly videos.

The toast popped, peanut butter was served and Aidan munched his way through two slices. Nicky ran upstairs quickly to get a shower and make herself look stunning. She made a point of always looking completely on top of everything when Lee came to pick up Aidan. In control and looking gorgeous. It would make him realise just how much he had fucked things up. As she swiped the mascara blade across her eye lashes for the last time the doorbell rang.

"Just in the nick of time," she muttered to herself, checking herself again in the mirror and smirking.

Chaos broke out down below.

"Dad," shouted Aidan, leaping from his seat, wiping remnants of toast from around his mouth on his sleeve, running for the door, swinging it wide open. A gust of wind caught it, tearing it from his hand, banging it loudly against the inside wall. Lee stood there beaming down at his son.

"Hey there Aidy. Great to see you," he reached out hugging his son and lifting him off the floor, whilst tickling him as hard as he could. Aidan giggled and wrapped his arms round his dad's neck.

"Mind my wall," snapped Nicky as she trudged down the stairs slowly, stretching her stockinged legs deliberately slowly in front of her. They were intended to be ogled by Lee, and he did not disappoint.

"Morning Nicky. How are you?" enquired Lee meekly. He always seemed to lose his bravado in front of Nicky these days. She leant her head to one side and watched Lee lower Aidan to the floor, a big grin sweep across her boy's face, grunting at him, "Fine. Don't be late back with him, he has school tomorrow."

Aidan grabbed his bag and took his coat as Nicky lifted it from the pegs. He kissed her and turned his attention quickly back to his dad.

"Where are we going today dad?"

"Hang on a second Aidy. Nicky, we won't be late. I see the gutter is leaking again. Do you want me to take a look at that some time for you?" he enquired gently.

"Oh! Is it? I hadn't noticed" she lied. "No its fine, I can sort it," and she swung the door closed quickly to hide the tears she could feel forming at the corners of her eyes.

Lee turned away from the house, the rain blowing straight into his face and he took Aidan's hand. "C'mon son, let's go have some fun!"

They headed to the car and climbed out of the inclement weather. Lee put the car into gear and they moved out heading towards the city centre. He glanced in the rear view mirror and for a second, thought he glimpsed Nicky looking out of the lounge window at them, wiping a tear from her eye.

"Right, Aidan. I thought we could head into the centre today as they have some celebrations on. They have made a beach, got some deck chairs and I even heard they have a Big Wheel in town. What do you think?"

Aidan nodded back at him.

"If the weather improves, we might even be able to get an ice-cream!"

Aidan looked up at his dad and smiled, "With sprinkles and a flake Dad?" They both smiled.

The traffic was horrendous for a Sunday going into the city and it seemed to take forever. However, the one advantage was that the rain had stopped by the time they parked the car and the wind seemed to be subsiding. Aidan had seen that the city was celebrating becoming the UK City of Culture for 2023 and had all sorts of events going on over the summer. The Old Market Square had a construction made like a pier outside the city council building to use as a stage for all the events. Around it they had poured tons of sand, with the square now acting as a beach, which was adorned with traditional beach huts painted in beautiful and dazzling colours around the outside of the square. In between the pier and the huts, were rows and rows of striped deckchairs for the city people to take a break and watch the entertainment. To the right hand side was indeed a mini big-wheel and a Helter Skelter, with the old hessian sacks enabling you to slide down the wooden construction at great speed, landing on a musty, thick bristle carpet, waiting to stop you dead in your tracks at the bottom.

Today, there was a heavy security presence. Armed police were in in obvious attendance both around the market square, but also hidden away on roof tops out of sight. Roads were closed off to taxis and buses as the Prime Minister was due to be in attendance, with a congratulatory speech to the Mayor and the people of the city of Nottingham, on being awarded the UK City of Culture.

Since BREXIT in 2019, the UK had no longer been allowed to participate in the European Capital of Culture. The last Tory government, in a bid to maintain investment and excitement in various UK cities, decided to replace this with their own local version. It was established to primarily recognise cities across the UK for their investment in local businesses and in particular, their commitment to pulling the UK nations closer together, whether this be through sport, music or art. There were other criteria that the cities had to submit a full, detailed dossier against, but it was not as substantive, time consuming, or of course costly, as the old European Capital of Culture entry. Nottingham had become the second city to win the accolade, taking over from Bristol as the previous winner two years earlier in 2021. If the experience from Bristol was anything to go by, it would bring further investment into the city, particularly around infra-structure and of course a media spotlight that would help to boost the economy with the impact on local shops and restaurants with informed travellers looking for new and exciting weekend breaks. Nottingham had a lot to offer and today the Prime Minister, Barnaby Aitken, would bring a new level of scrutiny and interest on the old city.

Chaos

Aidan and Lee walked up Listergate with the Broadmarsh Centre behind them. The streets were already busy with excited people and Aidan made a point of keeping his son close to him. Approaching the old market square, Aidan spotted the mini-wheel ride and a smile came to his face. He loved to ride up in the air with the wind rushing through his hair, looking down at the people below and how they turned from tall people into small heads with arms sticking out when viewed from above. It made him laugh.

"Dad, can we have a go?" enquired Aidan pleadingly. "OK son, if we must."

They made their way to the front of the queue where the attendant was adorned with gold chains and sovereign rings. Lee begrudgingly paid for the price-hiked fairground ride. As they clambered into the carriage and the bar swung over the top of their laps to retain them in the receptacle, Lee spotted some police activity on the other side of the square.

Armed police suddenly converged on either side of the road to prevent the public crossing. Wondering what was going on, Lee, pointed the activity out to Aidan, just as the Prime Ministers cavalcade drove up. They watched as the security services got out of their cars first and checked the area was secure, then they opened the door to the PM's car and Barnaby Aitken stepped out into the UK City of Culture. Those around who spotted him broke into cheers and applause. Something Lee had never witnessed with any previous PM in recent years. The crowds were actually supportive. Barnaby raised his hand to wave in acknowledgement. It did not go unnoticed by Lee that the PM wore a dark blue suit, with a crisp white shirt and of course a red tie. Red, white and blue. He wondered how long the blue would last.

Lee glanced at his watch, it was about ten minutes before the presentation to the people of Nottingham, they should be able to get a good seat and watch proceedings when they got off the ride. Aidan recognised the man from the telly and waved excitedly. Amazingly, Barnaby Aitken spotted them from the corner of his eye, looked up and returned the wave with a smile on his face. Aidan couldn't believe it. A celebrity, from TV had actually waved at him! At him! His friends would not believe it. Lee put his arm round his son's shoulder, realising the excitement this caused and squeezed him.

"Yo, catch you. Friends with the PM hey. Wow!" he laughed.

The Prime Minister moved off and shook hands with the Mayor who had approached from the Council House to greet him. They engaged in polite conversation and then headed back into the building out of view.

It must have been quite a challenge to conceal the pain in his face, presenting a smile as he'd shaken the hand of the Mayor, Bolek Kumiega. Bolek was born on the outskirts of Krakow in the mid nineteen eighties and had moved to the UK as an economic migrant about ten years ago. He was voted in as Mayor of Nottingham a few years earlier when cities were trying to highlight that diversity was critical for success in the gloom of the racist hatred that had been stirred by the BREXIT vote in 2015. It was people like Bolek, that the Prime Minister was trying to prevent from entering the country, increasing the burden on the already crippled infrastructure and services. Nothing against him personally of course, but the country could not go on like it had.

As the ride came to an end, Lee managed to get two deck chairs at the front of those laid out on the right hand corner, with a clear and unimpeded view of the stage. Aidan hadn't stopped jabbering since Barnaby Aitken had waved at him. Lee ruffled his hair and took in the growing crowd of people behind them. It was noisy and towards the back there was a group of protesters being shepherded by the police to prevent them venturing further forward. Most of the protesters were Europeans who'd built their lives for them and their families in the UK. There were handfuls of others from further afield, such as Jamaica, Thailand and the Philippines. Present, but in even fewer numbers, were white English. Those who were embarrassed to be associated with such a draconian approach. The volume rose.

Lee turned back towards the stage as a band started to play, bringing people's attention to the proceedings. As they struck up, banging out some summer tunes, pleading with the sun to come out from behind the murky clouds, Barnaby stepped out from the Council House and waved to the mass of bodies in front of him. He moved over to the left hand side of the stage facing the crowd, straight towards Lee and Aidan. He wanted to walk right across the front of those that had come to see him. As he approached them, he pointed his finger into the crowd and lifted his left hand to his heart as if to say, "I love you!" to those applauding him. It was more celebrity star than Prime Minister, but he was enjoying this. Barnaby leant over the railings at the front of the stage to wave down at those in the front rows.

As he did, a ground shuddering "BOOM" echoed out across the Market Square. The stage itself lifted off the ground in the centre, exploding upwards in a rainbow of splintered wood and summer bunting. Several police officers who had been stood in front of the stage to protect the PM were instantly killed as their bodies were flung out into the crowds, like a giant had taken a wrecking ball to them. The adjacent deck chairs with their once joyous occupants, erupted like a volcano. Blood stained corpses, limbs torn from torso's, landing on others who were lucky enough to escape the blast, instinctively cowering and covering their heads with their arms.

Barnaby Aitken had not been centre-stage, where he was supposed to make the address to the watching crowds. His minor action of walking to the left, instead of straight to the microphone had saved his life. He was out of reach of the immediate blast radius itself, but the force had thrown him over the barrier he was leaning on, landing with a thump in front of Aidan and Lee. The force had sent them flying backwards in their chairs. Barnaby's arm was bent underneath his body at an odd angle, his left ankle had smacked on to the pavement really hard and instantly ballooned and there was a gash to the side of his head with thick red blood already running down his face from the wound. The smile had been replaced with a grimace.

Barnaby Aitken instantly knew he was very lucky.

That was meant for him. He would later discover that the chaos had only just begun.

Chapter Five

Running

Smoke billowed outwards and up into the sky in a thick ball of grey. Silence was sucked into the vacuum created by the explosion for a short while, as the onlookers tried to make sense of what they had just witnessed.

Aidan screamed. Loudly.

Others around them burst into a cacophony of wailing, like a troop of baboons chasing away an intruder, as they realised the enormity of what had happened around them. It was carnage. Bodies strewn everywhere. Chairs, torn apart, wood splinters of varying lengths had punctured people at all angles. What was once the stage, had a huge semi-circular hole, gorged out from the front of the centre, about twenty feet in diameter. The edges were burned badly and the panelled floor was still on fire. Underneath, the metal frame that had supported the platform, was twisted and bent, broken into pointed shards, parts of which, also ended up embedded in the nearest unsuspecting onlookers.

Around the edges of the crowd, were those that cowered from the explosion, covering their heads and their loved ones instinctively with their protective arms, gradually moved them away to reveal the extent of damage laid bare before them. The protesters at the back had fallen silent, standing shell-shocked, placards dropped down by their sides. The police, who had been patrolling, keeping people at bay, had also dropped low for their own protection. Gradually they were coming to their feet, trying to make out what happened through the gloom, stunned into inaction for a short while.

Husbands; fathers; wives; mothers; elderly grandparents; who moments before had been smiling and laughing, sharing a special moment with loved ones, waiting for a unique point in Nottingham's history, were suddenly jolted, not back to reality, but to a scene from a horror film. Lives changed in the blink of an eye. Forever.

Dust started to descend on to the hypnotised crowd, who momentarily were incapable of thought or action. Barnaby winced as he pulled his arm out from underneath him, it felt like he had sprained his shoulder badly, but he didn't think he'd broken anything. His ankle was throbbing though. Lee scrambled to his feet, calling for Aidan, patting him down and checking him over. "Aidan, Oh! My God. What the hell? Aidan ... Are you ok? Are you hurt?" He spluttered, but he could barely hear his own voice.

His ears were ringing from the intensity of the blast and everything seemed to have gone into slow motion. Could he press pause? Rewind maybe? Make sure he was well away from here before the blast. Aidan, with tears rolling down his small puffy, dusty cheeks, didn't know what to say, so he threw his arms around his dad's neck. Lee hugged him tight whilst checking him over. After not finding anything protruding from his small body and, miraculously, no sign of blood, Lee took Aidan's head in his hands and kissed him. Instinct kicked in, he had to get Aidan out of here. NOW.

Lee turned to where the stage was, and in front of him, gathering himself, suit covered in dust and blood, red tie swept across his shoulders and trousers torn, was the confused face of the Prime Minister. "Sir? Are you OK Sir?" Lee asked Barnaby Aitken. He wasn't sure how to address him under the circumstances. Barnaby nodded slowly "I ... I ... Think so. My ankle hurts, but I think I am OK. You? Your son?" He said, lips starting to quiver and hands shaking.

"I believe so." Lee, holding Aidan's hand, offered his other hand to help the Prime Minister get to his feet.

"Ow, that hurts. I have hurt my ankle. I'm not sure I can walk." The PM was grimacing now as he lent on Lee heavily. Lee, looked around, trying to work out where the police and the PM's security service were. Over the shoulder of Barnaby, Lee saw the Mayor, looking directly towards them. He backed into the cover of the Council House, disappearing from view, to relative safety. Scanning around quickly, Lee noticed several groups of police officers who had regained their composure, not consumed by the blast itself and were starting to try and help those immediately around them. There were no police officers close to them. The PM had not been where he should have been. He had walked away from his protection, towards them on the stage. Amazingly, that small action had saved him.

Lee let go of Aidan's hand and waved at what looked like the closest officers on the other side of the square.

"Hey! Police! Help please!" He bellowed at the top of his lungs.

His shout joined the hundreds of others that were echoing out around the square, desperate for assistance. Each of course, more urgent than those around them.

It was like a whisper, lost in the Arctic winds, whipping across the unending ice, with nobody to hear it. Looking upwards, Lee noticed the armed units on the roof tops and raised his arms again in the hope that they would see him with the Prime Minister and radio for assistance.

Atop the roof of the Council House, an armed officer had been scanning the crowds through the scope on his rifle, assessing the situation. He spotted Lee waving wildly, taking in the small boy to one side of him. His telescopic sight settled on the dishevelled man next to him who was dressed in a smart, ripped suit, covered in blood and dust. Lee saw the man put his finger to an earpiece and speak into a microphone. The world went into slow motion for the second time that day. The man was lining up his rifle, taking aim directly at them.

"What the fu ..." He whispered to himself, staggering backwards a little, yelling, "Get down!" He pulled Aidan to one side roughly, whilst rolling himself into the PM, knocking him off his feet for a second time in a matter of minutes.

A bullet whistled past his ear, narrowly missing him and Barnaby. It hit a lady, who had been crying uncontrollably from the shock of the bomb, just behind them. The bullet entered a few inches below her clavicle, tearing straight through the left atrium of her heart, exiting on a downward trajectory, through her back. She died instantly, not knowing what had happened, dropping to her knees and falling forwards. With all the wailing and confusion around, Lee wasn't even sure if anyone else had even noticed what just happened. Panic was starting to take hold.

Barnaby was the first to react as the lady had fallen directly in front of him, the life gone from her eyes.

Running

"Bloody hell. They really want me dead." He crawled on his belly as low as possible through the bedlam, back towards the stage, away from the cold of the dead. Lee, did the same, pulling Aidan behind him. "Keep your head down Aidan. I don't know what's going on but it's not safe. We have to get you out of here."

Upon reaching the stage, Barnaby and Lee squatted with their backs to it, making sure their heads were below the level so as not to be seen again.

"I just saw that cop deliberately target us ... Well ... you actually. What the hell is going on? A bomb, a shooter ... Assassination attempt of our Prime Minister. Fuck. What did I bring you here for Aidan?"

"If the Police are targeting me, I don't know who I can trust. Do you have a car near here?" Barnaby responded, looking at Lee with desperation in his eyes. "I have to get out of here, so no one else gets hurt."

Lee, shaking his head in disbelief, was looking desperately around the square for someone else to take ownership of the leader of the country. It shouldn't be his responsibility. Aidan was his responsibility. But he couldn't leave the PM on his own in the middle of this. It wasn't his problem though, was it? It appeared, rather annoyingly, as if it had just become his problem.

He nodded quickly, "It's about a five minute walk from here," he said, looking into Barnaby's eyes. Lee turned back and lifted his head slowly above the stage looking to the roof tops again. Several officers were now scanning the area through their cross hairs. The same officer let off a second round and Lee dropped to the floor with splinters being torn out of the stage right in front of where he had been peeking.

"Shit. Follow me. Aidan stay low and stay close," he barked, adrenalin starting to surge through his body, the survival instinct well and truly kicking in. He was not happy about swearing in front of his son, or for that matter, the Prime Minister. What would his mother say? "Actually mum, I don't give a fuck right now," he thought to himself, "I think the situation allows a little swearing."

All three of them crawled to the right hand corner of the stage, Aidan sobbing uncontrollably and shaking violently. "Ok we have to make a break for it, round the back of the mini-wheel and down the side street. Can you run sir?" He enquired, looking at the PM's ankle with a furrowed brow, beads of perspiration forming.

"I'll have to," came the short reply.

"OK, follow me. One, two, three." Lee scooped Aidan in his arms, shielding him from the shooters above and sprinted for the side of the mini-wheel, Barnaby Aitken, the Prime Minister of the UK, following close behind, wincing from the pain of his ankle.

Three gunmen, all uniformed police officers, opened fire from above, taking several shots each at the moving targets. They could not be allowed to escape; the consequences would be too grave. Several bullets ricocheted off the metal frame of the support structure for the mini-wheel, thankfully deflecting in the opposite direction. As Lee, Aidan and Barnaby ducked around the corner of the fairground ride, Lee glanced back towards the Old Market Square. Through the panicking mass of the crowd, on the other side, he spotted a group of armed officers coming together, with one pointing over towards them. He put his hand over his ear piece and shouted some instructions to the rest of the group. They all turned towards Lee, starting to run through the detritus of bodies and deckchairs, pushing across the square towards them.

Lee turned back and looked down the street which had throngs of people, who were bizarrely rushing towards the Old Market Square. The nosiness of human nature driving them towards the madness, rather than away. Desire to know what was happening, stronger then the scent of safety. If they were lucky, they could potentially catch some of the really gory scenes on their mobiles, instantly streaming families despair on their social media accounts for others to like and share. People just died, but they didn't care, as long as it made them popular on the Internet. The bloodthirsty crowd however, may just help Lee and his entourage escape those that seemed intent on hunting them down.

As they raced down the street back towards the shopping centre, Lee dived into a turning on the right. Hundreds of people behind them now, blocking the view of the chasing pack gave them the chance to change course without being spotted.

"I know a short cut," Lee spurted, already gasping for breath. Barnaby was limping badly, but managing to keep up with Lee, who was burdened with the weight of his son. "Why are the police trying to kill you? They are supposed to protect you," Lee exclaimed, expecting Barnaby to immediately offer a rational explanation.

Barnaby didn't answer, but shook his head in response. As they rushed past people, they were half expecting to be recognised, but others were focused on the explosion fall out and the dishevelled man before them bore no resemblance to the normally well-groomed

Prime Minister, particularly when you weren't looking for him.

Turning into a narrow side street, the crowd thinned and Barnaby made the entry just before the armed officers sprang from the main street. Their pursuers carried on straight down, heading towards the shopping centre, looking hurriedly into the doorways of the stores they passed, for those they hunted. Sirens were blasting all around the city now, police cars and riot vans arriving, with more officers making their way toward the carnage on the square. Ambulances which had been stationed on the periphery of the City Centre hurtled in to the epicentre; not sure what they were descending on.

Lee was struggling now, but they were nearly to his car. He could hear a helicopter overhead and looked up to see cameras focused towards the city centre. They dashed out across the main road, sidestepping a few slow moving vehicles who slammed on the brakes, sounding their horns in disbelief. As they got to the opposite side of the road, they heard a gunshot sound again. This was becoming too frequent.

"How the hell did I get caught up in this?" Lee screamed to himself and it would not be the last time.

An officer had appeared out of the back end of the shopping centre, about a hundred metres further back down the dual carriageway. He was beckoning to his colleagues who started to burst through the doors in numbers now, all dressed in black with white checks round the rims of their caps and the waist of their bullet proof jackets, 'Police' emblazoned across the back, in case you couldn't quite tell.

"Quick," shouted Lee. "We're nearly there". They ambled across the next part of the road more easily as

Running

the traffic had stopped at a red light. Into the stairwell of the car park and up the first flight of stairs they hurried. Approaching Lee's car, he fumbled for his keys, opening the boot with the key fob. "You get in the boot," he shouted to Barnaby, who climbed in as quickly as he could, folding his knees up to ensure he could fit. Lee, put Aidan down in the footwell behind the driver's seat and dropped a coat on top of him. "Don't move little fella. We'll be out of here soon, I promise."

He climbed into the driver's seat and picked up a baseball cap that was lying on the passenger seat. Pulling it on his head, he locked the doors and drove slowly out of the car park trying to look completely normal. They'd be looking for three people in a car that was speeding surely? Just as the barrier lifted to let him out and he pulled away completely normally, he saw the armed police arrive in the car park in his rear view mirror. Lee could feel the sweat running down his temples as he swung out onto Maid Marian Way and drove up the hill. He didn't look back and thankfully, he did not hear anymore gunfire.

Behind him, the police started a slow sweeping search floor by floor. Guns targeted as one on anything that moved in front of them. A couple stepped out of the lift on the third floor to be confronted by three men aiming their firearms directly at their heads as they both let out a scream.

"Don't shoot," shouted the tall slim man, sporting a neatly trimmed beard.

The police lowered their weapons and turned away from them cursing. The lead officer spoke into his mic, "We lost them. Not sure what happened."

Chapter Six

Security

In the twelve years that Paul Buxton had led the protection unit for the country's Prime Minister, everything had gone according to plan. He'd protected three different PMs in his time and he, personally, oversaw hundreds of trips, both domestic and international. Liaising with security forces around the world, he was highly respected for the meticulous level of detail he demanded and the back up plans he always had ready. All run with military precision, incident free and most importantly, zero casualties.

Given the state of the attacks across the world in recent years, that was an amazing statistic. Until today that was.

An earlier career in the military had saw him rise through the ranks quickly, making captain in just over five years. Active service three times, over the course of the second Iraq War, picking up distinguished conduct medals for services to his country. The Military Cross was the first he'd received for leading a small group of soldiers back to save two allies, who had been part of an outpost that found itself ambushed. They had broken cover to reach them under heavy fire. Paul administered emergency first aid to stem the flow of blood from the femoral artery of the first soldier he reached. After ensuring he was taken to safety, he moved on under increasing rounds of heavy artillery fire to reach the second. Shrapnel was penetrating the soldier's abdomen from the side and he had passed out from the pain and loss of blood. Paul had signalled to his team to create a diversion and cover him with returning fire. He pulled the injured soldier over his shoulder, secured his helmet firmly over his head, stood and ran back towards his platoon, with covering bullets whistling past him, penning the enemy back for a few vital seconds. It was all been captured on his helmet camera. Miraculously, he avoided all the ordnance that was flying around him. Both the injured soldiers survived, albeit with permanent reminders of the conflict they had served in. The Army Generals had been so impressed with his bravery, they did not hesitate to reward his selfless act.

Other similar acts of heroism followed, accompanied with more medals in recognition. When he made captain, those in his command were openly delighted. They would follow him because they knew he would do everything in his power for them. Their safety and well-being would be his first priority. Eventually, Paul retired from the army for a new challenge. Highly decorated, highly respected, but he didn't think he could take another tour of active duty and still come out alive. He had ridden his luck for too long.

Taking up a post working for the security detail of the government, again he had worked his way through the ranks until the former conservative prime minister, David Cameron, had recognised his expertise and calm demeanour. When the previous incumbent had resigned,

Mr Cameron had asked Paul to step up to the role as the Head of the Protection Unit for the Prime Minister. Paul again did not hesitate. It was further recognition of his great work protecting democracy in a free world.

Today though, for the first time, something did not go according to plan and events had unfolded so fast, his back up failed him.

Planning for the event had gone like clockwork. Or at least, he thought it had. Just before the first explosion tore the stage apart, throwing the Prime Minister into the crowd, he was stood to the rear of the stage on the opposite side. His ear piece which kept whispering in his ear almost non-stop from the moment they arrived at the Old Market Square, crackled and suddenly went quiet. Enquiring if anyone could hear him, he received nothing but static in response. He'd looked towards the PM waving at the crowds and moved back towards the Council House entrance to check his communications, just as the bomb erupted.

The force of the blast threw him into the wall of the Council House head first. The impact knocking him unconscious. Only for a few short seconds, but he lost vital time in the response they'd practiced hundreds of times. He wasn't sure how long he lay on the floor, but when he came to, the scene of panic was all too evident.

Smoke swept around the stage, small fires burning randomly around them. There was a huge hole ripped from the front where the microphone had been, the crowd swept aside, like the old fashioned scythes taking out the corn before them. He scanned the crowd, trying to establish where the PM was, as he pushed himself up on to his knees.

"Can anyone hear me?" He shouted into his mic. There was no response. He needed to work out what was going on and quickly. People were screaming all around him, but his training kicked in and automatically blanked it all. Naturally he reached for his service pistol whilst getting to his feet, moving quickly now towards where he had last seen his boss.

As he looked towards members of his own unit, he beckoned them to join him, noticing that local police officers were already tending to the injured, trying to move people back from the scene. Major incident training that they would have all been through would seem completely unnatural, at this time, adrenalin, fear and instinct for their own survival and wellbeing would conflict against their orders.

A small group of armed police were running across the front of the market square towards the mini-wheel. Moving forward cautiously, he noticed that several of his team were missing. "Where is the PM?" Paul enquired of those that had gathered around him.

"Sir, he seems to have taken off down that passageway with another man and a young boy," blurted out one of Paul's subordinates, known as Smudge, pointing back past the fairground attraction.

"Was he hurt? Taken against his will?" shot back Paul.

"Hard to say if he was hurt badly Sir, but he certainly had blood on his head from what I saw. Don't think he was taken against his will. Looked more like a man and his son were trying to help. I can't say for certain, but it looked like one of the uniforms fired on them." The experienced security hand, was shaking his head in disbelief, telling himself he must be wrong.

Paul looked straight at Smudge, almost piercing him with his searching stare. Immediately his mind started processing all of the possible scenarios and what they were now potentially dealing with. Most people would start to panic in his position. The infinite possibilities and subsequent outcomes, too overwhelming to comprehend. Paul was not most people though. His years of training and experience propelled him quickly to a course of action.

"OK, teams of two, Smudge with me. We follow the trail and try to catch up with the PM ASAP to retake control of the situation. Anyone's coms working?" Paul was met with five shake of the heads. "Until we know otherwise we have to assume we have been infiltrated and we cannot trust those in uniform. Do not fire at them unless fired upon, but you have permission for shoot to kill. Let's go. I am not going to be the first security head to lose a modern day Prime Minister."

Immediately, the small security detail split into three groups of two and Paul led the way with Smudge, towards the alleyway the PM had been seen heading down. Unknown to them, the TV camera crews who had also recovered their senses, were now training their long range lenses on the small team and feeding it live on to TV screens around the world. Although the live audience did not know who they were, they could clearly see they had removed their guns from their holsters hidden in their tailored suits and were now breaking into a run as they took off to pursue their master.

Given the chaos and danger that had just hit the Old Market Square, Paul could not believe the tidal wave of people trying to come up the street towards the scene of death and destruction. The public's macabre interest

Security

always seems to drive them towards danger rather than in the opposite direction. It was like trying to run through treacle, impeded at every step, moving left to right, trying to force his way past the mass of general public. In the distance he could see armed uniforms enter the shopping centre, well ahead of them and beyond the gore seekers. Paul made a move to get as close to the walls and shop fronts as he could, but it was no better. After shouting several times for people to move out of the way, a few saw his gun and immediately moved to the side. The gaps were filled by people behind who could not hear the demand from the Head of the Security detail. He took his gun and fired directly into the air, bringing the entire walkway to a stop in its tracks, those closest to him dropping to their knees.

Paul and his entourage galloped forward, spotting gaps in the sea of humans, shouting warnings to the waves of bodies bent before them, "Get down and stay down". Immediately, wailing broke out from some, interspersed with screaming and the whites of people's eyes filled with panic. Bodies squeezed towards the edges of the alleyway, enabling Paul and his elite team to break into a sprint. Heading downhill they were able to get faster and faster, closing the gap to those ahead of them.

The noise of the gunshot had warned the uniformed armed officers of their pursuers and the two at the rear, turned to see the slick suited security personnel break into the sprint as they cleared the back end of the wave of humans surging towards the Old Market Square.

Dropping down to their knees, they took up position just behind the concrete pillars of the entrance to the shopping centre. With the doors propped open they both took aim with their automatic weapons and peppered a volley of shots up the hill of Listergate towards their pursuers.

The teams of two broke in different directions as the projectiles whistled past them. A couple of innocent civilians took the punishment on their behalf, not knowing what had happened as they fell to the floor, startled looks on their faces as their life was instantly snubbed out.

Warfare on the streets of Nottingham.

This was how Paul read the situation and a position he had found himself in many times in his career. Unfazed by the task ahead of him, he efficiently worked out the best way to approach it. Dropping to his knees, he signalled to the team on his left to move to the right as there was a slight bend in the street which would offer more natural cover. As they dived into the right, Paul and Smudge made a break for a shop front, heading inside and immediately making towards the rear exit. The shop assistants stood aside, arms raised in surrender to the gunmen in front of them, chins dropping down in disbelief. As they let themselves out the backdoor, they heard returning gunfire from their colleagues echoing down the walkway.

Paul broke out from the fire escape, finding himself in a small delivery area for the shop they had just exited. Breaking left, he jumped over a small wall, Smudge following close behind into the adjacent delivery area for the next shop closer to the shopping centre. Over the next three similar walls they went, until the came to the last in the row. Now they had to do the reverse through the shop. With no handle on the outside to open the door, Paul banged hard with the side of his clenched fist and the butt of his pistol.

Security

After a few seconds, the door opened slightly. A scrawny looking teenager, shaking with fear from the events unfolding outside the front of the shop, pushed open the door towards them.

"Thanks," Paul offered as he barged past the teenager. "Stay back here, get people out the back of the shop to safety," he beckoned others towards him with his arms as he moved forward, putting his finger to his lips. Several shoppers were hunkered down behind clothes rails and display shelves, fear etched on their faces, seeking any protection they could from the melee out the front. Paul and Smudge made their way steadily forwards until they had line of sight to the front of the shopping centre doorway.

Dropping onto his belly, Paul crawled forwards and pulled himself against the shop door, protected from view by the pillars supporting the frame. From here, he could clearly see that there were two gunmen firing up the street towards his colleagues. The youngest, of his crew, nicknamed Junior, had made his way out into the middle of the street, tucked in behind a large concrete planter, autumnal blooms filling it with colour. Peering out to the side slightly, he caught sight of Paul who signalled to him with two fingers and thumb down that there were two gunmen that he could see. Paul spoke quietly to Smudge who positioned himself just to the right of the doorway, where he was only able to see one of the gunmen from his position. Working in perfect harmony, they both edged forward slightly to ensure a clean shot without having to fire through the glass of the door in front of them as it may change the trajectory of the bullet slightly.

They had to connect with this first, and possibly only, opportunity.

As they took aim, Junior lifted himself to his hands and knees and sprang forward, sprinting for the opposite side of the street, diving into another shop front. The uniformed officers that were holding them back, both opened fire at the moving target, their bullets trying to catch up with the blur in front of them. This was enough of a distraction for Paul and Smudge, who both released their single shots across the path of each other, almost laser guided to their targets.

Paul's victim took the single gunshot to the back of his head, tearing the bottom of his skull away, resulting in instant death. He slumped down and to the right with grey matter and blood splashing across the tiled floor. The uniformed infiltrator that Smudge was aiming for, was immediately taken out of action with the bullet piercing through his left lung and exiting through his back, leaving a large exit wound that blood gushed from, like a dam giving way under pressure. His death was not instant however. There was time to feel the pain, knowing that he would die before help arrived. Blood filled his lungs, crushing his chest with fluid, ensuring vital oxygen could not be sucked in for his limbs and organs to perform. Death took him before the Prime Ministers security team could break their cover and make it to the gunmen.

The six regrouped quickly just inside the shopping centre, looking down at the uniformed officers, wondering what the hell this was all about.

"No time to ask questions now," stated Paul, "We're losing time," and he broke into a run again, heading for the exit onto the main ring road. All six were now in pursuit again.

Security

As they broke through the doorway on to the ring road, guns held in front of them ready to return fire, they automatically covered each other's backs and were looking up and down the road. There was no clear sign of where the uniformed officers had gone, so they split again. Two to the left, two straight ahead and two to the right.

With oncoming traffic all around them, Smudge was just ahead of Paul and shouted, pointing over towards the car park, lifting his gun and aiming. Just outside the exit of the car park, a white transit van was moving slowly. Several policemen were jumping into the side of it. Paul ran towards them pointing his gun and releasing a round from the chamber. It punctured the metal of the side as the door slid shut and the van took off at speed.

"Shit," exclaimed Paul. "Who the hell was that and where the fuck is the Boss?". He dropped his arm to his side, knowing full well that things were now well and truly outside of his control.

Paul became the first Head of Security to have lost The Boss. The Boss, just happened to be the Prime Minister of the UK.

He would have to call it in.

Chapter Seven

Friends

With Aidan out of the house, Nicky always felt like the place was empty. It was relief from the constant demands of a small child, but she missed the noise of his TV programme, his laughing at silly jokes and of course his little arm reaching for a cuddle round her waist when he wanted something.

It was her time to relax supposedly. Instead she found herself cleaning the house, finishing the ironing and tidying Aidan's bedroom. As she picked up his pyjamas from the floor, tucking them under his pillow, she noticed Beano just underneath the bed. He must have thrown it there as he raced to get ready. She scooped Beano up and rested him on Aidan's pillow, with the quilt pulled up to his chin, like he had been tucked in to bed for the night. She gathered the other cuddly toys into some semblance of order, if indeed you could order pandas, bears, pigs and other assorted animals, at the bottom of the bed.

Nicky moved to her room and rolled her stockings back down her slender legs. "No need for them now," she whispered to herself. "They've done their job!" Nicky pushed them back into the top drawer and started reviewing her wardrobe, searching for something suitable for the afternoon's barbecue. After changing in to

Friends

her favourite stretchy jeans and a simple purple blouse, Nicky fixed a chunky silver necklace and found a slightly slimmer version for her wrist which jangled softly as she moved.

Looking in the mirror again, she caught herself off-guard. Her hair was swept across her face and looking back at her was an image of her mother she had nurtured in her memory for years. A sharp intake of breath as she thought of her beloved mum. Where had she gone? Why did she leave? Was she safe? Had she met someone else and had another family? Was she even still alive? So many questions that her and her brother Ben had stopped discussing with each other a long time ago. It was too painful. Her dad rarely bought his wife up these days. Only on her birthday each year would he mention Jenny. He would always go back to the place that they married and leave a single yellow rose for her, taking time to remember the vows they said to each other in front of their family and friends. Still a romantic to this day, holding out in hope for his one true love to come home. Chivalry.

Not for the first time that day, Nicky wiped a single tear from her cheek. Flicking her hair out of her eyes, she headed downstairs and heard her phone ping. It was Leslie, "Do you want to stay tonight? No work tomorrow!!"

Nicky smiled and was about to respond "Yes," when she realised Aidan would be coming home and she had to get him to school in the morning. "Soz, No can do. Aidan at school!"

"However, I might get a taxi back though as I fancy a few wines with the girlies," she thought to herself.

heading for the kitchen, she pulled two bottles of wine from the fridge, along with the defrosted sausages from the sink and put them in a bag by the front door.

A couple of hours later, Nicky pulled up outside Leslie and Dan's house just as the clouds were parting to let the sun warm the cool air. She was early but they wouldn't mind.

"Hi gorgeous," purred Dan as he answered the door, slipping his arms round her in a tight embrace and kissing her on the cheek. "You smell wonderful, what is that?" he enquired.

"Pork and apple!" she retorted quickly, giggling as she spoke, "My favourite barbecue perfume. Hello Dan, lovely to see you. Where is your better half, I have wine and we need to bond?"

"She's upstairs finishing her beauty regime. Come on through and I'll pour your first for you. Prosecco of course," he joked as he made his way to the kitchen at the back of the house.

The folding patio doors looked out over a long rolling lawn, lined on either side with vibrant colours from the flowers that Leslie lovingly tendered on a regular basis. Not a weed in sight, the grass had dark lines in a criss-cross fashion. It wasn't real though. Artificial lawns had taken off in recent years and looked just like the real thing, but without the butterflies or other small insects that bought the birds into the garden. Leslie took perfection into the home as well, with clean, simple lines, natural tones on the walls and oil paintings, rich in colour, matching that of the fresh flowers on the kitchen table.

Dan poured the Prosecco as Leslie came bursting into the room, squealing with delight. "So glad you could

Friends

come, Nicky, you may have saved my day. Dan's invited some folks from the golf club and they can be such a bore!"

"That's not fair!" started Dan as he handed his wife her glass. "They are just a little more reserved than you two, that's all."

"Always happy to help a friend in need," called Nicky, raising her glass to the air and clinking it against Leslie's. "Anyway, I don't like being in the house when Aidan isn't there, so you've done me a favour as well."

Dan slid out the door to go and light the barbecue, as Leslie gave her best friend a big hug.

"How was Mr Slimeball this morning?" she enquired.

"Couldn't keep his eyes off me as usual. Was offering to fix my downpipe if I wanted him to," replied Nicky with a grin.

"The dirty sod. He can't stop himself can he? He should have tendered your pipes a little more when he lived there," cackled Leslie bursting into a fit of giggles.

"You are so naughty Leslie, but I like it. You know that's not what I meant. My drain pipe is leaking and he very kindly offered to fix it." She shrugged her shoulders. "I think he misses me. Misses us actually. He adores Aidan and he is really good with him. I probably shouldn't give him such a hard time," sighed Nicky, leaning back and looking down the garden towards Dan.

"You absolutely should! He treated you with no respect my lovely. Keep it hard on him," retorted Leslie looking stern. "And kick him in the balls if you get the chance. Just for good measure," she cackled, as Nicky laughed, taking another sip of her drink.

Friends started to arrive as Dan, now adorned in his favourite apron, was taking food outside to cook the feast. Leslie left Nicky to go and answer the door and Nicky stared down the garden towards Dan, watching him turning the meat periodically and dancing round trying to avoid the smoke getting in his eyes. The ritual of man at a barbecue was one she always found amusing, yet annoying at the same time. The hours of preparing the food, marinating, chopping salads, boiling pastas, making breads, sweets, folding napkins and dressing the table was usually carried out by the lady of the house. The guys would get out a few chairs from the garage, organise a tub of water to keep the beer cold, burn off the mould on the barbecue, declaring it 'clean', then spend an hour turning meat to avoid it burning too much, whilst drinking beer and laughing with friends. Hardly a chore. Then they would take all the glory for the event! Gits, the lot of them.

Laughter filled the kitchen as old friends mingled with strangers. Nicky found herself chatting with a lady from the golf club, who was enthusing about the latest female number one. She had no idea what, or who, she was talking about, but smiled and nodded occasionally at what she thought was the appropriate moment.

A dark haired hunk with his ear pierced and day old stubble on his chin, rushed into the kitchen. "Have you guys seen the news? There's been an assassination attempt on the Prime Minister. Bombs gone off and there are loads of people killed and badly hurt. It's right here in Nottingham. Insane man. Can you turn the TV on Leslie?" He looked stunned, but reached for a beer he'd bought with him, cracking the cap off the bottle, taking a deep slug, then setting himself up for a perfect view of the large screen on the wall.

Nicky had not heard the first part of his comment, but as the room fell silent and the TV kicked into life, she read the ticker tape reel across the bottom of the screen as the image portrayed a chaotic scene from the Old Market Square in the centre of Nottingham. It read 'Breaking news: Assassination attempt on Prime Minister, Barnaby Aitken. Large bomb explodes in centre of Nottingham killing dozens and seriously wounding many more. PM missing as police try to establish what happened'.

There were exclaims of "OH! MY GOD!" from several, lifting hands to mouths.

The image above showed the gathering in the square moments before the bomb went off. The PM coming out of the Council House, walking across the stage to wave to the crowd. He bent over the railing just as the bomb exploded. The stage was thrown upwards, then the TV image was cut as they said the scenes were too harrowing for viewers to witness. Bodies were apparently everywhere. Serious injuries with blood covering many people. Mass murder and carnage lay before the press of the UK. They had just captured it live on TV. Death and destruction damn near equalled 'Liquid gold'. A ratings winner.

Reporters gathered their wits relatively quickly, seizing the opportunity to report 'World Exclusives', live from the scene of devastation. Although the public will have been live streaming the events on their social media accounts, people still turned to traditional media for these types of atrocities. It had to be terrorism, didn't it? No longer a scene of celebration, now an enquiry on the horror unfolding before them. Speculation on who was responsible had started within minutes. Trial by press had intensified over the last ten years and guilty or not, if the papers believed they had a story and you were in any way suspiciously linked to the events, you were never going to get a fair hearing.

As the reporter's words filled the kitchen, the silence from the guests was ghostly. Dan wondered back into the kitchen with a tray of cooked meat and stopped in his tracks. "What's going ..." but before he finished speaking, he too was drawn to the calamity unfolding in front of him. "Fuck me!" he exclaimed without thinking.

The TV reporter was desperately trying to convey the enormity of what they had just witnessed, but was clearly shaken himself.

"So, so... so it looks like the assassination attempt on the Prime Minister may have failed, but we really aren't sure at this moment in time. After the explosion, police officers on the roof were seen taking aim at what we believe is a man, possibly grappling with the Prime Minister himself." As the cameraman restored the picture after the explosion, it immediately zoomed into the area where Barnaby Aitken had been standing. The smoke was thick and black, but sure enough a man in a torn dark suit was seen to be pushing himself up from the ground. He looked so dishevelled and covered in dirt it was almost impossible to say if it was the Prime Minister.

"BLOODY HELL," pronounced the dark haired hunk with the stubble. The room of people were transfixed. Food and drink forgotten.

Next to the Prime Minister, another man got to his feet, patting himself down and then grabbing a small boy, checking him over. Nicky stared at the screen intently, the hairs standing up on the back of her neck. She recognised the man and the little boy instantly,

Friends

"Oh! My god!" she let out in a whisper and her grip on her wine glass failed. It fell to the stone floor, jolting the room out of its trance.

Nicky walked closer to the telly as the footage showed the two men starting to run away from the stage, one carrying a small boy. Out of sight of the TV cameras.

Dan moved towards her, but Nicky's legs gave way and she collapsed to the floor before he could get there.

Chapter Eight
Missed Target

His mobile phone rang. He looked at the incoming call and wasn't sure he wanted to answer. The client would not be pleased as the target had escaped death. Many things went through his mind, but he knew it was no use putting it off. He slowly swiped right to answer and bought the phone to his left ear.

Lifting a small silver vape machine to his mouth in his other hand, inhaled the bizarre mix of nicotine chemicals and toffee flavourings, inducing a relaxing effect at the same time his blood pressure was about to rise drastically. Blowing out a smokeless cloud of vapour into the room, he listened intently to the client without responding or interrupting.

"I've heard about the events of today and it sounds like the plan went wrong. Months of preparation to remove our problem and it seems to me that you were not up to the job. I paid a lot of money to ensure that this was carried out professionally. Am I to believe that I employed the wrong team?" The voice on the other end was very calm. Serene, even. Like it were laying on a beach in the Bahamas. An effective and convincing response was required.

"No, you did not employ the wrong team. Unfortunately, the puppy strayed from the path that was chosen, breaking free from the leash it was on. We will retrieve the puppy and ensure that the training is finished." There was a strong accent to his voice as he spoke, deliberately slowly, ensuring he pronounced everything he could in his best English.

Both client and customer knew not to say anything that could be connected with the events of the day themselves. The atmosphere was alive with listening devices. The airways were in no way secure and they could not risk being identified, or further jeopardise the plan they had initiated.

"I hope for your sake, the puppy doesn't bite back," came the calm response. "I want an update when you have located it. This number only, no text messages. If you fail to deliver on our agreement, there will be consequences, you know that."

Silence followed. The call was terminated from the other end.

"Short and to the point as ever," the vaper said under his breath. Wiping his brow with his vape hand, he realised he was sweating a little. His client clearly unnerved him in ways he daren't consider. Although he himself had a murky past, he'd heard of gruesome consequences for those that had failed to deliver. Particularly in relation to this client.

He knew they must locate the target quickly, before he was recovered by the real police. They had infiltrated the local constabulary, including the armed response units, relatively easily over the past few months, laying a few sleepers low in each section that they knew would be deployed for the Prime Ministers arrival at the Council House. Paid hit men who had no affiliation to any cause or country in particular, they expected to be rewarded richly for their endeavours.

A rotund, slightly oily character, he was obsessed with computers at an early age, he had often found more friendship on the web than he had in his local neighbourhood and as a self-taught programmer, it meant he was always able to find work, but it usual lay outside the realm of civilised society. Hacking the security system, laying out clear unblemished backgrounds for employees with exemplary references that all checked out, had been a piece of cake for him. Once in, the sleepers were tasked with the PM's protection and they had all of the inside information they could possibly want, from route's to be taken at various times, down to the details of the Metropolitan Police protection that would ride with him.

Instead of searching for possible devices around the Council House, several of the sleepers had been able to plant the carefully timed device right under the microphone on the stage, which they knew the PM would walk to and the precise time he would walk to it. They had gone with a timed device as they had learned they were harder to trace back to anyone than triggered devices. On top of that, security services around the world had started to use sophisticated jammers at important events in case remote devices had been hidden. He had as of yet been unable to master hacking those systems without being detected.

Drains were sealed off, declared safe after searching and bins removed from the locality, as they could be used to hide possible threats. The deadly device had been pinned to the underside of the stage by a sleeper, dressed in police uniform. Hiding in plain sight was what all security forces dreaded. It was a relatively small package, but designed to be deadly. It had been programmed for the precise time that Barnaby Aitken was supposed to walk to the microphone and was certain to kill him instantly. It would probably take out the unsuspecting, front few rows of the audience with him. Collateral damage was not part of the fee that had been paid, but it was unavoidable. A small price to pay for the target being taken out.

However, the bastard had not stuck to the plan though. 'The Puppy' had walked to the other side of the stage, away from the device and towards relative safety.

He walked back into his control centre, where two other men and a young Asian women were hunkered down over a row of computer screens. The control centre was located in an old garage at the back of some flats and a run-down house they had being using in Sneinton, a suburb of Nottingham. Wires were hanging from the ceiling and trailing across the floors and the team had to be careful not to dislodge overloaded plugs when they moved around the room. It was cramped and hot due to the heat emitting from the back of the electrical devices. From here they were able to access and view every CCTV camera across the city and beyond.

All were expert hackers, sought by various governments in several countries, known only to each other by their professional names.

'Toad'. 'IPFree'. 'Sloth2000' and 'HaPee as Larry', were the best in the business and the vaper, known as Toad, had sought them out specifically for this mission.

"I want eyes on every camera over the city. Check back on the camera tapes for all cars coming out of that car park. He had to be inside one of them. I want him found quickly." croaked Toad.

Chapter Nine
COBRA

COBRA, the emergency committee to deal with the countries security at a time of crisis, given the target of the attack were summoned to meet, literally minutes after it all started. It was the second time they had met in as many months since the EIP had come to power. The name COBRA sounded far more exotic than it actually is. Cabinet Office Briefing Room A. It doesn't evoke the same kind of emotions from the press or general public than COBRA.

Having been on a state of high alert, or 'Severe' for many years now, things had just escalated to the highest level, 'Critical' meaning an attack was imminent. Or in this case, had just occurred. Given it involved the country's highest ranking official, other than King Charles, there should really be another rating, possibly entitled 'Panic'. The country's highest-ranking officials in charge of our safety and security sat round the oval shaped walnut table, sharply dressed in tailored suits, crisp white shirts and hand stitched ties for the men, whilst trouser suits adorned most of the ladies. Serious faces all around, with chins being rubbed and strong black coffee the order of the day.

A foreboding silence fell across the room.

The meeting was being chaired by the Home Secretary, Helen Langley, less than two hours after the bomb had exploded in the Old Market Square of Nottingham. A graduate from Oxford with a first in Economics, still in her early forties, Helen had made a fortune in real estate when the markets disintegrated in 2008. She had invested every penny she had when the market hit rock bottom, at a time when others pulled out. Over the next ten years she had seen her net worth go stratospheric. With a brilliant mind, she was destined to lead the English Independence Party at some point in the future, but now she had to act swiftly to locate and recover the prime minister unharmed. Once that was sorted, they would make sure the perpetrators of this barbaric act were dealt with rapidly and severely. Every level of force would be used to ensure those responsible were bought to the courts to face justice. Or possibly annihilated in the process. That was a consequence that many would want to see play out.

"What the hell has happened and what do we know about the prime minister's condition and current whereabouts?" demanded Helen, searching the room for the heads of MI5 and MI6. Marcus Poole led MI5 and was the first to respond.

"Ma'm, it appears to be a well-executed and direct attack on the prime minister himself. Using a timed device, we believe at this stage, rigged to detonate at the precise time Barnaby was due to start his speech. Thankfully, he took a slight detour on stage and was just outside of the immediate blast radius. From what we can tell, it looks like he has sustained a cut to his head, possible a lower leg or ankle injury, but other than that it does not look like he has any more serious or life-threatening injuries". Whilst Marcus was talking, images of the explosion were being played out on large screens around the room and he was highlighting the PMs head wound and the way he was limping.

"We understand there were twelve members of the public that were killed instantly, along with four police officers. At this time, an unknown number with injuries ranging from mild cuts and abrasions to life-threatening and life changing," he paused, surveying his audience inviting questions. None came, so he continued. "The prime minister was then seen to talk to a man and his young son. What is concerning at this point, is from TV footage, it looks like at least one of our own uniformed officers on the roof of the Council House, fires directly at the prime minister."

He paused the TV footage to show the scene to the room.

"It is not clear exactly. He may have been aiming at the man by his side, perhaps panicked by the situation unfolding, possible believing the PM is still under attack. However, we have been unable to locate that officer and as we now know, Paul Buxton and his team who set off in pursuit of the PM, the man and his son, were fired upon by at least two other uniformed officers. Those men are now deceased and we are currently trying to identify them. From Paul's own account, there were at least four others who climbed into a transit van and drove off. This man," he pointed back to the screen at Lee in the Old Market Square, "has been run through our criminal records facial recognitions database and we do not have a hit. However, old passport records have an eighty-two percent match with a man called Lee Bevan who lives here in Nottingham. We think he is probably trying to help the PM escape from the attack. We are sending teams to his address now and we are trying to locate Barnaby's mobile as we speak Ma'm."

The teams had already discovered so much in a short space of time, but there was fear in the room that they were still not acting swiftly enough. The Head of M16, Irm Brown, watched her companion closely, but did not add anything else to the commentary. Irm was of Indian descent, second generation British, in her late fifties, married to an English entrepreneur and had become the second woman to head MI6, but the first of Asian descent. Since the EIP had come into power, she had wondered how long it would be until she got her marching orders from the role she had worked incredibly hard for. Her face did not seem to fit in with the new regime. Overt racism was becoming commonplace across the security forces, despite the thousands that were employed, who were not white British. It would not be able to function without these people and, yet here they were, in the twenty-first century, being made to feel like second-class citizens. She knew she would have to prove herself all over again to retain her position, but Irm was not the sort to give in without a fight.

Helen had been listening intently and her first response was straight to the point. "I want you to ensure that Maureen has her security tightened and does not leave Chequers. Locate Barnaby's daughters and their families ASAP and ensure they are taken into protective custody. Notify our special forces that they are to be deployed immediately to Nottingham, to locate and secure the safe extraction of our prime minister. As we do not yet know what we are dealing with here, we will operate a shoot to kill policy if fired upon. Given we are potentially at war, does anyone have any objections to that proposal?"

Helen looked with an icy glare directly at the deputy PM and the governments legal counsel, almost daring them to defy her. All around shook their heads.

"We will declare a state of emergency and our armed forces are to be made available at major cities across the UK. No flights in or out of our air space, with immediate effect. Those en route are to be diverted to neighbouring countries where possible. Transatlantic flights to land in Ireland at this stage."

Britain was going to be on complete lockdown, a situation never experienced in the modern day.

"Ma'm, I would suggest that our surveillance teams also step up their cover of the airwaves for any coded messages and try to work out how these guys are communicating. We need to try and get ahead of their next move, if indeed they have a next move, but my instinct tells me they are not yet done with the PM," stated Marcus, moving his gaze from the home secretary to the deputy PM. They both nodded approval, without feeling the need to consult more widely. That had to be a given.

"From what you have described Marcus, it sounds like our police forces have been infiltrated. This is what the EIP have always been afraid of and we should have closed our bloody borders years ago. Look at the chaos we have now. I want answers from the police commissioner in Nottingham to understand how we work with them, who we can trust and then I want to know what the hell went wrong. Use secure networks only with our teams and no phone calls to non-secure lines. Everyone understand what they need to do?"

Determined nods were delivered by the attendees as they gathered their belongings and briefing packs and rose to get to work.

"I want hourly updates and to find the PM before they get to him," Helen fired a parting shot to all, to ensure they knew what was at stake. As if they needed a reminder. What happened over the next few hours would determine not just the fate of the country's prime minister, but possibly that of the country itself.

Marcus and Irm fixed eyes firmly. Irm knew she would have to work with him for a successful outcome, but was not convinced he would be wholly co-operative. He broke free from her gaze and left the room, contempt written across his face.

Helen headed out the door to go and brief the deputy PM, Sebastian Horner. With the PM missing, he would have to face the world's press at this unprecedented time of a national emergency and, who knew; possibly a war.

Where the enemy was and who they were, at this moment in time, was completely unknown. Given the events over the last few years, but particularly the last twenty-four hours, it was highly unlikely that any allies from Europe were going to come to their rescue.

Britain was on its own.

Chapter Ten
Lady Bay

Lee was panicking. How the hell did he end up involved in this? He'd never been caught up in any sort of atrocity before. They happened to other people, didn't they?

Over the last ten years, random terror attacks in the UK had become more common place. London had seen the majority, with vehicles used for mass murder on regular occurrence, including those outside the Houses of Parliament and across London Bridge. The rest of the UK hadn't escaped the mindless murder and mayhem. It was like a return to the eighties, when no event was ever deemed entirely safe and people always had a nervousness about them. The threat of the IRA hanging over the mainland, like a smog, suffocating joy from the supposedly free people. Now it was a different threat.

Extremists intent on disrupting normality, frightening civilians, all supposedly in the name of religion. Although many cities had been targeted by lone wolves, hundreds of members of the public had been killed or maimed by suicide bombers, none had, as of yet, targeted the establishment directly. Despite that, our normal police force still did not carry arms. There were armed response units everywhere these days however. You did not have to wander far through a large gathering, sports event or gala to see machine-gun wielding cops. Of course they were armed, they had to be.

The Government over the years had naturally been blamed for its foreign policy, inciting hatred in young men from the wars of the early noughties in Iraq, Afghanistan, alongside the bizarre choices that were made in the Syrian conflict. The refugees came in their droves, many thousands drowning in the sea as they made the perilous journey across the Mediterranean. Many were genuine refugees, looking for a better life, free from persecution and war, taking enormous risk to move their family to the western world. Leaving their beloved, yet destroyed homes, behind them.

Many other single men, boys in many cases, set off with a different intent. To deceive. To plead for support from the west, accepting the helping hand that charity offered. Lying low, living off the state it was determined to see torn apart. Sleeping. Sleeping, so that one day they could be awoken and spurred into action for a cause. A cause that infidels would never understand. Every religious group rejected the actions of these terrorists. These acts were not committed because of religion. They were committed out of hatred.

Was it possible that one of those sleepers had been responsible for this attack on the prime minister? How had the security services failed so badly? So many questions filled his spinning head. A quiet sob from the rear foot well behind him bought him back to his senses. "Ok Aidan. We're OK. Don't worry, I'll get you home safe to your Mum," he whispered back towards his frightened son. He wiped the sweat from his brow and adjusted the cap again, ensuring he covered his head properly.

Lady Bay

As he drove slowly around the city, he spotted the plume of smoke that was still moving upwards from the Old Market Square. Sirens were going off in all directions and a cavalcade of ambulances had started to arrive, queuing now to get into the chaos. The public servants desperate to get the aid and attention to those who had borne the brunt of the attack. Many with life changing injuries, and in several cases, on the brink of death. Lee had to get away from the city centre, soon you would not be able to move through the army of worker ants.

Turning left, with the square directly behind him, he headed towards the outer ring road. "Think. Think," he muttered under his breath, still hyperventilating. His hands were shaking as the shock of the last thirty minutes caught up with him, adrenalin starting to wain after his exertion. Lee held his breath and then started long slow breaths to get a hold of himself.

"We need to be undercover. Hang on Aidan, it will be about ten minutes and then you can get out son."

Lee drove the rest of the way in silence, finally passing Meadow Lane, Notts County's football ground as he headed to an old haunt of his. It was long past its prime, but in years gone by, Lee used to come here for some solitude, to lose himself, as he practised some climbing moves. Lady Bay was a metal bridge spanning the River Trent, where many years back, lots of young, lithe climbers, came to practice holds, master overhangs and build their strength for when they could tackle the real rock faces out across the Peak District. Plastic holds bolted to the underside of the bridge, allowing climbs of escalating difficulty, traversing the construction, cars and lorries still thundering past overhead, shaking the bridge almost constantly.

He pulled the car to a stop and jumped out to open the wooden gate, allowing him to move up the lane and get the car off the road out of site. He felt like a fugitive and yet he had done nothing wrong. Moving the car up the lane, he called to Aidan that they were here. Climbing out the car, he returned to the gate and carefully closed it behind them. They were hidden from the view of the road and under the shadow of the bridge itself. There was no-one around and it was eerily quiet after the deafening noise from the Old Market Square. Despite that, he still checked around him before he pulled the jacket off of Aidan and scooped him out the footwell.

He hugged him tight, with tears running down his cheek. Slowly, he released his grip and pushed him away slightly, so he could look at him. Aidan's eyes were red, cheeks puffy from the tears that had been burning their way down his face. Lee could see fear there.

"It's alright Aidan. We're safe. Let me check you over and make sure you're not hurt. Does anything hurt?" He said softly to his little boy. Aidan shook his head.

"My ears are ringing Dad", Aidan spoke as Lee cupped his face in his hands.

"I know, mine are too. It will pass soon enough. Let me check the rest of you," he replied and started to scrutinise his little lad from top to toe. As he moved his hands over Aidan's legs, checking for cuts and bruises and any shrapnel that might have penetrated his body, a thumping noise on the boot of the car startled him. Aidan went stiff at the noise.

"Oh my God! The prime minister. I forgot he was in the boot."

Lee sprang towards the rear of the car, releasing the catch and allowing the top to lift upwards. A groan came from within, as a long leg poked its way into the open air.

"Thank you," Barnaby groaned as the blood rushed back into his cramped limbs. He lifted his head clear of the boot and placed his feet on the ground. Rubbing his thighs, he went to stand, but the now swollen ankle, would not take his weight. Where his cut face had lain against the carpet in the boot, a deep stain now ran.

"That looks bad Sir. You should rest, don't try and walk on it. Here let me help you," Lee pulled the Prime Ministers arm around his shoulders to support him as they moved towards an old shed under the bridge. "There used to be some chairs in here you should be able to sit down."

Aidan opened the door at the front of the small wooden building. Paint was flaking from the sides of the rarely used outbuilding and the lock which didn't look like it had been fastened in an eternity, was rusted in position. Inside, it was very dusty, smelling of damp and mould spores. The small window did not allow much light in as it was covered in grime and cob webs. Home to more spiders, wood lice and a various assortment of other insects and invertebrates than it had seen humans in many a year. Propped up on the side were several mats, used in their prime for climbers to fall onto should their move or grip let them down. The side of the shed was covered in hooks, on some of which still hung small, screw gated safety locks, used to attach safety harnesses to ropes. It had been a long time since they had seen any climbing action.

In the corner were two wicker chairs stacked on top of each other. Lee propped the prime minister up against the side of the doorframe and went to pull the chairs apart. He shuffled Barnaby back towards them and the prime minister slumped back into the seat which groaned under the weight, but thankfully held firm. Lee lifted his swollen ankle gently up towards the other seat, and taking off his jumper, placed it underneath the damaged ankle. He carefully removed the shoe and pulled the sock down to examine the ankle. A large, purple mound had formed.

"Can you move your toes Sir?" Lee looked up at the prime minister.

"I think so," responded Barnaby, crunching his toes together slowly. "Thank you ... for saving my life." He lifted his gaze towards Lee and nodded slowly. "It was obvious that was all meant for me. Innocent people just got massacred, yet I survived. Because of you. I don't even know your name?" He enquired of Lee. "I know your son is called Aidan. Are you OK Aidan?" Barnaby glanced towards the young boy who was still stood near the doorway. Aidan nodded his head as Lee smiled for the first time in what felt like days, but he knew was only a short time.

"My name is Lee, Sir. Lee Bevan. I think we all just had a very lucky escape." Returning his eyes to the prime minister, Lee spoke softly. "I didn't know where to go, given the police themselves were trying to kill us."

As he spoke, he noticed Aidan's face fall and tears gather in the corner of his eyes again. Reaching out, he gathered Aidan in his arm to comfort him. "Then I remembered this place. Out of view and very quiet. I can't remember the last time I came here when I saw other people. It'll give us time to think and work out what we need to do. What is the protocol Sir? Who do we contact? Who comes to save us?" Lee threw lots of questions at the leader of his country. Barnaby Aitken did not respond straight away as he looked at the young man.

"I wish I knew the answer to that Lee and please, no need to call me sir. You have done plenty for me already. My name is Barnaby."

He nodded towards them both to offer his thanks again. "It seems those that were tasked with protecting me from this very type of event, were actually the ones who carried it out. My own inner circle should be the ones to protect and extract me, but they were nowhere to be seen. I should call them. My personal secretary as well. He will know who to contact to ensure our safety."

Barnaby reached for his mobile in his inner jacket pocket. As he pulled it out, he noticed several text messages and missed calls displayed on the locked screen.

Barnaby scrolled though the list of missed calls first. Two from his personal secretary, one from the head of the security service assigned to protect him and one from his wife. There were three messages left, so he dialled his answerphone.

"Sir, this is Paul Buxton, are you OK? We are not sure if you are injured, kidnapped or otherwise. Please confirm using the dial code we agreed. Get in touch ASAP. We have the full force available at our disposal Sir."

Barnaby was pleased to hear Paul's voice. There was strength there that heartened him. Next was a message from his personal secretary, Mike Lightfoot.

"Barnaby, this is Mike. What a nightmare. Are you OK? Call me, you know the protocol. We are worried. Not sure who we can trust and the who the enemy is."

There was genuine fear in Mike's voice that was palpable. Finally he heard the voice of his wife Maureen.

"Honey, its Mo here. Are you OK?" came the enquiry. A tear welled in the corner of his eye. "That looked really bad on TV and Mike called to say they didn't know where you had gone. Get in touch honey, we need to know you are safe. Speak soon."

His wife's voice was calm. She was always calm in a crisis. Unflappable in all circumstances. Barnaby held his phone against his chest as he considered what to do.

"Sir let me have a look at the cut on your head," said Lee, moving back towards him. "The bleeding has stopped but it's quite a deep wound by the looks of it," he said, holding Barnaby's head to one side. "I have some water in the car that I can clean that up with. What should we do Sir? Who should we call?" He enquired of the countries eminent minister again.

"I'm calling my wife first," came the response as Barnaby pressed the mobile to the side of his head. He listened to it ring several times before Maureen answered. "Honey are you OK?" enquired his serene wife.

Lee turned towards the door with Aidan to go and retrieve the bottled water from his car.

"Hi sweetheart. I'm OK. I'm not sure what's going on, but I'm OK."

"It looked like you got kidnapped after the explosion. What happened? Where are you? Can the security team come and get you?" A load of questions fired directly at him, machine gun like from his spouse.

"Mo, I have no idea where I am and I have not been kidnapped. There is a young man helping me out, called Lee, with his son Aidan."

At the mention of his and his son's name, Lee stopped in his tracks, turned and glared at the prime minister. He did not need to be put in even greater danger.

"My ankle hurts pretty bad, but other than that, I am OK. I need to call Paul Buxton, tell him to come get me so we can sort this bloody mess out. Someone is going to pay for this. I'll call you again as soon as I am somewhere safe honey." Barnaby knew he had already broken with protocol by calling Maureen first, but she had to know he was alive and safe for now.

"Barney, don't you put the phone down on me ..." she shouted down the phone. It was the first time in ... he couldn't remember ... since she'd lost her temper.

Next, he called Mike and with Lee's help explained where they were and the extent of his injuries. Mike was relieved to hear his voice and know the man he served was alive.

"Have you dialled the code Sir?" enquired Mike.

"Not yet Mike," came the reply.

"Sir you have to dial the code – it's protocol. They need to locate you and send the extraction team before this gets any worse."

Barnaby drew a breath. His head was starting to pound now, but more from the thinking he was having to do than the damage to it from the explosion. "OK Mike, I'll call now" and he hung up on his friend and personal secretary. Barnaby's eyes dropped to the wooden floor, the dust holding his gaze. Before he could look up, a faint whirring noise stirred the air, over the gurgle of the gently moving river Trent.

Lee looked up at Barnaby and gestured for him to put his shoe back on, then turned his attention towards the door. He moved rapidly towards the exit and Aidan followed. Moving outside from the relative darkness of the shed, the sunlight seemed so bright they had to shade their eyes with their hands. They continued forwards, out from under the shadow of the bridge towards the bank of the river. As their eyes adjusted, the noise of traffic heavy overhead, the sound of whirring got louder.

Lee scoured the sky, but looking into the sunshine made it difficult to focus. Gradually two objects came into view. Eight rotors supporting the weight of each device suspended underneath. Several cameras attached at the bottom, giving them complete three hundred and sixty degree vision for the person controlling it. The DroneCam was moving over the river towards the bridge and descending to get a view underneath.

"What the heck are they?" Lee said to himself, but knowing the answer as he spoke. These were the types of device that professional photographers had been using for a number of years, giving a new perspective on the world we lived in from above. Allowing viewers unparalleled observations from the air, out to sea, or off the sides of cliffs and gorges, where man could just not venture. These were similar to the type of device that Amazon had once looked to use for home deliveries. After many disasters, law suits from shopping dropped inadvertently on cars and people, thefts from goods left outside homes, it had been abandoned as a 'Great idea, that society just wasn't ready for'. Apparently, the human race wasn't as civilised and law abiding as Amazon had thought. The technology also occasionally let them down.

But what were drones doing here? Aidan was mesmerised and gazed upward in fascination. Lee was wary and summoned his son to come back behind him.

Lady Bay

The drones came ever closer, about ten feet apart, the noise of their blades getting louder. One started to drop down towards them and Lee could see that the cameras were zooming in on him and his son.

They were searching for something. Or someone.

The door creaked behind them and they both turned to see Barnaby in the doorway to the hut. "Stay back Sir. I'm not sure what's going on," called out Lee.

As he returned his gaze back to the drones, beyond them, across the river, past the City Ground, to the edge of Trent Bridge, a small bright flash of light burst upwards.

It was the unmistakable flash of a gun firing its round.

Chapter Eleven

Frantic

Nicky was sobering up quickly, but she could not stop shaking. Fear and adrenalin were still surging through her body. Her breathing was erratic, her pulse racing and she kept feeling faint and dizzy.

Given the enormity of the incident and how Nicky's separated husband and son seemed to be caught up in it, Dan had cleared out the rest of the party attendees. A silence had fallen over the house and Leslie was making sweet tea to aid Nicky's recovery. He didn't know what to do to help, so he just sat and hugged Nicky.

"They'll be Ok Nicky. The security services will get to them soon enough."

Nicky was looking to blame Lee for taking Aidan into danger. How could he have been so stupid to put our son at risk like that?

"What was he thinking?" sobbed Nicky. "My poor little boy ... was he hurt? Could you tell if he had been hit? Was he bleeding?" She asked in between tears and mouthfuls of tea.

"It's difficult to say," replied Lesley, "He looked Ok, I think, and Lee was carrying him when they left the Old Market Square. I am sure they will have got somewhere safe by now. Call his mobile and see," she suggested.

Frantic

Due to her frantic state, Nicky hadn't thought clearly enough to even consider that as an option. Her eyes widened. "Of course! Why didn't I think of that?"

Jumping from the sofa, she raced for her handbag, rifling through to locate her mobile. Plucking it out from the depths, she swiped right and started scrolling through her numbers to locate Lee's. Pushing the green phone button, she listened to the dialling tone. The call did not connect to the phone, but diverted straight to voicemail.

She heard Lee's voice on the message, sounding softer and friendlier than she remembered it of late.

"It's Lee, but you know that. Pleeeeeease leave a message and I will call you back as soon as I can. I promise to as I don't get many these days. Thanks."

The beep sounded and Nicky almost burst into tears.

"Lee, it's Nicky. Where are you? Is Aidan OK? Call me. I have to know he is alright. What have you got into? Call me." She pressed the off button and lowered her head to her hand, sobbing. Leslie put her arm round her to comfort her.

"Maybe he has headed home," suggested Dan. "It's where I would feel safe and whoever is after the prime minister wouldn't know where he lived, would they?"

Nicky raised her head and sprung upright. "Yes. Let's go. You're right, he would head there, he doesn't have anywhere else he could go."

Dan reached over to grab his car keys, "I'll drive, you are in no fit state to be behind the wheel of a car right now". Leaving Leslie behind, they jumped into the car.

As they headed through the streets of West Bridgford, Dan kept checking on Nicky who had sat in the back seat. She was looking out the window in a daze, tears running down her cheeks and constantly looking at her mobile, willing it to ring.

Not wanting to disappoint her, it burst into life.

Chapter Twelve

Surviving

The shot that had been fired at them across the river at Lady Bay Bridge, smashed through the wood just above where the prime ministers hand was resting on the door frame, sending splinters and shards into the shed and across the pathway. Barnaby was knocked backwards into the shed with the shock of the exploding woodwork.

"Where the hell did that come from?" barked the PM. Lee turned in slow motion, aware that a projectile had just whistled past him, narrowly missing his shoulder and appeared to be aimed, yet again, at Barnaby Aitken.

Lee pulled his son to the ground and they crawled around the concrete pillar. The buzzing of the drones was still coming towards them and it was clear now they had been used to closely identify their target for the gunmen on the other side of the river. Like a demonic wasp hovering over your dinner in the garden, ready to wreak havoc on the next victim should they dare to stick around. Seeing a short wooden board on the ground in the dust, Lee picked it up, testing the strength against his hand. He pushed Aidan back against the wall and shouted to Barnaby to stay inside the shed. Aidan sat with his back to the wall, knees drawn up towards his chest. How he wished he was back in his bedroom with Beano. Watching videos on his kindle was so much nicer than getting shot at. Who would shoot at kids? his mind asked involuntarily.

The buzzing got louder and in the muted reflection of the dusty shed window, Lee noticed the first drone was nearly upon their position, but the second had disappeared. He waited another few seconds and then burst into action. Springing forward from his position, he jumped up into the air, raising the piece of wood high above his head and smacking it down as hard as he could.

It connected with rotor blades made of rigid plastic, instantly bringing an end to the rotation of them. Swatted from the sky, Lee followed this up with a stamp, landing his size eight feet heavily on the drone as it hit the floor. He wasn't sure if the cameras were still working and he didn't want the operator to see the fear in his eyes. Plastic snapped. Thin bars of metal twisted and the drones flying days were definitely over.

Noise of a second shot rang out, just as another bullet entered the ground right at the base of the twisted flying wreck, narrowly missing Lee's raised leg as he went to stamp again. He shuddered and dived back for cover. Where was the other drone? He could hear it. The operator must have sent it round the back of the pillar supporting the bridge for a different perspective. He crept along, sticking close to the concrete, in the shadow of the bridge itself. Aidan was hugging himself and crying again.

Lee had to get Aidan out of here and to safety, fast. The second flying camera came round the far pillar. Lee ran forward, again raising the wooden weapon to the left above his head and this time swinging right. The force of the impact connecting, knocking it out of control and downwards, hitting the water at an angle. The rotor blades let out a fizz as they tried to extract themselves from the River Trent. With its electrics dipping into the river, the machine gave out and with one last spin, it descended into the depths of the murky, cold water, leaving its operators blind again.

Lee ran back to Aidan. "It's ok, they are gone," he wrapped his arms round his son again, picking him up. Under cover of the bridge he moved back towards the car, knowing he had to get out of there as fast as he could. He put Aidan in the foot well again, reassuring him as he was closing the door.

Turning, he sprinted back to the shed to get the prime minister, taking care to stay out of the previous line of sight for the gunman. Leaning against the pillar, he shouted "Are you Ok? Can you open the door, but stay out of sight?"

"Yes, I'm alright," came a faint response as the door swung open a little. Lee dived in, expecting another bullet to be exploding across the river, but nothing came. Perhaps their pursuers had decided they were moving to come and get them before they could really escape. This thought urged him on.

"We have to get out of here fast," he said putting his shoulder underneath the PM's arm again. He lifted him from the ground, "Ready?" he enquired and Barnaby nodded in response. His face more serious than ever before.

They moved quickly back towards the car. Still no sound of gunfire, but this frightened Lee even more. As he pushed Barnaby back into the boot of his car, lifting his legs up over the lip, a thought entered his head.

"Give me your phone Sir. They tracked us down so quickly they must have tapped your phone, followed it somehow. The police themselves appear to be trying to kill you; us. They must be able to track it."

Barnaby pulled it out his jacket, looked at it with disgust and hesitated, but passed it over. He knew it was his lifeline to his security forces.

Lee sprinted back to the river and slung it as far as he could out into the meandering river.

Returning to the car, he fired the engine and his wheels squealed as he took off as fast as he could back down towards the road, flinging it left as the rubber hit the tarmac. His phone linked into the hands free kit and he realised he had a missed call from Nicky. He did not listen to the message, but instead gave a voice command to dial her. The number connected.

Lifting the phone to her head Nicky almost screamed down the line. "Where are you? Is Aidan OK? What the hell is going on?" Questions machine gunned at him, but fear surrounded her short sentences. Fear of a mother, frantic for her son's safety. Lee knew from the sound of her voice and the machine gun firing of questions at him that she was fully aware of the events of the morning. He didn't know if she knew the prime minister was with him.

"I don't know what the hell is going on, but someone is trying to kill the prime minister and he is with me right now. Where are you, I need you to take Aidan and get him away from this."

Given what Lee had experienced over the last few hours, he spoke very calmly. Most would have been a quivering mess, unable to communicate with others around them.

"Listen carefully Nicky. Don't go to my flat. They seem to have been able to track us so far. They must have worked out who I am and presumably where I live. Go to the place where you told me you were pregnant with Aidan. I'll meet you there as soon as I can."

"What?" shouted back Nicky. She was confused. Couldn't think straight. "Where is that? I can't remember ..." she sputtered, but the end of the line had gone dead.

"No!" she wailed out loud, looking at the phone in desperation. Dan pulled over to the side of the road, not sure what had just been said in the short call.

"Is Aidan OK?" Dan reached back towards Nicky.

"My poor boy. What's he caught up in?"

The tears came thick and fast again as she wracked her brain to remember where they had been when she told Lee she was pregnant.

Chapter Thirteen
Tracking

Toad and his team of hackers had been busy. They were able to review all of the CCTV cameras surrounding the car park at the time the prime minister had disappeared into thin air. The young Asian lady, known as 'IPFree', had short cut hair in a bob, her nose pierced and anti-establishment tattoos on her shoulders. She played six different videos at once on small screens in front of her and quickly established that there were two cars entering the car park and only one leaving, at the time the false armed police entered through the stairwells.

"Go back. Stop. Zoom in on that one," directed Toad. "Bring it up full screen". All the hackers turned to look at the image in front of them. It was a white, Nissan Qashqai with a 2015 plate. The image was a little grainy, but still pretty clear. There were no passengers in the car and it would be easy to overlook, given they were hunting three. The driver looked out to the right with a baseball cap pulled down low. He looked intently at the face. He wasn't sure.

"Run facial recognition against the man seen leaving the square with the target," he blew out the sweet smelling vapours as he spoke.

Tracking

"We only have partial image matching here, but the estimate is seventy-two percent match. I'd say it's him," returned IPFree.

"Get me the number plate and I want it tracked wherever it goes. Where are his passengers I wonder? HaPee, I want the PM's mobile located and all calls or texts I am to know about. Understand?" Toad knew that not just his reputation was at stake, but potentially his life, if he did not turn this around sharpish. 'HaPee as Larry' nodded as he had already started to establish the connections.

It did not take them long to locate the vehicle, just as it was nearing the Lady Bay bridge. Their nearest unit was on the other side of the river. Relaying messages that the PM had been in communication with his wife and personal secretary, the armed sleepers pulled into the small road before Trent Bridge. The van parked facing back to the main road to ensure a quick getaway should they need to. The rear doors were opened and two expert drone operators emerged from the back and readied their flying equipment.

"I want eyes as close to the bridge as possible. We need confirmation the target is there and we must not miss this time," Toad had relayed to the team on the ground.

"Understood," came the brief reply from the drone lead. Lifting off the ground they set off over the water towards Lady Bay, aware that beyond, across the city, the sky was littered now with police helicopters and air ambulances. It was against the backdrop of the sirens sounding out continuously as the real police searched for the target too.

Next to the van, a third sleeper set up her sniper rifle. She had been trained by the Russian military and had a terrific ability at long range. Moving her right eye towards the scope she was already able to see people moving towards a small shed several hundred yards away on the other side of the river, further downstream. A few minutes later the drone operator confirmed the PM was indeed present as he had been spied coming back out of the doorway. Eying the once well suited, but now rather shabby looking PM, she had breathed slowly out, squeezing the trigger, firing her shot without hesitation. She was about to become infamous for assassinating the leader of the UK.

"You fucking missed," spat the drone operator as he viewed the close up action from his vantage point in the sky. "What the f ..." he suddenly shouted in anger as he realised his drone was being attacked and taken out the sky. "Shoot that son of a bitch," he shouted at the sniper. Squeezing her trigger a second time just as the new target had lifted his leg to crush the fallen drone. She couldn't remember the last time she had missed twice in succession.

As the second drone went down, Toad was shouting obscenities down the line as he watched it all unfold before him.

"Get round there now and close them out before they escape again."

The van took off at speed, racing over Trent Bridge to find a way to get their target back.

They could track the car anywhere, but now the PM had dumped his mobile, it would be harder. They had to find out who the person was helping the PM.

Sloth2000 had just hacked the government database. "His name is Lee Bevan. Lives down Radcliffe Road in

Tracking

West Bridgford. Sending details through now. I'll locate his mobile number as soon as I can."

Toad smiled. "Coming to get you Mr Bevan. I'd like to pay you back for the trouble you have caused."

He moved his hand across his throat to signal to the team that Lee should be terminated as soon as possible.

Chapter Fourteen
Just Cause

Irm had been busy since departing the COBRA meeting. Her instinct had served her well in crisis situations previously. She mobilised her team to find known critics of the PM with international connections to fundamentalist and any other possible terror groups. Those who may have the capability, and lack of humanity, to carry out such an attack.

Undoubtedly, Barnaby upset many people in the run up to gaining power and certainly since taking office. He'd been resolute in his stance on immigration, with a derisory attack on those who were less fortunate in life. His view of the European Union autocrats and their stubborn approach to Britain's negotiation to exit from the EU, had riled him massively. He'd almost seemed hellbent on destroying all links to the 'lap dogs' of Brussels as he referred to them. Instilled was a steely determination to see it fall on its knees and stop the 'rape of the resources from Britain.' Wasn't that quote taken directly from Trump?

There were many European Country, and Business Leaders, who would want to see Barnaby 'move on'. Motive was not difficult to establish. It was whether they could do something like *this* that was the question they needed to answer.

"What have we got?" she enquired quietly of her team of analysts across the light open office, sun streaming through the large windows.

"Well Chief ... there are several groups that we believe could have carried this out. The usual ones including the British Muslim Movement and of course ISIS. But at this stage we have no reason to believe they are responsible," responded a young man wearing thick rimmed glasses. He looked away as he mentioned the British Muslim Movement, uncomfortable to hold the gaze of his boss.

"Why not?" came the curt reply.

"There has been no intelligence from any of those groups and we have resources well placed to feed us that kind of information. Their members are well known to us and it is highly unlikely that they'd have been able to place sleepers in our police without us picking something up."

"Ok. So who is behind it?"

"We believe this is likely to be a new organisation that is starting to operate from the fracturing European Union. There are several that are operating now from Germany, Italy and of course, Spain. However, there is a hard-line, pro-European group with eastern European connections, who believe they have a lot to lose should the EU fail. Our intelligence suggests they are pretty pissed that Barnaby is closing our borders and trying to prevent free movement of people. At this stage, little is known about them and we certainly don't know who leads them. They operate remotely, mostly via the dark web, with links in many countries, including Hungary, Poland, Bulgaria, Romania and the Ukraine."

"What intelligence do we have?" Irm's questions were short and to the point, but her tone and pace did not change. She had an amazing ability to remain calm and focussed. Don't get distracted with emotion. Keep to the facts.

"At the moment very little. Several months ago, we picked up some traffic on line. Coded, that took us a long time to crack. Cipher we haven't seen before. It came out of Hungary and appeared to be some kind of instructions." He looked at his screen more intently and relayed the few short messages that were displayed:

Everything is in place
It has to end. Our financial security is threatened
Sunday 11am, NG. Mobilise the connections
The Puppy must be put to sleep, Toad

The group exchanged quizzical glances. "Have you established their meanings?" enquired Irm.

"We think there are some obvious elements. "*Everything is in place*" said Glasses, now pointing to a screen at the front of the office, all eyes transfixed. "If it is related to this incident, suggests that they have all the plans laid up, resources in position, bomb primed and they are ready to go. Presumably they have also been able to confirm the prime ministers movements."

"Go on," waved Irm, moving her hair from her eyes and reaching for more hot coffee.

"*It has to end. Our financial security is threatened* is kind of obvious," suggested another member of the team. An older man, sporting a neatly clipped beard, tattoos covering his exposed forearms. "That has to be in relation to the approach that the PM is now taking

Just Cause

with the EU. Closing the ports, preventing movement of people, reducing or annihilating, trade with other European countries. We know there are some concerned wealth creators, making noises in eastern Europe, who can sense their life blood being stemmed. Maybe they want to take decisive action to retain those channels of business." It was a bold leap of faith, but not impossible for the others to follow.

"*Sunday 11am, NG.* We can clearly see a link here that was not obvious before. Sunday 11am is the time the bomb exploded and we know the PM should have been stood exactly over the device. Given that *NG* is the postcode for Nottingham, it now seems highly likely to me that we have some connections here to what has happened this morning." Glasses, pushed them back up his nose, tapping the screen intently, the veins in his temples starting to pulse with increasing vigour. Irm, leant forward on her elbows, clasping her hands together over the desk.

"So, *The Puppy must be put to sleep,* is how they are describing the plan to kill the prime minister? Seems innocuous on its own. People have to put puppies down all the time. Is *Toad* the code name for whoever is behind this?" Irm looked around the room enquiringly with her gaze.

It was Tatoos who answered. "We aren't sure at the moment" he started slowly, holding her gaze. "It would seem logical, but we don't have anything else we can reference at this stage. It may be what they called the prime minister, or *The Puppy*. There is no intelligence we are aware of, on anyone referred to as Toad."

Irm, pushed her chair back from her table and stood up, walking towards the front of the room. She was asserting her authority in her usual calm way. The team knew it was time for them to listen.

"Ok. I want all the intelligence you can find on eastern European terrorist groups. Everything you can gather regarding trade routes that might be cut off with the prime ministers current position. Those who have most to lose, I want names, business ventures and connections to the underworld." Her eyes fixed everyone around the room, individually imploring them not to fail her.

"I want to know of any other references, coded or otherwise, to *The Puppy*, that have been made over the last two years. This kind of hit takes a while to plan and we have to assume that whoever is behind it, has connections everywhere." Irm was in her element now. "They appear to have been able to place operatives in our bloody armed police force to enable this to happen. I want to know everyone involved in clearance of the armed officers, trained and recruited, in the last two years. I want to know the names of all armed police officers on deployment in Nottingham today. Who were the rogue officers that appeared to have fired on the PM from the roof that we can't locate? Start with the two dead ones that Paul Buxton managed to eliminate."

After pacing the room a little, she retook her seat. "If we can establish connections, it may lead us to whoever *Toad* is."

Her finger was tapping on the table, in time with her speech. "We have to find those responsible for this atrocity. The future of the UK depends on us right here, right now. If we can determine those that had just cause, we will find those responsible. In time, it may be clear that our actions not only led to catching those responsible, but preventing the UK going to war. We cannot afford to fail. Those intent on this cause of action must be held to account." Irm chose her words carefully now, determined to inspire positive action from those around her. She knew there were some recently who were starting to question her authority.

Not because of her ability, but because of the colour of her skin.

"Oh! And one final thing," exclaimed Irm, "isn't the Mayor of Nottingham Polish? It may be nothing, but bring him in for questioning. We need to establish if there is any possibility of a connection between him and this event." She pushed back her chair, rose and walked out the office without looking behind her.

Glasses and Tatoos looked across the office at each.

Why hadn't they spotted that?

Chapter Fifteen
The Arboretum

The car slowed down and pulled into the small parking area just above the gardens. Dan turned the engine off and twisted to look at Nicky. There were a few other cars randomly scattered around, waiting for their owners to return from their latest adventures.

"You sure this is where you told him about Aidan?" he enquired, looking left and right.

"No," snapped Nicky, "But it's the only place I can think of. I think we came for a walk after lunch and I had the test in my pocket. It must be, but I just can't think straight." She undid her seatbelt and reached for the door handle as Dan touched her elbow.

"I'll come with you," Dan uttered reassuringly. Nicky nodded back at him, not wanting to be left alone. They climbed out and scanned the car park. She couldn't see Lee's car so started to walk towards the garden entrance, Dan striding alongside her. The flow of tears stemmed for now and she had calmed down very slightly, adrenaline starting to taper off.

Striding towards the main bandstand at the top of the hill, her gaze was drawn out across the city. There were some lovely views of Nottingham from up here. Or at least there would be if it weren't for the activity of the

The Arboretum

helicopters circling in the distance. Sirens still sounding out sporadically across the streets. Her knowledge of the mindless murder that had erupted on the Old Market Square earlier in the day, completed a dark and foreboding image. It was contrasting with the memory of warm, sunny days of summer, with heat hazes twisting the air.

Her pace gathering, she headed straight for the metal structure. Its copper covered dome had tarnished over the years, stripping it of its once grandiose appearance. There was no band playing today and although the clouds had broken and the wind died down, the leaves were starting to turn colour on the trees surrounding the outside of the park. Curling up, as the fauna prepared for autumn. Warmth was returning to the day, but the striking colours, deep crimson reds, greens turning yellow, reminded everyone that the last days of summer were leaving them fast.

"They're not here," she exclaimed. "I can't see them ... where are they?"

A sense of urgency, desperation, in her voice. Dan looked around, walking right around the outside of the stand to ensure they weren't concealed by one of the uprights somehow. As he came back to her, he noticed some movement over to the left hand side, where small laurel hedges lined the neatly cut grass. The leaves parted slightly and someone peered through the thick bush, straight towards them.

Dan caught Nicky's hand and beckoned her towards the bush. They walked slowly, unsure who was the other side, but convinced it would be Lee, Aidan and possibly the prime minister in tow.

"Thank God!" exclaimed a relieved Lee from the other side of the hedge, before he stood, looking Nicky straight in the eye. She stood frozen on the spot, gazing at his dishevelled appearance, transfixed by his forlorn look.

"Where is Aidan? Is he OK?" she started sobbing, tears cascading down her cheeks.

"He's here, he's fine love," Lee bent down, concealed again by the hedgerow and when he reappeared, Aidan was clinging to his side.

"My baby ... Aidan," she blubbered, pushing her way through the hedge to claw her son from his father's side. Lee passed him over, knowing his mother was where he wanted to be. Aidan reached for her, needing the reassurance of her soft stroking hands and the warmth of her embrace. Lee naturally leant forward and put his arms round his son and estranged wife.

He felt her tense. Standing up straight he moved back towards the shadows.

"Man, are you OK?" Dan took his old friend in his arms and gave him the support he needed. Lee felt his emotions beginning to stir. He couldn't remember the last time someone had hugged him other than Aidan. He'd had to be the strong one since all this had kicked off this morning. Strong for his boy, strong for the prime minister, strong to survive. As his lungs sucked in air, his chest heaved and he felt a wave of relief surge through him. He was no longer doing this, whatever this was, on his own. Lee gripped Dan tight, pulling him closer and patting him on the back as he felt the tears stream down his face.

"Good to see you Dan. Thanks for bringing Nicky. It's been crazy. I can't say much because it freaks Aidan out, but presumably you've seen the news."

It wasn't a question. Lee had composed himself and was realising that they were not out of danger. Wiping the tears from his face, he left grey smears down his cheeks from the dirt that had been battering him throughout the day.

Lee turned around and introduced the prime minister who was lying quietly on the ground observing a family and an old friend reunion. He'd noticed the awkward interaction between Lee and Nicky, as they both realised the other was OK and yet, of course, they weren't supposed to care. Sharing a child meant you never really let go of your partner completely. Love and hate. Both deeply held, guttural emotions. If it hadn't been for the fact this reunion was taking place under the bushes, in the old gardens of the Arboretum in Nottingham, where they were hiding from the madness of the world, it would have filled him with joy.

Lee turned towards Barnaby and started to speak. "This is my wi ... Aidan's mum, Nicky, and my best friend Dan. I think you know who this is," exclaimed Lee, gesturing back towards Barnaby Aitken.

Nicky looked uncomfortable as she moved towards the Prime Minister to shake his hand.

"Very nice to meet you Nicky. Your son is a rather remarkable young boy," he said, wincing in pain as he moved his body upwards to shake her hand. "And your husband, Lee, has saved my life on more than one occasion today. I can't thank him enough."

Nicky was breathing deeply, cheeks red from the sting of fresh tears and slightly embarrassed at meeting the leader of the UK in such bizarre circumstances. "Hello" she spoke softly, reaching out a hand whilst wiping her face with the back of her other. "You look hurt Mr Aitken. Let me take a look." Before Barnaby could respond, Nicky was on bended knee, examining his wounds.

"Nicky is a nurse Sir," explained Lee, before continuing. "A second generation, French immigrant nurse, Prime Minister …" he left it hanging in the air without further explanation. Nicky shot him a look to make sure he said no more, the whole situation was awkward enough as it was. The prime minister already felt uncomfortable in the hedgerow, before Lee introduced that to the mix. He dropped his gaze, but repeated "It's still very nice to meet you Nicky."

Nicky had no hint of a French accent, so no-one would know of her French ancestry. Her mother's family had moved here and were, for all intents and purposes, English. Although her mother had been called Jenny, it was short for Genevieve. Nicky could not even speak French.

"Nice to meet you Mr Prime Minister" said Dan, flustered under the circumstances. "You all look like you have been in a war zone," he continued. "It looked terrible on the TV. I can't imagine what it must have been like to be … to be there in person." His gaze flicked from Lee to the prime minister as Nicky bandaged the PM's ankle with a scarf from her bag to try and give him some support.

"Do you think this is about what you did yesterday Sir? Closing the ports?" Nicky shot him a glance through her hair, his foot still in her grip.

"Impossible to say at the moment," Barnaby winced through gritted teeth, the throbbing getting stronger with the handling. "If it is, it reinforces to me that we need to manage our borders more effectively and keep those hellbent on terrorism from coming in."

The Arboretum

"Forgive me Sir, but *not all* immigrants are terrorists," Nicky pulled tightly on her makeshift bandage making the prime minister contort his face whilst trying not to allow any noise to leave his lips.

"The NHS would collapse in a heartbeat without immigration. God knows it nearly has several times over the last few years. Most of my colleagues are from overseas. Talented professionals, caring for the sick, young and old. We shouldn't stop everyone coming here because of the mindless acts of violence of a few. If that's your view, we should kick half the Brits out as well!" she exclaimed, her tone full of intolerance with the bigot in her care.

Lee and Dan both looked on a little uncomfortable at the tension building in the bushes around them.

"What do we do sir? Where do we take you, or who do we call?" Dan jumped in to rescue them from the awkwardness.

"I am not sure where you should take me, as I don't even know if the local police are secure. Indeed, I think it safest for all of you, if you leave me and I will call my head of security, Paul Buxton. He'll make the necessary arrangements to have me extracted as soon as possible," Barnaby looked directly at Dan as he spoke.

"Sir, we can't leave you here on your own. That's just not going to happen." Lee retorted quickly. "Nicky can take Aidan away from here to safety with Dan and I'll stick with you to make sure you are Ok. You can't even walk properly on your own." Lee gestured towards the newly strapped ankle. Nicky was nodding in agreement, wrestling with the torment of her son's safety over that of the prime minister.

"That sounds sensible," quivered Nicky's soft voice. "We can't leave you all alone Mr Aitken."

Dan was nodding in agreement as well. "I'll take Nicky home, make sure her and Aidan are Ok. Call me if there is anything else that comes up or you need me to come back and get you both. Take you somewhere else maybe."

"It's Ok, I have my car nearby," replied Lee. He pulled out his mobile. "Bugger! My phone is nearly out of battery and I have no charger with me," he held it up to the others to inspect. Dan reached for his own and passed it to Lee. "Take mine. Pass code is 135790, it's almost full so should last a while for you." Lee nodded his thanks and exchanged it for his own.

A soft voice made them all look round. "Dad," called Aidan, wiping more tears from his face. "Come with us Dad. Please come with us." Aidan's gaze lifted to his father's face as Lee took his young boy in his arms again and hugged him tight.

"Hey, don't worry Aidan. We'll be Ok. I have to get Mr Aitken here to the hospital so someone can have a good look at that ankle for him. I'll be home before you know it and maybe I can even put you to bed tonight. If Mummy will let me?" He glanced upwards to Nicky, who nodded slowly, choking back a lump in her throat. Reaching out her arms to Aidan again, he moved towards her as Lee squeezed his shoulder.

"Come on young man," said Dan as he scooped Aidan into his arms and all three turned to look at Lee and Barnaby.

"Stay safe Lee" said Nicky, gazing into his eyes. She moved forward and kissed him gently on the cheek. "Thank you," she whispered gently. "Good bye Sir," she held out her hand to shake with the prime minister, "Good luck."

The Arboretum

"Thank you, Aidan," smiled Barnaby, "You've been an amazing young man."

Aidan nodded, then waved gently to his new friend. Then they turned to head back towards Dan's car. Lees instinct kicked in as he felt fear course through his veins, causing him to call after them. "Dan, could I take your car? They ..." he stuttered, "I think they know what I'm driving." His eyes locked into Dans imploring him for a positive response.

Dan turned back towards him as Nicky shook her head in disbelief. "Oh! My God. How ... What the hell is happening?" Tears ran silently down her cheek again.

"Of course mate. We'll call an Uber or something. They aren't looking for us. We'll be fine." Dan reluctantly handed over the keys to his pride and joy, a blue Lexus GS. "Take care of it fella, you know that's my baby!"

They turned and headed towards the main road, Nicky dialled for the driverless taxi to come and pick them up. Ubers latest business model of their driverless car technology was starting to catch on. People couldn't quite let go of the control aspect of their own cars, but if you needed a taxi, sometimes having one without a driver was a blessing in disguise. Particularly if you didn't want someone to see you, engage with you and possibly remember you. If people came asking.

Lee couldn't help but wonder if that might be the last time he would ever see the love of his life. And their son.

Chapter Sixteen

Questions

In the space of only a few hours, mobile units had already been established to deal with the immediate aftermath of the bomb in the city centre. Hundreds of legitimate, on and off duty police officers, fire fighters, ambulance crews, paramedics, GPs, surgeons and other medical personnel had swarmed to the Market Square. Like ants rushing to defend their own nest when it was under attack from predators.

Over fifty percent of them were non-British nationals. Working professionally. Empathetically. Resilient and caring.

Cordons were put in place with tape, marked "Crime Scene". The public and press were moved back from the perimeter of the initial blast. Makeshift tents erected with some lighting and limited medical equipment, enabling those that could not be shifted by ambulance to hospital, to be treated. It gave an element of privacy from onlookers keen to capture more suffering on their mobiles. Live personal broadcasts to the public, slaking their thirst for drama and violence.

Inside the tents, it was reminiscent of a scene from the field hospitals of a war zone. The screech of pain sounded like animals being tortured. Blood covering almost every

Questions

surface, smeared across the mottled skin of those injured and those helping. Gashed heads. Limbs missing. Flesh torn from bone. Ligaments and muscle hanging. Wooden splinters protruding from those clinging to life by fine, gossamer threads.

Agony was evident. Morphine couldn't flow fast enough through plastic tubes, piercing veins, dripping into blood streams to relieve the suffering. Euphoria washed over them as sedation took them quickly to more pleasant lands.

With volunteers helping wherever they could, the authorities moved to regain control. It was becoming a very fast moving investigation that went all the way to the top of the British Intelligence. Irm's team worked quickly to establish who could be trusted in the local police force in Nottingham. Secure lines of communication had been established and already the local police had taken in the Mayor of Nottingham, Bolek Kumiega, for questioning.

The two dead uniformed police officers from the shopping centre had been fingerprinted, their blood sent for DNA analysis and facial recognition run. They had nothing on either of them, other than some very ordinary police background checks of 'ordinary or family man, dedicated to upholding the law ...' Both of them seemed to have completely unblemished pasts.

"The first is a thirty-two year old, white male, of Belgian descent, according to his employment record with the police. Moved to the UK in 2020, joined up in 2021, after many years serving in the Belgian Army. Name is Lucas Jacobs and he was a first class soldier with an exemplary record. Passed all the relevant checks to join the police force. Never married and no children as far as they knew. He was clean. Almost too clean" Tattoos updated the team. "The second victim died from a shot to the chest …"

"Let's hope it bloody hurt before he died," interjected Glasses.

"Indeed," retorted Tattoos, before resuming. "As far as we know he is a family man, lived in Mapperley, with a wife and young daughter. His name was Fabian Pichler. Again, early thirties, moved to the UK in 2016, from Austria. Vienna specifically. Nothing in his background came up that would cause alarm. Trained in Computer Science in France at the *Ecole Normale Supérieure, Paris*" he tried in a poor French accent. "Appears to have joined the police in Nottingham just after the start of 2017 after signing up originally as a Community Support Officer." Looking up from his screen, he noticed Irm gazing out the window whilst he talked.

Her gaze turned towards him. "Have his wife and daughter picked up immediately. I want them in custody and grilled to see what they know. I agree with you, there is something amiss here. Two exemplary records don't suddenly assassinate the prime minister, or anybody for that matter, unless they have some underlying psychosis. It would be unusual for one in the armed police, without them being identified before it got too serious. It's bloody impossible for two in the same unit I would think. Who are they really? Pichler can't have been planning something like this without his family knowing anything. I want both their houses turned inside out. There has to be something to help us establish a motive.

"I thought you said earlier on that you thought this may be a group connected with eastern Europe? Belgium is not in eastern Europe. Admittedly Austria is

Questions

closer, but even that's not classed as eastern. What's the connection?"

"Not sure yet Ma'am," offered Glasses meekly, turning his attention back to his own screen.

"Well find out quickly. What links these lowlifes together? Who else were they working with, because clearly there were more than two. On the TV, it looked like at least six were chasing after the prime minister and that young man and his son. What was his name?" she asked.

"Lee Bevan lives in West Bridgford. The ground team have been to his flat Ma'am. No sign of him or the PM. His place had been ransacked. Whoever is behind this, presumably found out who he was faster than we did."

Irm turned to look at him, shaking her head in disbelief. "How the hell ..." she started.

"Neighbours are being spoken to in case they saw anything, but given what is unfolding today, they may choose to stay quiet, even if they did see something. His car is not there and we have flagged it for pick up an all automatic number plate recognition cameras and CCTV across the city. They seem to have disappeared right now, although we do know there were reports of shots fired outside the football ground a while ago now. It's on the other side of the River Trent to where they went under the Lady Bay Bridge and we believe it may be connected. The team is looking into it. The last pick up we had of the car on CCTV was on the other side of the river."

Glasses then nodded at Tatoos and gestured towards their boss.

"Ma'am, you should know that all CCTV has stopped working. About fifty minutes ago..." he began.

"What do you mean stopped working? Across the whole of the city? That's impossible!" Irm was starting to disbelieve everything she was being told.

"Yes Ma'am, we believe it's across the whole of Nottingham. It's unlikely to be a malfunction, much more likely to have been infiltrated. Hacked Ma'am. The team are trying to establish how and regain control of the cameras as a matter of urgency," explained Tatoos.

The pressure was rising in the room. They could feel the heat increasing all around them. Operating blind and others trying to reach the prime minister before them was not a good position to be.

"Get me Marcus Poole, let's see if they've had more luck than us. We need to work with them on this, though it pains me to say so. Tell me at least, that the fucking Mayor is in custody?"

It was the first time ever that her team had heard her swear. It stopped them in their tracks.

"Yes Ma'am. Bolek Kumiega has been taken in for questioning. The IT guys are busy trying to re-establish control of the CCTV and we'll keep you updated."

Irm strutted out of the office towards the coffee machine. She needed a fix and she needed it quick. The room breathed a sigh of temporary relief behind her.

At the Central Police Station on Maid Marion Way, Bolek Kumiega sat at a table with his head in his hands. Across the table, two suited detectives opened files and flicked through photos and videos on the iPad in front of them.

"What the hell happened out there?" the first looked up from the iPad. "Our Prime Minister narrowly avoided death, whilst in your presence, and now he is missing. He seems to be on the run, with our own local police

Questions

force intent on taking him out. We need some answers Bolek and we need them quickly." He passed the screen over the table for Bolek to see the footage of the PM walking out over the stage before events started to unfold.

Bolek raised his head from his hands, shaking it in disbelief. "I don't know, it all happened so fast," he started, in exceptional English, coated in his native Polish accent. His eyes never left the screen as he watched the Prime Minister lean over towards the crowd. A flash of light exploded in the corner of the screen and the camera shook, losing its focus. As the operator recovered from the shock of the blast and searched the scene for the prime minister, Bolek's eyes widened. He hadn't seen the footage before and it was a disaster zone.

The second detective stopped the footage. "Why weren't you outside with the Prime Minister?"

"What? Erm, one of my team called me as we were about to walk out from the Council House. I stopped to answer him and Mr Aitken carried on outside, on his own." His hands were remarkably steady as he moved them down towards the table.

"What was so important, that it stopped you being with the prime minister at the precise time the bomb exploded?" growled the second detective, already convinced that the Polish Mayor was inextricably linked to these events.

"Um ... they asked me if the prime minister's wife was going to be joining for dinner in the afternoon. We were of the understanding that Mrs Aitken was supposed to be attending the event as well. There must have been a miscommunication, so I told them we would continue without her. I then went to follow the prime minister outside. As I did, I could see he was off to the side and as I was about to step outside ..." his voice trailed off. Bolek moved his hands upwards and outwards, "Boom!" He looked down at the table again, a sad look on his face. "It was carnage. There was screaming and dust everywhere. It was difficult to see anything, or make anyone out specifically."

"Why did you not go to the aid of the prime minister?"

"I did not know where he was. I er, I was ... afraid." Bolek hung his head down, as if ashamed at his actions.

The first detective put another screen in Bolek's line of sight. "You see what concerns me," he said, "is the way you reacted to the whole thing." He pressed play and a second camera angle picked up the Mayor of Nottingham.

It showed Bolek standing in the entrance to the Council House. He looked at his watch and seemed to hesitate. Before he could take a step forward, the hidden bomb exploded. The camera shook and moved quickly over the scene of the explosion. As the controller of the camera had regained his composure and seemingly failed to locate the prime minister in his search, they had swung it back towards the Mayor of Nottingham. Bolek Kumiega had remained in exactly same spot. He appeared remarkably composed, looking out across the stage.

The detective stopped the video playing and tapped the screen.

"You see to me, that looked like you checked your watch and deliberately did not follow the prime minister. It was almost as if you knew what was about to happen. Did you?" asked the detective leaning across the table towards Bolek.

Questions

"No ... No, I didn't" came the reply, Bolek shaking his head in disbelief.

"I don't believe you. You know why I don't believe you?" he continued.

"Because I am a Polish immigrant who became the Mayor of Nottingham," replied Bolek, looking straight into the detectives eyes.

"That's a good reason, but it's not THE reason," he exclaimed. Tapping the screen, he continued. "There, that's why I don't believe you. Because you are looking right at the prime minister. You can see him from where you are standing. You can see he is hurt and yet, you do nothing to help. You turn around and walk back into the safety of the Council House. What I want to know, is why?"

The second detective had stood and walked behind Bolek, making him feel very uneasy. Bolek looked around, turning in his seat, then turning back and pointing at the recording device in the room. "Why are you not recording this interview? I should have a solicitor present," he said gruffly.

"We don't have fucking time for that," spat the first detective, back across the table, "Somebody tried to kill the prime minister and he is still missing, being hunted by the people who are behind all this. We need answers and we need them now."

Bolek shook his head and looked back down at the table. "I told you. I was afraid and I did not recognise the Prime Minister after the blast. I could hear gunfire. It was awful ..." he began.

The detective behind him could restrain himself no more and rushed at Bolek from behind, pulling his head back and smashing it down on the table. "Don't mess with us Bolek" he spat in disgust. "Tell us who is behind this and where the fuck the prime minister is. If you don't cooperate quickly, you will regret that decision."

Bolek lifted his head from the table, feeling the blood ooze from above his left eye. "What the hell are you doing? I don't know what happened and I don't know who is behind this," his voice wavering as he spoke.

The first detective leaned back in his chair and examined his own watch. As the second detective pulled his head back again, Bolek grimaced and put his hands out this time to try and stop another impact with the table.

Law and order was definitely losing its way.

Chapter Seventeen

Internal Affairs

Helen Langley was back at her desk, keeping a close eye on the reports of her press briefing. It had been hard. Lots of questions from concerned and, for once, frightened reporters.

Not since the Brighton bombings in the early 1980's had there been a direct attack on the British Government. The media were having a feeding frenzy.

"How could the Prime Minister have gone missing? Was this incompetence of MI5 and MI6?" from *The Independent*.

"Do you know who is behind this? Has it been claimed by any terrorist organisation? ..." and so, it went on. The final question nearly threw her off course.

"Is this a declaration of war?" asked the journalist from *The Huffington Post*.

"At this stage we cannot confirm that." Helen's ice cool stare never broke from the journalist. For the rest of the press briefing she had given short answers, not speculating at all on areas where they had no intelligence. "No comment at this stage ... as you will appreciate, it's our main priority to locate the Prime Minister and ensure his safe return ... We ask the public to remain calm and vigilant."

It went on for around twenty minutes. Camera flashes firing constantly. Reporters normally quite calm, yet looking smug, were writing and typing furiously. Shouting over the top of each other, desperate for their question to be heard. Helen was feeding the sharks with live bait, from the safety of a small aluminium cage dropped in the water. They smelt blood from several miles off and rushed in to join the kill.

They had to wait though. Without faltering at all, Helen completed the briefing without showing any signs of distress, or nervousness. Some would later say it was the display of a future prime minister. Unflustered, even though she was dealing the worst possible scenario.

Her office was no respite from the frenzy though, as people were in and out, updating her on events since the Cobra meeting had finished. The prime minister's wife was secure, still at Chequers with her security detail doubled and the surrounding area on lockdown. Barnaby's daughters and their families had been located and were on their way to secure locations.

The phone rang on her desk and Langley snatched it up to her left ear. "Yep? Ok. Send them in please."

The oak door swung inwards and Mike Lightfoot, Barnaby's personal secretary, walked in just in front of the Head of MI5, Marcus Poole.

"Well done Helen, you handled that mob brilliantly," congratulated Mike as he extended his hand. "They're a nightmare at the best of times, like rabid dogs, ready to tear you apart in a split second. But today ... I've never seen them behave like that before."

"Hmm. Thank you Mike. I guess it's an unprecedented time. I hope you have some good news for me?" Helen enquired as they all sat around her desk.

Internal Affairs

"I understand we have lost control of the CCTV cameras, so we're operating blind. Couple that with Barnaby ditching his mobile and we have very little to help us here. I understand he called you Mike?"

"Yes. It was a brief conversation. He said he was Ok, explained where he was, so we dispatched the team to go get him. Unfortunately, I think they came under attack again and by the time the SAS got there, no sign of them."

The SAS had been deployed to the streets of Nottingham and it was they, that had gone to the home of Lee Bevan in West Bridgford. To Helen's knowledge, not since 1980 had the SAS been deployed on the streets of the UK. Terrorists took twenty-six hostages at gunpoint inside the Iranian embassy in South Kensington. Six days later, it was bought to a dramatic end when the SAS dramatically stormed the building, under operation Nimrod, as it was broadcast live across the globe. An operation that resulted in millions of school children re-enacting the scene in playgrounds across the country for weeks, as small children dreamt of becoming masked heroes.

Helen Langley was barely walking at that time and certainly did not remember the events herself, but she was well aware of the historic use of the SAS on home soil. If they had been utilized on the streets of the UK since then, she had certainly not been made aware of it.

Initially, they had been dropped by helicopter at the Lady Bay bridge. The place that Barnaby had described to Mike Lightfoot. They found the shed, bullet holes in the door frame and the smashed drone lying on the floor outside, cameras wrecked from the battering Lee had given it. Blood spots were found inside and they knew this was the right place. They were just too late. A van picked them up and they headed across the bridge towards the only other place they had a lead on at this stage.

Finding the home of Lee ransacked, the SAS called it in and took to the road. The report of the shooting, just back up the road near Trent Bridge, was presumably the shots fired at the PM and his saviours. With little else to go on at this stage they headed for it.

Five men and one woman. Highly trained. Killers.

"Any idea what the hell is going on Marcus?" she redirected her gaze.

"At this stage it's very difficult to say. There are a couple of the usual suspects who are claiming responsibility for the attack. However, it's not their usual *modus operandi* and the two bodies we have, courtesy of Paul, have no connections to them that we can tell."

Marcus, opened a briefing folder in front of him and took out some pictures of the two from the shopping centre, presenting them to Helen. "We have a Belgian with an exemplary record as far as we can tell, by the name of Lucas Jacobs. Lived alone, ex Belgian armed forces. The second is a family man from Austria, Fabian Pichler. Local police are on the way to his home to pick up the family. Both houses will be torn apart to see what we can find."

"Any speculation on motive?" Helen looked up from the folders at both men in turn.

"There is a feeling that this could be related to the stance Barnaby has taken on Europe. The hard line he has had with them recently, following the '*Soft BREXIT*' debacle the bloody Tories insisted on. Many don't like it, we know that much. Barnaby has received a lot of abuse about his stance. But of course, he also got voted in because of that same stance" offered up Mike.

"Marcus?" Helen shifted her gaze.

"Well, it's plausible. There are plenty of people with motive at the approach the government has taken." He was careful not to single out Barnaby. "Many political and business leaders have been climbing over each other to highlight the detrimental effect of the UK closing its borders completely. That goes for those in the UK as well outside of it. Although we had the transition period ahead of the complete pull out, it meant for many that nothing changed. Now you finally pulled the plug," he looked at Helen, "I am sure there are many that can see their livelihoods, careers they have worked hard to build, and possibly their homes, going up in smoke."

Helen observed Marcus as he spoke. She knew he would be honest about this, hiding his personal opinion on the matter, lest it cloud his judgement.

"Closing the borders was possibly a step too far that may have pushed them, whoever they are, over the edge. But, given the planning and sophisticated attack we are seeing, this will have taken months to plan effectively, so I don't believe it's a kneejerk reaction to such draconian measures." His eyes never left Helen's as he spoke.

"Have your intelligence teams seriously not picked anything up in the last few hours that will lead us to the bastards responsible for this?" Her voice remained calm, but Marcus could tell she meant business.

"All sorts of things are coming up Helen. Smokescreens often. The teams are working under intense pressure to get this resolved and the prime minister located safely, as soon as possible. Extra agents have been drafted in.

Thousands of hours of surveillance videos, suspects movements, e-mail and mobile traffic to sift, code to decipher and undercover resources to link up with. It's an enormous amount to wade through, coupled with random calls from members of the public telling us their *'foreign neighbour is acting suspiciously'* and can we *'look into it'*. Nobody trusts anyone right now and the government, quite frankly, are the cause of that Helen." Marcus held her gaze.

"Ok. Work with Irm …"

Marcus' head dropped at the mention of her name.

"Put your differences to one side Marcus and get me some answers as quickly as you can. That's not a request." Helen stood, indicating their meeting was over.

"Do you trust her? I mean really trust her?" asked Marcus, already knowing the answer.

"Yes. Absolutely. Without question. She may be of Indian descent, but Irm has been a first class leader of MI6. Work with her. Understand?"

He had not always been against working with her.

Their work had bought them close together. So close in fact, that they ended up as passionate lovers. Irm worked in his team many years ago, when he became mesmerised by her. Often lost in the moment and unable to make clear decisions around her, it had started to impact on his results. His previous good character, judgement, sharp mind and dedication to the cause was not quickly forgotten though. He promised to leave his wife for her, but suddenly a promotion he'd sought for a long time came his way.

It came with conditions. Given it was the secret service, everyone in the department knew it had been going on. The most difficult part had been keeping it from his wife. The ultimatum he'd been given, forced him to make a choice. Marcus Poole, then in his mid-forties knowing a chance like this would never come his way again, chose his wife and his career, over Irm.

It broke Irm for a short while. The affair had distracted her from a career she had been building for herself. No longer under the watch and care of the man she had fallen for, Irm focussed back on rebuilding a name for herself. A move sideways out of the British intelligence service to the foreign intelligence office enabled her to make a fresh start. Ignoring any personal or social life, she spent five years handling undercover operatives in all corners of the world. Changing their identities. Passing high level intelligence on to various security services, and in some cases the country's leaders. Irm had lost count of the potential coups, civil wars and possibly even full scale wars, that she and her team had helped to prevent. Small pieces of information, names, dates, locations and times passed to the local security services, who swooped in time to prevent murder, treason and anarchy.

No recognition externally. No glory in the public eye. Irm not only served the UK, but served large sections of the world. Her skill and demeanour eventually landed her the top job: Head of MI6.

Opposite her old lover, Marcus Poole. Head of MI5.

"Irm hates you. Hates the English Independence Party and everything you all stand for. She thinks you are all racist bastards and will remove her from her role at the first opportunity you have. Not only that, but you know she doesn't like me and I can't imagine she will want to start working with me now," retorted Marcus, standing up himself and leaning over the desk towards Helen, to look her straight in the eye.

"Well, that's a problem you created Marcus," said Helen focusing on the second part of his statement. "You'd better find a way to work with her and do it quickly. I need to go and update the deputy PM on what's been happening." As she moved towards the doorway, she stopped and turned. "Remind me of the code name we used for this kind of scenario?"

"Big Ben," answered Marcus. "The prime minister is Big Ben. Anything to do with him being attacked, targeted or blackmailed." Marcus picked up the folder and left the room, leaving Mike alone with Helen.

The door swung shut with a soft thud. Mike stepped towards it sensing it was time for him to depart.

"You Ok Mike? I know you are very close to Barnaby, this must be traumatic for you." Helen reached out to embrace Mike now they were alone.

"It is. Thanks. Is there anything I can do to help?" responded Mike, nodding his head rhythmically.

"If he gets in touch again, you let us know straight away," Helen stroked his arm affectionately. Mike froze. His arm stiffened and Helen sensed his unease. "What's up Mike?" she smiled warmly at him, tilting her head to one side. She had often heard that having power was an aphrodisiac. It certainly seemed to be turning her on right now, despite the fact that the country was in crisis.

"Nothing Helen. I'm fine. I'll let you know if I hear anything." He stepped away from her, turned and opened the door.

As Helen moved back towards her desk, he looked back at her. Did Helen just hit on him? He wasn't sure. But in this time of crisis, when you would think that she would have her mind full of more important and pressing issues, he was sure she just made a pass at him.

Times had definitely turned around from a few years ago.

He was flattered. She was attractive, of that there was no doubt. If he wasn't attached already, he might be interested.

But Mike was loyal; Mike, was very loyal.

Chapter Eighteen

Cameras

Dan had instructed the taxi to take them back to his house. The address was displayed on the screen at the front for them to accept. A monotone, but friendly female voice, came from the speakers in the doors of the cab. "Thank you for choosing Uber. Your taxi is ready to depart. Please fasten your seat belt."

Nicky buckled her son in to the centre seat and sat next to him with her arm around his shoulders, pulling him towards her and stroking his hair. "It's alright sweetheart, you're safe now," she cooed at him, tears still fresh on her own cheeks.

Dan turned back towards them and patted Aidan's knee as well, but kept quiet. He felt like an intruder, but Nicky needed the support. What a crazy day.

As they moved off, the electric car gliding into the traffic, keeping a fixed distance from the car in front, they all felt relief and gradually started to relax.

"We'll get you home Aidan, run you a bath and put your favourite show on TV. Maybe do you a hot chocolate hey?"

Dan smiled at him trying to warm his spirits. He looked down at Lee's mobile in his hand, only three per cent energy left, and a message displayed saying

'Emergency Calls Only' and laughed. 'Yeah right!' He showed the screen to Nicky "And who would we call?"

There wasn't enough energy to make a phone call. There was just enough however, for the phone to be located. If you knew how to look for it.

Not far from where they were, Sloth2000 had finally got the details on the phone number for Lee Bevan. Sloth retrieved it from a highly encrypted database, where millions of phone numbers from the largest network provider in the UK were located. Young, old, famous or insignificant nobodies. He could get them all.

'Your personal data security is our priority,' was the companies mission statement. It had taken Sloth just forty-two minutes to crack the algorithms that kept 'personal data secure'. Forty-two minutes. He was a highly autistic individual with a gift for numbers, patterns and solving problems. Years back, people wouldn't have known how to respond to him, he was so socially inept. These days, people paid lots of money to have him on their team.

Sloth2000 was not only capable of breaking into massive databases with the highest level of on-line security, but he could cover his own tracks very discreetly. No one had much chance of even knowing he had been there, unless they were looking very carefully, on purpose. From the US originally, Sloth had resided in Europe for the last few years as the FBI had been closing in on his identity after he made a mistake. He'd got careless, cocky possibly. He felt the only way he could escape that mistake was to leave his home and unsupportive family behind. Now he worked for the highest bidder at the time and he did not care what their cause was, or who might get hurt in the process. As long as he made money.

"They're moving, I have a signal." Sloth relayed to Toad.

"Good. Pick the car up on any street cameras it passes. I want to know exactly where it is and what direction its headed," spat Toad back at him.

"Locating the cameras now, relaying to the big screen. The signal is just coming up towards camera three six five." Their heads turned towards the big screen as they searched the oncoming cars for the white Nissan Qashqai.

"That's strange. It's not there and the signal has passed the camera, heading towards the next at the bottom of the hill ... Camera three six six....." Sloth ran his fingers through his thick dark beard and pulled at his left ear repeatedly. A tic from a young age. It helped him cope when he felt stressed.

"Zoom in all cars coming towards that camera," Toad inspected the screens in front of him again. This time he spotted a taxi, the Uber sign clearly identifying it from above, with a number on top of the car. "HaPee, get me eyes inside that Uber cab now."

A smile started to spread across Toads face. "Mr Bevan must have ditched his car and called himself a cab."

A few clicks on the keyboard in front of HaPee as Larry and another screen sprang to life. Three discrete security cameras hidden in the interior of the cab revealed crystal clear images from several angles of the occupants. As they switched between them, the images that appeared before them, showed them that inside the cab was not Lee Bevan and the prime minister as they had expected.

Cameras

Sloth, Toad and HaPee looked at each and then back at the screen. "Who the fuck is that?" growled Toad, looking up at his hackers.

It looked like a couple. A couple with a young boy.

Chapter Nineteen

Delivery

Armed police arrived at the end of the street just as darkness was falling. The temperature was dropping quickly, as the chill of an autumn evening started to make its presence felt. A stone's throw from the golf club, with the gloom descending, the last of the golfers had departed the fairways for the day.

The road was cordoned off at both ends, with police vans blocking the street leading out on to the main roads. Single file, they moved down the road. A delivery driver moved to the side, raising his hands to let them past as he walked back towards his van. The rest of the street was quiet. Families settling down for the night, surrounding their TVs to soak up the latest on the extraordinary events of the day in their own city. Sunday dinners eaten on the sofa. Eyes transfixed on the drama of the day, unaware of the ordinarily, unusual intrusion, right outside their own front doors.

Heavily protected officers, passed down the street quickly, counting the numbers until they arrived at number thirty-one. Coming from either side of the property, several of them moved towards the back of the house to ensure there was no escaping. This was the home of Fabian Pichler, the second assailant killed by

Delivery

Paul Buxton. They were here to pick up his family, take them for questioning, then send in the forensic team to pull the place apart.

Silently, they moved towards the front door, a man holding a metal battering ram, moving to the front of the team. Lights were coming from several of the windows and the curtains had not been pulled. They signalled each other by hand and listened intently. Nothing could be heard coming from within the building.

Stepping forward, he lifted the battering ram to swing for the door, right next to the frame. In the fading light he paused, noticing that the door was not quite closed. There was a very small gap, a shaft of light passing between the edge of the door and the wood against which it should firmly nestle. Signalling back to the lead officer, he stepped back and allowed the others, with their weapons at the ready, to move ahead of him.

Stepping firmly towards the entrance, the door was swung open as one of the officers dropped to his knees. Another stood right above him and a third to his side. All three had guns, safety catches off, pointing in different directions, poised ready to take out potential assailants. A long tiled hallway stretched out in front of them, bathed in darkness, light emitting from the room at the end.

"ARMED POLICE!" they bellowed. "Stay where you are and do not move," they continued to shout ahead of them. There was no response from anyone, but they could hear the sound of running water. All of them moved swiftly into the house, one taking straight to the stairs followed by several of his companions. The other two proceed down the corridor, one heading for the source of light, more of the team following his lead. The third moved to the right as they came to the first doorway, opening into the lounge at the front of the house. All with small cameras on their helmets, a live feed through to the control centre. Continuous recording of potential evidence should the need arise, to be used in court at a later date.

Within the lounge, light from the street lamps outside was filtering through, enabling them to see the room was unoccupied. Toys strewn across the floor, blankets on the settee and the TV screen was black before them.

The lead officer heading towards the light at the back of the house slowed. He could smell something sweet. He knew he'd smelt it before, but he just couldn't place it. He stopped in his tracks as he got to the kitchen doorway. His scope of view increasing, as he left the hallway to take in the whole of the long, thin, kitchen diner. Plates and cooking utensils were piled next to the sink, hot water still pouring into the bowl from the taps. A large parcel lay on the kitchen table, mats and condiments had been moved to accommodate it.

Sprawled across the floor, hidden from view of the front door, was a young women on her back. She was of a slim build and he guessed, in her mid to late twenties. Her brown hair splayed in fine threads across the tiles, held together in the sticky blood that was pooling underneath her head, slowly expanding in size. He recognised the smell now.

The sweet smell of warm blood. Freshly exsanguinated, from the human body. The woman's eyes were fixed and she had a small hole in the middle of her forehead. There was burned skin around the edges, indicating where the bullet had entered her flesh and instantaneously, ended her life.

Delivery

A classic assassination.

The kitchen scene was all picked up on camera and those in the control room watching on screens in front of them gasped. Simultaneously, the live feeds for those that ventured upstairs, relayed the body of a young female, about four years old. Looking just like a smaller version of her mother downstairs. Again, a single bullet hole had extinguished the life of the innocent little girl, before hers had barely begun.

Taken in the same way her mother had been. Did she wait in fear after hearing what had just happened to her protector? Kneeling to pointlessly check for her pulse, the officer spoke to confirm the girl was dead. Although he was a burly man and had seen much in his time in the police, his voice faltered slightly. "Sir, her body is still warm. I would say this only just happened." The operatives behind the cameras raised hands to their mouth, chins dropped as tears welled in eyes that had already witnessed much today.

"No …" came the soft response.

"Same here with the wife … girl's mother. Check the rest of the house, the assailant may still be here."

All operatives were immediately back in strike mode, combing the rest of the house. Room by room they were declared "Clear," and the teams gathered downstairs, deflated with their findings. "Why would you?" started one, but he was cut short.

"The delivery guy we just passed on the way in. There's a parcel on the kitchen table. He was here. Perfect cover to get someone to open the door. Did anyone see which house he was coming from?" called the troop commander. Shaking heads all around. "Well it's all we have right now, get after him."

Several of them left the building, breaking into a run towards the end of the street he had been seen headed towards, neighbours now peering out of windows. Hearing the police shouting on entry to number thirty-one, some had ventured outside the safety of their front doors to investigate. You didn't want to miss out if something was going down in your neighbourhood.

"What's going on?" a middle aged, overweight man called out.

"Get back inside sir. For your own safety. Lock your door and we will come and get you when everything is OK," one of the uniforms shouted back. Several scuttled back to the relative safety of their own homes. Others stood firm, holding their phones aloft, recording every step the police took. Their own safety was clearly not as important as getting a few likes on social media later.

Moving rapidly towards the blockade at the end of the street, they confirmed with their colleagues which way the delivery driver had gone. "Thought it was odd. His van was parked down there and not in the street where he was dropping off. It was a white transit van with a DPD logo on the side, I think the number plate started with LA95. Didn't catch the rest, but it was only a minute or so back, turned left at the end onto the main road."

"Let's go," demanded the chief. Four armed officers jumped into two squad cars and took off at high speed, their lights flicking a bright blue, luminous glow, out into the now dark sky. He relayed the information to the control centre.

"We can't help with location because all our cameras are off-line. We'll put an alert over the secure station for other officers to converge on the B684." came the control room. "We are looking at the helmet cams to see if anyone got a good pick up on the delivery guys face. We'll let you know. Go get this fucker, don't let him get away."

Professionalism from the controller slipped. Nobody noticed.

The two cars sped down the main road through Mapperley, sirens blasting to warn the cars ahead of their arrival. Cars moved left and right, like a zip unlocks its links, moving out of the way as fast as they could, mounting kerbs, owners staring in rear view mirrors. Gathering pace, they sped past a supermarket on their right hand side, the car park empty, shutters down for the night. The occupants were calm, but the adrenalin levels were off the chart.

Up ahead, they could see a white van, slowing for some traffic lights, but couldn't make out if it had the correct logo on the side. The sound of the sirens made the driver look in his rear view mirror. Instantly he knew it was him they were after. It hadn't taken them long to find the bodies of those he had just murdered, but it had given him a very slight head start. It may not be enough, but he had to make it count.

He swung the van out to the right to avoid the car in front, pressed the accelerator hard to the floor and flicked through the gears, weaving through the traffic coming towards him. Swinging it back to the left, just managing to avoid a head on collision, but his back end crumpled as it collided with a stationary vehicle. Other drivers hit their brakes and then their horns, gesticulating wildly at the driver of the van.

The police, chasing from behind, knew they had called it right. They were not going to let him escape.

Over the next ten minutes the squad cars chased the transit van at high speed. They mounted pavements, trying to get past the van to cut it off. Shots were fired at the wheels, but at high speed and being jolted around, accuracy from the firearms officers was lacking. The van driver swerved constantly, pushing them towards a wall and they had to back out. Round side streets single file, back on to the main road and finally headed down the A60. The van was touching speeds of eighty miles an hour. With the wider road, the two police cars tried to go each side of the van, but were again forced to back off by the dangerous swerving of the escapee.

Approaching a large roundabout up ahead, they could see other uniformed colleagues lying in wait. A row of vehicles parked across the road, blue lights evident all around and armed police, positioned behind the metal barricades, guns trained on the moving target. Stingers were deployed across both sides of the carriageway and as the van sped over the top, the metal spikes pierced the tyres, allowing the air to escape rapidly. The driver lost the forward momentum he had, his ability to steer, disappeared rapidly.

Knowing his vehicle could take him no further, he yanked the steering wheel sharply to the right. The van flicked over on to its side, bounced down the road, sparks flying out behind it. Pieces of bodywork breaking off, launching projectiles across the street as the thin metal of the bodywork tore free from the pillars supporting it.

It came to a stop on its side, about ten feet from the first of the barricades. Officers sprang into action,

Delivery

moving quickly towards the stricken vehicle. Rounding the front of the van, they could see though the smashed windscreen that the driver was hurt, blood running from his forehead.

Suspended in his seat by his belt. He was alive.

Fighting to get his belt off, the man looked up realising he was trapped. Like a snared wolf, he growled at those closing in on him and reached for his gun. There was no way he would get out of here alive, but he could take some of them with him. As he raised it upwards, one of the officers shouted a warning, but fired at the same time.

The bullet tore through the assailant's right shoulder, breaking his scapula into small fragments as it exploded on its way through his flesh. The pain was intense and he instantly dropped the weapon, stifling a scream.

They squad cars that had been chasing him, squealed to a stop and the occupants jumped out, running towards the man they had been pursuing. "We got him Sir. He's alive" said one as they pulled the man clear of the van and pushed his head into the ground, forcing him onto his front, pulling his arms behind him and locking the cuffs on. The man squealed in pain.

"You bastard. That was a little girl and her mother you murdered in cold blood back there. Read him his rights. We have some talking to do."

Pulling him to his feet, a photo was taken with a mobile phone and relayed instantly to the team at the control centre. Bending his arm up further, they touched his fingers to the screen and the scanner mapped each of his fingerprints in turn. They could start work on his identity before they got him to a secure unit.

They had to discover how he was linked to Fabian Pichler and why he murdered his family. They seriously needed a breakthrough, as they still had no idea where the prime minister was and how many of these murderous thugs were trying to kill him.

Pushing the captured man into the back of the squad car, his phone pinged an update through from control.

They had a match. This time he was alive.

Chapter Twenty

Leverage

Toad recovered his composure quickly, knowing he had to start making some progress. His client would be calling again soon for an update he was sure of it.

"Can you take control of that cab?" He looked at HaPee.

"I should be able to. We have the ID code. Give me a minute," and HaPee turned back towards his keyboard and started inputting code instructions as quickly as his fingers could move.

"Sloth, IPFree. Could you please run facial recognition on that boy when he looks up? He looks like the kid that was with Mr Bevan and the bastard prime minister earlier."

His fellow hackers looked at the screen again and then nodded in unison. "He sure does. I'll check," purred IPFree

"It's him Toad. You're spot on!" responded the Asian female. "Ninety-eight per cent match. I never seen that high before. It has to be the Bevan kid."

Toad clenched his fist and pulled on his aromatic vape machine again. It had been starting to feel like a long day. Several hours had elapsed since the initial explosion and the sun was starting to go down over a sombre, forever scarred, Nottingham. He felt a resurgence of energy though as he reformed plans in his mind. He knew exactly how he was going to get the Puppy back on the right path. This time it would not escape.

This time, he would pull the trigger himself if he had to.

"I'm in Toad. I have control of the car," called out HaPee.

"Wonderful." Toad gave a sarcastic round of applause. "Could you please add a stop off *en route* for our travellers? Make sure the doors are securely locked beforehand though, we wouldn't want them getting wise and trying to escape. I'd like to find out what happened to Mr Bevan and his famous partner."

Vapours escaped from his mouth as he spoke.

HaPee tapped a few keys, confirming the doors were locked. He inputted a new address as a stopover for the cab. Watching the screen, they saw the man inside the cab look up. Reaching forwards to the passenger control screen. He tapped it as if something had gone wrong. Although cameras were allowed in these cabs, to have microphones was still illegal. It was 'Ok' to have video of occupants, as that was for the customers safety. But to listen in on passengers, was considered an invasion of their privacy. For the moment at least.

The cameras had microphones of course, they just weren't activated. Until HaPee turned them on.

"Somethings gone wrong," said Dan, tapping the screen. "It's taking us to a different address for some reason. Somewhere in Sneinton! What the hell ...?" He pressed the button that was supposed to allow you to communicate with a human, should you feel the need. Nothing happened.

Leverage

"Hello. Hello. Is anyone there? Can you hear me?" Dan looked back towards Nicky who was starting to get unsettled again.

The hackers were mildly amused, watching the passengers become distressed. A few clicks of a keyboard from anywhere in the world and they could literally take over someone's life. No need to put oneself in physical danger. They could do it from the safety of their own hub, unknown to the world. That was real power.

"Will they be able to hear me?" enquired Toad of his team. HaPee nodded confirmation.

"Hello Sir. We can hear you loud and clear," responded Toad, holding a microphone to his lips. "Please relax, everything is OK. Your cab has just been selected for a routine security inspection. You will be checked at the address displayed on your screen. Once everything has been completed, you will be free to continue your journey. There will be no charge for this ... Uber cab ride, due to the inconvenience it may have caused you. Please, sit back and enjoy the ride." The microphone clicked off and Toad gave a broad grin, inhaling deeply on his vape machine again.

Dan looked perplexed. He had never heard of this happening before. Maybe it was because of what had happened today in the Old Market Square. Nicky relaxed back into her seat. The voice on the line had been very reassuring and Sneinton was not too far away now. It wasn't an area of Nottingham she normally ventured to. There was no real need. She certainly had not heard great things about that part of town, but the council had been working on improving the situation. Hadn't they?

Darkness descended over the streets of Nottingham. In the distance, the sound of sirens still filled the air.

The cab slowed down and pulled up outside the address it had been given remotely. It was next to a row of small rundown garages and the street lights weren't working. Bins littered the streets; foul smells rose from the heavily clogged drains and stray dogs barked in the gloom. The occasional orange and white light could be seen through windows, thick with years of pollution, pumped from the exhausts of passing cars.

"You have arrived at your destination," came the monotone voice of the cab for only the second time.

"Surely this can't be a checkpoint for Uber?" questioned Dan, looking out of the windows rather nervously. "This doesn't feel right Nicky." He leant forward to try and tap on the screen again just as the doors clicked to unlock and the interior light flooded the car. Nicky jumped and Aidan tensed, grasping his mother's hand tightly.

Shadows moved from the side of the house and between the garages. Suddenly, the car door was opened from the outside and the interior light sprang to life.

"Could you step out the vehicle please Sir?" A gravelly voice commanded.

"Who are you? What's going on? This ..." but Dan was cut off as the muzzle of a machine gun was pushed into the cab with its occupants. Dan scuttled backwards, putting himself between the gun and his friends. "What the f ...?" He started, raising in his hands automatically in response.

"It's not a request. Get out the cab and do as you are told, or this will become very uncomfortable for you." Using the muzzle to motion to their captors, Dan moved slowly for the door, unable to think of any alternative. As he reached his hand for the door frame, he could see it was starting to shake violently. He hoped Nicky and

Leverage

Aidan couldn't see he was shit scared. Stepping out from the car, he was grabbed quickly by two people with their faces covered. They too were carrying machine guns. Moving his hands behind his back they wrapped them together with black cable ties and pulled a cloth tightly around his mouth.

Nicky kept Aidan behind her in a protective position, but knew she could do nothing. "Please ... don't hurt my boy ... he's only a kid ... he's had a really bad day already," she begged those in front of her, tears back again, streaming down her face.

"We know," came the short reply as they bound her hands, then grabbed Aidan from behind her. On hearing their comments, Nicky tensed, immediately understanding they were in the hands of those responsible for everything that had happened today. Fear coursed through her body as she realised they were now at the mercy of their captors. Mercy had not been their forte today. Aidan kicked out, petrified at what was going to happen. "No, leave me ..." but his scream was cut off abruptly with a gloved hand over his mouth as they lifted him clear of Nicky, taking him between two of them.

The captives were brought into the back of the house that the team had used for their base. It was next to the shitty, run down garages that nobody would ever pay attention to. There weren't many neighbours around here. Drug dens had ruined the community a long time ago and many had moved out. Those that stayed, knew to keep themselves to themselves.

Fear has a smell about it. Animals have a sixth sense, exploiting it to locate their prey. Humans detect it in the faces of those that are before them. Little flickers of the eye. Pupils reacting to tiny triggers. A bead of sweat breaking out on a forehead. A temple pulsing rapidly. Aidan, Nicky and Dan reeked of it and could do nothing to hide the tell-tale signs from their captors.

Toad was both human and animal. He loved fear in others and now his day was coming back on track. The prime minister would soon be dealt with.

His phone rang and Toad smiled as he answered.

He had some leverage.

Chapter Twenty One
Collaboration

Marcus Poole and Irm Brown were sat on opposite sides of a broad walnut desk in her office. The walls were all plain, block colours, with the occasional picture breaking the monotone backdrop. Alone together for the first time in a long time. This time, they did not want to embrace each other as lovers do. Desire to paw at each other's clothes ferociously had dissipated long ago. it was replaced with contempt from one side, atonement from the other.

Locking eyes, hostility obvious from Irm, Marcus was taken aback at the strength of feeling he still had for the woman before him. He did not love her anymore, but it wasn't true that he hated her. Marcus wanted to tell her how proud he was of her achievements. How happy he was to see her achieve the accolade of the position she was now in. He shared none of that with her.

"Given the unprecedented events of today, it's clear we need to work together on this, to get the prime minister back safely. If we don't, I suspect it will be both our arses on the line. We'll be picking up our P45, probably dishonourably let go, and it wouldn't surprise me if our pension pots are cancelled too. I'll share what we have so far, but it's shifting sands. Things may well have changed before we leave this room," started Marcus in a bid to break the ice and get things moving.

"Marcus," acknowledged Irm. "A fine mess we're in. One of us has dropped a bollock here and I'm damn sure it's not me," she started, face emotionless, arms crossed over her chest and straight to the point.

Marcus decided to ignore the comment and get straight to business, so he turned a large screen on at the end of the room, flicked the contents of his tablet up to it, where some images came to life before them.

"A lot of traffic has been picked up since the explosion this morning. Most of it dross, not leading anywhere. However, we have been sent some coded information from a hacker. Apparently, they are appalled at what has happened here today. They seem to be particularly irate at the killing of the lady, when the shooter on top of the Council House, opened fire on the PM." Marcus turned towards the screen as some cipher was unscrambled in front of them to reveal a message:

Concerning Nottingham atrocity. Not HAppy so many innocent people killed. Particularly pissed that lady in thE square was shot after the bomb went off. WTF?

Don't know who is responsible, but as a professional hacker on thE circuit, I was contacted a long time ago about getting involved in something concerning Nottingham. Didn't accePt and until today, did not know what it was about.

Glad I reFused.
REspEct

Irm leant back in her chair, her arms uncrossed as she read through the message several times, her lips moving as she sounded it out to herself.

Collaboration

"What do you make of it?"

Marcus pointed to the message, "Well, I am sure you can see there are a few letters in capitals where you wouldn't normally capitalise? They stand out and you don't need me to point out that they spell "HAPEE" and "IPFREE". Clearly, it's not how you would normally spell happy," he continued on, "A quick database search and we have a hit. 'HaPee' otherwise known as 'HaPee as Larry', is another hacker. We believe to be based in Russia normally, possibly male, but we have been unable to identify him.

"The second one, IPFree, is also a known hacker. As the name says, IP, we assume refers to *Internet Protocol,* as in IP address. Free, well maybe they just think everything should be free, or they are free, who knows! Barking mad most of them. Brilliantly talented, but barking mad."

Marcus was moving his arms in the air, methodically highlighting the capital letters with a pointer and then pulling them out so they could be assembled in to the names he spoke.

"Both of them are sought by a number of governments for hacking sophisticated, supposedly watertight systems, including national power supplies, defence and missile launch centres. So far, we have not been able to identify either of them. IPFree, we do believe is female and most of the activity from her, has been in the far east, specifically Hong Kong, so we think she may be Asian, but no guarantees."

Irm, put her hands together and bought her fingers to her chin. "Or could it be that the person sending this is letting you know who they are? Perhaps they are actually HaPee Larry, or IPFree, or both, but they don't want to get fingered for this particularly murderous act."

"We did ponder that ourselves to start with," nodded Marcus in response. "However, each of these IT whizz kids tends to leave a personal signature, as you know, encrypted in the message itself. Sometimes hard to detect, but it's almost like a badge of honour to them and they feel compelled to leave it. A bit like serial killers, if you find the clues they leave, it taunts you. Makes them think they are smarter than you, because although you think you know and you're getting closer to catching them, you really don't know a thing. They can't resist."

"Who is it then?" asked Irm, putting her hands on the table, clearly wanting to speed things up. "

In the bottom left hand corner of the message is a small bow tie, with an eyeball and a capital E. Bow-eye-E, otherwise known as 'BOWIE'. Previous interceptions have revealed that the player is a massive David Bowie fan and has had clips of his music playing, or inserted lyrics from one of his songs. You know, 'Ground control to Major Tom' type of shit."

"Why are these people always so frickin weird?" Irm asked of no one in particular.

"Anyway, we know this is an operative based in the UK. So far, we have pinned it down to the South East, but as of yet, we can't be more specific." Marcus finished his short overview, but really it hadn't helped them move much further forward. "Have your team pulled anything up on either of those characters at all?"

Irm swung her chair back round to face him again after being drawn to the screen. "I'd have to check, but they don't spring to mind from what they've been talking about so far. Hang on." Irm leant forward to her desk and tapped a quick message to Glasses asking him to pull anything they had on HaPee as Larry and IPFree.

Collaboration

Turning back to him, Marcus challenged Irm, "So what have your team managed to pull today? Clearly they have been busy since this bomb exploded, I noticed a lot of stressed faces and people who already looked like they had been on long shifts when I came through."

"Our initial intelligence suggests its connected to a really hard line, Pro-European group with eastern European connections. Undoubtedly, they believe they have a lot to lose should the EU fail. Some field operatives reported contacts across Germany, Spain, Hungary, Romania, and so on, are pretty annoyed that Barnaby is closing our borders, trying to prevent free movement of people. Something of this level of ferocity and planning has not just happened on a whim though. It will have taken a lot of meticulous planning beforehand. As well as a lot of money.

"A message was intercepted a few months before the attack," Irm displayed the same message that Glasses had shared with her earlier in the day, whilst explaining the extreme cipher that had been protecting it.

Everything is in place
It has to end. Our financial security is threatened
Sunday 11am, NG. Mobilise the connections
The Puppy must be put to sleep, Toad

Marcus looked at the screen with a high level of curiosity, then turned his attention back to Irm and fixed her with a steely gaze. Raising his voice slightly he started "Why did you not share this earlier? This is ... this could have been used to intercept the perpetrators and prevent the attack from happening." The normally calm exterior slipped for a second.

"The code was only broken in the last week or so and the team were trying to work out what it meant. Of course it seems to be an obvious connection, with hindsight of the events of today. Everything is more obvious with hindsight Marcus, you of all people, should know that." Irm was not about to be admonished by Marcus. Her tone and delivery did not change as she fixed his gaze.

"With hindsight, you wouldn't shag your boss and fall completely in love with him, just in case he got offered a promotion and dumped you. Breaking all the promises he ever made. Along with your fucking heart. With hindsight!" she finished.

Her point was made and her old boss, lover, looked to the floor, clearly embarrassed, at what had been a long overdue reprimand, for the way he had behaved towards her. Gradually he raised his head and nodded slowly.

"Ok. I had that coming. I'm sorry for everything Irm; I really am. It was an ultimatum. I wanted the promotion which I'd worked so hard for ... I knew it would not come my way again", he paused and drew a deep breath as this was going to hurt no matter how he phrased it. "The service did not want an internal scandal on their hands. I was torn. I loved you Irm, you know that. But I was forced to let you go." His eyes flicked between hers before he looked down at his hands.

Irm stood and moved round the desk towards him. She sat on the edge of the desk, lifted his chin with her right forefinger and looked him straight in the eye. "I get it Marcus. Collateral damage is an accepted risk in this game. It was the fact you never felt you could come and tell me why you made the choice you did. That hurt so much."

Irm, moved her head back, stood and turned her back on him. "But I'm over it, and I am over you. Let's say no more about it and find the prime minister before we are toast."

Marcus let out a long slow deep breath as the tension subsided in the room. "Ok. Have your team got anything else to go on?"

Irm, waved through the window to Glasses who had been periodically checking whether he was required. He and Tatoos came into the room with another tablet device and a couple of folders that had already grown substantially in size.

"You know who this is?" she queried as they both returned nods, but neither bothered with pleasantries or introductions. It would take up time they did not have. "Please update us with everything you have so far" commanded the Head of MI6.

Tattoos started to speak first, again relaying information from his tablet up to the larger screen in the room. Firstly, addressing Irm he said, "We are checking on the hacker names you just sent through," then he turned to face Marcus. "As you know, the two perpetrators killed by Paul Buxton and his team seemed to have clean records. Our first victim was killed by a bullet to the back of the head. He was identified as Lucas Jacobs, who had an unblemished record with the Belgian army. Well, the Belgian armed forces have no record of him at all." Tattoos looked up to see Irm and Marcus exchange glances.

"How the hell did he get ... hacked?" Marcus realised, before he completed his question.

"It would appear so Sir. After his image was shared by the media earlier today, it spread very quickly. We were cross checking with the Belgian authorities. There was no record of a Lucas Jacobs ever being in the army within the time frames on our database. Anyway, someone got in touch after seeing his face on social media to say they recognised him." Tattoos again looked at Irm for confirmation to continue.

"Apparently, he is actually a young Belgian called Victor Jansens, with connections to the farming industry. Armed with that information, we've searched again and indeed found him on our systems, but there was no facial imprint that we could have checked against previously."

Glasses picked up the stream of information from Tatoos. "Jansens had a conviction back in 2018 after a peaceful protest about BREXIT got violent. This was in Belgium, outside of the European parliament, where a number of industries were protesting that the EU should be doing more to either keep the UK in the European Union, or get them to pay a hell of a lot more money in the divorce bill."

"Like we didn't get shafted enough," huffed Tatoos. Irm shot him a glance and he turned his gaze back to his laptop.

"Anyway, the protest got heated, minor scuffles broke out with the police. Politicians were getting pelted with eggs, bottles started to be thrown. Then some intent on harder action, or just violence, got really rough and a full scale riot broke out. Makeshift weapons were used, many were injured and police bought in the heavy defences. Batons, tear gas and tasers. Jansens was caught red handed beating a fallen officer with a shortened scaffold pole. It was later proven he hadn't just picked it up at the scene, he bought it with him to the protest, presumably intent on causing trouble. Got nine months suspended sentence as it was a first offence." Glasses looked up again from his screen at his audience. The solemn, silent thoughts, of those before him were obvious.

"That's a big step, in terms of scale of planning and violence used. Scaffold pole, protest over BREXIT, to armed attack with guns and bombs? Infiltrating our police department. Trying to kill the prime minister of the UK? What the hell happened to him in the last five years? More to the point, how the hell did he get into our armed police unit without all of this coming up in the screening? We must have known. Who the hell cleared him for service?" Irm placed her palms on the desk and pushed herself up from her chair. She began to pace around the room. "What is the link to farming here, or is he one of those that likes to protest for the thrill of the fight?" she asked.

"That may be true, but apparently he had been very vocal for the Farmers Unions in Belgium claiming that if the UK leave the EU, then the subsidies that farmers in Belgium receive will be cut significantly, threatening their livelihoods. Maybe he got carried away on the day?" responded Tatoos this time.

"You don't move to assassinate the PM of the UK because you are losing a bit of money," came a calm response, from the Head of MI5 this time. "Could this really be related to BREXIT and the breakup of the European Union," Marcus continued. "What have you got on the other, the second body?"

"Our records identified him as Fabian Pichler, innocuous background in computer science with family living in Mapperley. Armed police went to pick them up earlier, where they discovered his wife and young daughter had been assassinated."

Everyone in the room sucked in a lung full of stale air, shaking their heads in disgust at how someone could do such a thing. Glasses pushed them back up his nose, then pressed on. "We presume they were making sure there were no loose ends. Remove anyone who could possibly give them away. However, the officers realised the murders had only just happened, gave chase to a delivery driver they believed may be involved. After a high speed pursuit across Nottingham, they arrested the man they believe to be responsible."

Marcus sat up and for the first time that day, felt a surge of positivity. "A breakthrough! Well done local law enforcement. What do we have on him, I haven't caught up with my team yet on that?"

"I'll come to him in a second, but before I finish on Pichler, you should know we've nothing yet on his real identity. His house is being torn apart as we speak and if we find anything we will let you know," finished Glasses before leaning back in his chair and turning to Tatoos.

"The ground team there can have their resources increased if they need them. This is of paramount importance and we must find something, if there is something to be found. Tear the walls out, if there is nothing obvious. If he has been living there for a number of years, there must be something." Marcus became the most animated he'd been all day. Although he was clearly in a very serious business, he loved it when there was some kind of opportunity, or breakthrough, to get the grey matter stimulated. The chase was definitely on and he intended to be leading it. Even if he did have to work hand in hand with his old flame.

Collaboration

Tattoos picked up from Glasses. They were like a wrestling tag team. When one was getting tired, or thought the crowd needed rousing again, they would exchange an unsaid word, seamlessly allowing the other to take centre stage and finish the task at hand.

"So, let's come to the exciting part; our detainee delivery driver. We had an immediate hit on his fingerprints." Tattoos, pushed his sleeves further up his arms, interlocked his fingers and stretched them backwards, allowing a couple of his knuckle joints to pop, whilst a smile rose slowly across his face.

Tapping a couple of keys on his tablet, again some images sprung to life in front of the others and they started reading some of the headlines next to an old police mug shot and a photo taken earlier in the day when the man was captured.

"This is Jack Lumley. Born in Paignton, Devon early 1990." Marcus and Irm exchanged a quizzical glance, both confused a little, as the fast moving investigation seemed to be moving further away from eastern European connections again.

"The photo on the left is from 2008, when he was just eighteen years old," continued Tattoo's, "when he was arrested after being caught breaking into a shop with a couple of other reprobates. Hence, his prints on record. It was the only offence he was ever arrested for, although police records show they suspected him in a string of burglaries across the local area over the next few years. His father operated a small, local fishing company and it's believed that Jack started working for him around 2011, when he turned twenty-one."

"Maybe his mother wouldn't let him out to sea until he was a man?" suggested Glasses, "And, interestingly, the local burglaries almost dried up overnight."

"Petty theft is a long way from mass murder and attempted assassination of the prime minister. Come on, what's the story in-between," pushed Marcus starting to get a little frustrated.

"Well, this is where it gets really interesting. Jack went missing from a fishing vessel that left Paignton harbour in late Spring 2020. A heavy storm hit the boat in the English Channel and his father said he was thrown overboard. Guess what? He wasn't wearing a lifejacket and despite the coastguard searching for him for several days. They never found him, or recovered his body later on." Tattoos put his hands on the table and signalled to Glasses he should go for the killer blow.

"So, after a lengthy battle with the courts, he was finally declared dead in the autumn of 2021. The insurance company paid out four hundred and fifty thousand pounds to the family." Glasses was peering at his audience over the top of his own, who remained relatively stony-faced and focussed on the two doing the talking.

"Coincidentally, the company records show they had been running at a loss since 2019. Not massive debts, but it was the first time in over fifteen years the company did not turn a profit. I am sure it doesn't need me to point out the fact that in 2019 was the official exit of Britain from the EU. All subsidies to the British fishing industry came to a stop." Glasses again stopped and observed his audience.

Marcus was the first to respond to this information, but he had a question. "So, Lumley has been 'dead' for three years and then resurfaces, caught up in this. Where has he been for that time and how the hell did he get involved with this?"

Collaboration

"Don't know the answer to that yet Sir, but the ground crew in Nottingham are working on precisely that," responded Tatoos.

Irm had been looking through some of the information that was in the folders. "I'd get someone down to Paignton and pick up Lumley's father. Gauge his response when you inform him his dead son has been found alive and well. We need to know if he has been involved. Not only a potentially fraudulent claim, but more importantly if he is involved in whatever his son is part of now."

"There is a connection here, Irm," stated Marcus, rubbing his temples. He stood and moved to a glass screen at the back of the room, with marker pens close at hand. He started to capture names, dates and the key information they had for each of those they had been able to identify so far.

"We have Jansens, real name, from Belgium, background in farming, protesting at loss of UK withdrawal from EU and the size of the subsidies," he circled 'FARMING'. "Then we have Lumley. English, with links to the fishing industry. Family in debt – reason? UK withdrawal from Europe and loss of subsidies from the European Union. You said he wasn't in debt by much, but people start to do funny things when the money dries up."

"There are plenty of people losing out because of BREXIT that's for sure, but people don't turn into homicidal maniacs. It's tenuous Marcus. At best!"

"Maybe. But tenuous is all we have right now," turning back to the small group in the Head of MI6's office. Behind him, circled in the same way to 'FARMING', were 'FISHING', 'EU SUBSIDIES', 'BELGIUM', 'UK', 'AUSTRIA', 'HaPee as Larry', 'IPFree' and 'BOWIE'.

Standing back, he ran over the words on the board again and then added another: 'MONEY?' and sat back down again.

"It may be tenuous Irm, but the two people we have identified so far are not ordinary people are they? Victor Jansens we know has a violent past with his arrest in Brussels. Since then he has laid low, cover placed for him by a professional hacker. He has led a double life since then. I would class him as a sleeper. A sleeper positioned in a perfect place to help carry off one of the most audacious terrorism attacks in modern history. The attempted assassination of our prime minister.

"Jack Lumley made himself disappear for some reason. Normal people don't do that. Has he been making connections to this group? Learning to become a hardened criminal? Has he killed before he assassinated this poor mother and her daughter?" Marcus tapped the board on each call out and then leaned towards Glasses and Tatoos, raised his arm and pointed back at the board.

"We need to find out who gave the cover for Jansens and his sleeper friend, 'Fabian Pichler'. Which hacker was it? HaPee as Larry, IPFree or someone else? They must have been given clearance codes to enable them to approve them for the police force. I want to know what those codes were and then we may be able to tell if they have had help from the inside."

They looked at Marcus, taking notes and nodding in complete agreement.

Irm added to the list quickly. "Establish who the hell 'BOWIE' is as well and we need to know the IP address of the person who did give them cover if you can get it. If you can get anything on their identities and whether they are in Nottingham, connected directly to this."

Collaboration

She froze, "We need to find out how the hell, and who the hell, took control of the CCTV cameras in Nottingham and whether it was one of those three. OK?"

They both nodded and responded with a, "Yes Boss," pushing back their chairs to move towards the door.

"One last thing," she added as they opened the door. "Pump Lumley for information and do anything required to get all he knows. Understand?" Glasses and Tatoos smiled and left quickly to get moving on the tasks at hand.

Marcus turned towards Irm, a smile rising at the edges of his otherwise stern expression. It felt good to be working with his old protege.

He felt like they had moved forward.

In more ways than one.

Chapter Twenty Two
Big Ben

Lee and Barnaby were not sure where to go. With the cover of darkness and the change of car, it would undoubtedly make it harder to be discovered by those chasing them. However, given the events through the day, particularly the drones and the targeted shooting in the shed under Lady Bay bridge, they felt distinctly uneasy.

Deciding to head out of town in Dan's Lexus, they positioned Barnaby behind the back seats this time, in a bid to make it slightly more comfortable for him. Concealing him with a travel rug, Lee moved the front seat forward to give him more space, and Barnaby hunkered down as low as he could.

As the adrenaline wore off and darkness was descending, Lee suddenly realised how hungry he was. Searching the glove box to see if there was any food that Dan may have stashed for later, the obligatory tin of hard boiled sweets was all that offered itself up. The sugar would keep them going until something more substantial was available. Reaching back, he held the tin open to the Prime Minister.

"Sir, would you like a sweet? Probably need to get some sugar in both of us."

"Thanks," replied Barnaby, taking two from the tin. "I really can't thank you enough for what you've done today Lee. Do you mind me asking, what made you help me, back there in the square?" he enquired.

Lee shrugged his shoulders, returning his gaze to the road, headlights picking out bends and junctions ahead. "Instinct, I suppose. Shock of the whole event ... You were hurt. Anyone would have done it." He was slightly embarrassed, not wanting to offer more up.

"Many people would not have done so, faced with such a ferocious attack. They would have thought of themselves and their families and decided not to get involved. Just in case. We've lost the sense of right and wrong in this country sadly. People generally wouldn't intervene in the way that you did," retorted the prime minister.

Lee glanced backwards. "Sir, not everyone is bad. I know you think that we have a country full of foreigners who don't care and they'd take whatever they can for their own gains, that they don't value our society, but that's not true." Lee surprised himself with his strong rebuke. "The media portray all foreigners as lazy leeches, feeding off our benefits system. Either that, or they are all criminals. They depict them in such awful ways," he paused to breathe deeply, almost in disbelief at what he was saying to the publics choice to lead the country.

"You of all people should know the media is run by complete fascists who don't have a handle on reality. It's wrong. So wrong." Lee could feel his face starting to redden as the anger simmered within him.

"I realise the media twist things, Lee; God knows, I've had enough of it myself whilst I was running to be elected. Those that are aligned with your views, never print the bad stuff. We *all* have bad stuff in our past. The ones that are against you, literally go to the ends of the earth, paying people to invent things, to dig things up, twist them around, tease them apart and distort the facts. It's like getting pips out of an apple and then presenting the pip as the whole fruit!" Barnaby pulled the blanket round his body more as he spoke.

"But, the bottom line is, there are too many people in this beautiful country of ours. We have to get a handle on it. BREXIT was supposed to put a stop to the human avalanche that the UK was under, but it didn't. They kept coming in droves," Barnaby shook his head.

Lee was shaking his head and burst into argument again. "I voted for BREXIT," he offered, "But it wasn't because I wanted to stop immigration. I see the good that people from overseas do here Sir. They work in our overstretched hospitals, work alongside Nicky, Aidan's Mum. If it wasn't for them coming, despite the hostile environment they come into, we would not be able to staff our hospitals. The injured people from that horrific scene in the square today …" Lee felt his stomach tighten as he thought back to the earlier carnage, "they will be treated by doctors from Spain and Germany. Nurses from Hungary and Austria. Talented individuals, who come to work, in what used to be, the best health care system across Europe.

"They'll work into the small hours, to make sure everyone is assessed and treated in the best way possible. That's not *'lazy foreigners, leeching from our benefits system'* as the media would have you believe. They are highly trained, highly skilled surgeons from around the globe. Coming here, because they like our way of life and they want to help others."

Big Ben

Lee sat up in his seat to look into the rear view mirror at an angle so he could see Barnaby's face. Fixing his eyes, he continued. "It's restaurant workers with long hours and low wages. But it's work that they can't find in their own country because their economies are weak. Its cleaners in office blocks, cleaning our toilets across the UK, because the British don't want to bloody do it. The Brits are the lazy ones. We have generations of families who haven't worked - EVER. Benefits paid, roof over their head and they have no aspirations, because they earn more than our fu ... teachers do. They are sat at home on their arse, playing with virtual reality games and watching daytime TV." Lee was getting up a full head of steam now. "Too many have this *'it's our right to be on benefits'* mentality and aren't prepared to do those low skilled jobs that are essential for our society. Many of those travelling here, Sir, to do those jobs, do so because it offers more than they have at home and they don't want to be sat on their arses doing as many of our own nationality do."

Barnaby was listening intently to Lee's monologue. They were arguments he had heard from others before. This personal insight seemed different, it was spoken with passion and real conviction. He could tell Lee believed what he said and wasn't outlining these issues because he thought it was the right thing to say.

Lee continued, "I voted for BREXIT because I was sick of the non-elected autocrats that really run the European Union. The Jean-Claude Junkers of this world, undermining the British government all the time. It was almost pointless having a government in the UK, they had no mandate, because it had not been approved by some jumped up little arse, who used to run Luxembourg.

I mean Luxembourg for God's sake! It's not exactly the centre of the universe! And he's telling France, Spain, Italy and the UK what we can and can't do. It's ridiculous!" Lee flung his arms up from the steering wheel in frustration.

At this point Barnaby raised a smile. It was something close to his heart. He was starting to like Lee rather a lot. "I am definitely with you on that point, young man. They cost me my life's work. A great business, employing many local people, up in smoke because of some decision made by the European Union, that did not reflect the reality of the situation."

It was Lee's turn to nod in agreement. He took up the conversation again. "I'm sorry Sir, but anyone who voted BREXIT to curb immigration in general, was never going to be happy with the outcome. The bloody media for you again, twisting BREXIT to be about immigration rather than sovereignty.

"I understand why you closed the borders Sir, but in my mind, it was an overreaction. Foreigners continuing to come here, is a good thing for the British economy. They contribute, they pay tax. They bring skills and attitude that we desperately need." Lees anger was turning to excitement, he was on a roll. He couldn't believe he had the ear of the one person who could actually do something with his point of view.

"So Lee, if you were me, what would you do?" probed Barnaby, trying to sit up a little in the footwell and lean forward to his young counsel.

Lee flinched. He had effectively just been asked how to fix the problems of the country. It was one thing to discuss with friends and family at the safety of your dinner table about what you would do if you were in charge. It was distinctly different when questioned by the country's top politician, sat in the back of your car injured from a terrorist attack. Slowly he scratched his chin with his left hand, keeping his right gripping the steering wheel.

"Well, really it's about the Government finances available to provide the relevant services and, as ever, you don't have enough money in the pot. People continue to come to the UK, that says to me our economy is still performing well. That is, if you'll forgive the language, two fingers up to the EU, who were adamant that the UK would fail if we left their little men's club. Well we haven't failed Sir" a wry smile came to Lees face.

"The UK is thriving! On top of that, the EU continues to be met with criticism across a wider Europe now. Look at what has been happening in France, Italy and even Germany. Ok, none of those have voted to leave just yet, or have majorities that will allow that to happen, but the ground swell of populism has been evident for some years.

"If I were you Sir, I would play to the fact that the UK is thriving. Rub the noses of the Eurocrats in it. Reinforce the point, that despite them doing everything possible to prevent us from being successful outside the European Union, we have been. Our growth rate is nearly double that of the EU. Trade around the world has beaten even the most optimistic forecasters predictions. BREXIT is a success!"

Lee felt a surge of pride as he spoke about his homeland. He'd never been that interested in politics, but he understood more than he let on.

"Well, that is certainly a different spin on the situation," Barnaby was quizzical at the response he'd been given. "So, you'd reopen the borders?"

"Absolutely! Has it entered your mind that this attack on you may well be because you closed the borders yesterday? What if it's the European Union itself behind this?" Lee almost couldn't believe he'd just suggested such a thing. Now he'd said it out loud, he realised it sounded ludicrous. Didn't it?

"It did. However, I think it was too organised, planned and thought out, for it to have been a spur of the moment reaction to the announcement yesterday Lee. Look at the way they found us so quickly, with drones. As for the EU itself behind it ... that would be a declaration of war against the UK. I don't believe they are that arrogant, or stupid enough, to start down that road." Barnaby leant forward to stretch his back and rub his ankle as he spoke.

"Did the security services not have any warning about this? There has been lots of hostility recently across the country. It's got worse since ... since *Your Party* came to power." Lee felt uncomfortable saying it, but it was true. "It's almost like when Trump came to power against the odds. That was *cart blanche* for racists to come to the fore, white supremacists beating up the black community, police officers shooting them for seemingly no reason. It's awful."

Barnaby was again listening intently, but could no longer bring himself to look at his protector. To be compared to Trump was like a knife in his heart. Twisted to make sure he felt the pain.

Lee went on. "That is not what many people I've spoken to voted for when they said they wanted out of Europe. They voted out because they were fed up with paying billions, yet not understanding what they got back, except interference in the laws of our land."

It fell quiet for a while. Barnaby deep in thought. Eventually he spoke in response. "M15 and M16 have been so busy trailing Islamic extremists over the last decade, that there hasn't been any attention paid to other potential threats. The resource has just not been high enough to delve into these kinds of things," started Barnaby, "but maybe we were looking in the wrong areas. It was never our intention to provoke racism or hatred amongst the British public. That is a terrible outcome, for which I am ashamed."

He looked up, his eyes dull, expressing the sadness he felt. "I understand your comments Lee, but with so many people flooding into the UK, mainly from Europe, what do we do about the continued housing crisis? What about the pressure on our beloved NHS? Our schools can't cope with the amount of foreign nationals that don't speak English as their first language. How do we cater for that? The only sensible way is to stop people coming and reduce the pressure. We can't afford to keep adding endless numbers of people into the system to give them free education, free health care, child benefit, pensions ... the list goes on" offered Barnaby.

Lee shook his head in disbelief. "Mr Aitken, I am not a politician and I don't have all the answers," he started, "but there are some things I think you could do to ensure more people contribute to the system, without excluding those coming here to seek a better life for their family AND contributing to the wider society.

"Listen," he demanded, suddenly full of authority, "I work in the healthcare industry, have done for many years now and there are massive inequalities in the way healthcare is delivered to patients. If you have asthma, unless you are a child, you have to pay for your inhalers. People die from asthma and that is no fault of their own. But, and this really pisses me off," he took a deep breath, "if you have diabetes, type II diabetes, a reversible condition, in fact a preventable condition," Lee could feel the pressure rising in his temples and his face starting to redden as he continued, "you get ALL your medication, not just that for diabetes, free of charge! Free of charge! Why? Diabetes is reversible. People can do something about diabetes themselves, but they '*can't be bothered*' because their medicine is free."

He was tapping on the steering wheel as he lectured the Prime Minister. "It's a major public health issue that continues to grow and costs the health service billions every year. People need to get off their couch, put down the chips and the *diet coke* and go and do some exercise for God's sake. If you made them pay for their medication, I bet you, they would take it more seriously, lose some weight and probably, *possibly*, rid themselves of the sugar disease. Bizarrely, people aren't motivated by the fact that they might lose their eye sight, or have their feet amputated. They want to eat their cakes." Looking forward again at the road ahead, he realised his tapping had turned to banging on the steering wheel as his anger continued to surface.

"Hit them in the pocket and it will change their behaviour," he stopped the drumming, resting his hand back on the steering wheel. "Many of the problems people complain about are access to their GP and yet we still have thousands of no shows at GP surgeries across the land on a daily basis. Its scandalous, but people don't turn up because it costs them nothing. They are probably the same ones that complain about the lack of appointments." He glanced at the mirror again, flicking his eyes backwards and forwards.

"If it were me, Sir, I'd charge people twenty pounds for an appointment with their GP, have their debit cards on record and charge them automatically. But, if they need a prescription, that twenty pounds covers the usual cost of any prescription charge. Effectively your making people pay up front for their medication."

Barnaby looked perplexed by this suggestion. "But that's denying free health care to those who are most vulnerable, or can't afford it," he stated shaking his head as if to instantly dismiss the idea.

"Fair enough. So only charge those that usually pay for their prescriptions. Once you've sorted the inequality of which diseases are covered and which ones aren't. If you are pregnant, a child, elderly, on benefits, then you don't get charged. Simple." Simple to Lee, but of course it could be a difficult sell to the general public. Whilst he had a captive audience, he decided to move on.

Lee suddenly felt empowered.

"As for the housing crisis, stop international purchase of houses under a certain threshold, say three hundred thousand pounds. Only make them available to UK based citizens to buy. The mansions, and ridiculously overpriced property in London, is out of reach for those wanting to get on the property ladder, so let them continue to buy them. But charge them extortionate amounts of stamp duty. The Russian oligarchs and the Chinese billionaires can afford it. Win: Win. On top of that, you could cap the amount of properties an individual or company is allowed to buy for rental purposes."

Lee sensed that Barnaby was listening intently to him. How about that! An audience with the injured prime minister, in the footwell of his best friend's car.

"Those property magnates are so rich, they don't need more property. All they are doing is driving the prices up to make it unaffordable for others. They then control the price they can charge for rentals as well. People can only afford them, if they have multiple people or families, living under one roof. It's not right."

The car pulled to a stop at some traffic lights and Lee spotted a bright sign up ahead indicating that a garage forecourt was still open on the other side of the junction.

"Do you want some food? There is a garage ahead."

"Oh! Yes please. I haven't eaten since about six this morning and I'm ravenous," responded Barnaby.

Lee pulled into the garage forecourt but moved away from the well-lit areas to minimise visibility into the car. Instructing Barnaby to stay under the blanket, he pulled his baseball cap low over his head and stepped out locking the car door as he left, walking towards the convenience store within the garage.

A few minutes later, he emerged with sandwiches, crisps, chocolate bars and soft drinks. He returned with a sugary feast. Enough to induce diabetes for about eight people. Lee decided he didn't want to go into public areas too often and he wasn't sure how long they'd be on the run for. He smiled at the irony, given his recent discussion with the prime minister.

Climbing back into the car, he put the food stash on the passenger seat, then passed some behind him underneath the blanket. For a couple of minutes, all that could be heard was the quiet sound of hungry mouths. Chewing. Swallowing.

"Thank you, Lee. Again. I really am indebted to you in many ways," Barnaby extended his hand towards Lee from under the blanket. Lee turned and shook it firmly.

Big Ben

"You're welcome Sir. We need to get you somewhere safe as soon as we can."

Taking out Dan's mobile phone he entered the passcode he'd been given and the screen sprang to life. "Sir, you said earlier about calling your security team, but the attack on us in the shed prevented you. I think you should call them," he passed the mobile over.

Barnaby looked at the screen and for the life of him he could not remember the number for his Head of Security.

"I'll have to call it in to the main team" he said tapping numbers on the screen. This number was ingrained on you from the moment you took the highest office of Number Ten. Lifting the phone to his ear, he heard a female answer

"Security clearance required?" came the short response, voice recognition automatically aligned with the call.

"Umm, Big Ben" replied Barnaby. It was the code name that had been allocated to himself. Only to be used when the Prime Minister was under attack or a direct threat placed against him. It was the highest level code that the British secret service used. Apart from the King.

The other end of the line went quiet as the operative tapped in the code word. Instantly, warnings were triggered across the security services network. People in the highest offices, including Irm Brown and Marcus Poole, were about to be contacted and told that the Prime Minister had called in.

At last.

"Sir. Good to hear your voice Sir?" spoke the female operative, raising a hand to her head as she realised the importance of the call she was now handling. She made a few quick enquiries to ascertain the extent of his injuries and who he was with, whilst logging the mobile number he'd called from and instantly triangulating it to enable them to locate him.

"Are you still being pursued Sir?"

"No, we switched cars and phones and we haven't seen any of those responsible for a couple of hours at least now." Barnaby sighed with relief as he realised the threat was slowly diminishing.

"OK. I can see that you are on the A60, just north of Redhill, so you've been heading out of Nottingham. Stay where you are Sir, I'll mobilise the troops to come and get you, we have the SAS just a few miles away. They will be with you before you know it and take you to a safe location."

As he terminated the call, it suddenly sprang back to life with an incoming call. It was Lee's own mobile number displayed on the screen. They must be home and have charged the phone, Lee thought.

He took the handset from Barnaby and answered, closing his eyes, he said, "Hi Nicky, you guys OK?"

It wasn't Nicky's voice on the other end of the line.

It was the voice of a man. A man he did not know.

The colour drained from his face and he felt the hairs raise on the back of his neck for the second time that day.

Chapter Twenty Three

Progress

Jack Lumley, the delivery driver, come hit man, had been taken to a little known about, secure unit, separate to where they were holding Bolek Kumiega, the Mayor. If these two were connected in some way, they wanted to be sure that there was no chance of messages being relayed to each other. They also wanted to be convinced they could extract everything this scumbag knew. The building was well outside of Nottingham, hidden behind the facade of, 'Dangerous - Keep Out' signs. High fences deterring any from accidental entry. It was an old prison, that had the persona of an abandoned facility. It was anything but.

A different team had been assigned from those that arrested Lumley and they were led by M15 this time. Experts at working with suspected terrorists and organised criminal gangs. This team worked their prey with precision. Intolerable pressure, applied in the right places, to get them to open up. Mentally, and physically, if required, although that was always denied by the authorities. Once the hard exterior of the suspect had been removed, the layers of bravado peeled back, the soft under belly exposed, information was extracted at will. It was like watching an eagle using its claw, disembowelling a small mammal it was about to devour for lunch.

The room they bought Lumley to, contained no furniture other than a solitary chair he was secured to. It was bolted to the floor, two cast iron rings either side of the rear feet protruding from the polished, painted concrete floor. There was no two-way viewing screen and no recording devices that were usually present in police interview rooms. Thin grooves were cut into the concrete and Lumley noticed the chair was on a slight incline. His eyes followed the grooves down towards a grill covering a deep drain which ran directly to the sewers via a bleaching tray. He wasn't to know it, but it had been used to gain information from uncooperative suspects on occasion.

A tap, with a hose attached to it in the corner, allowed any evidence of 'ill treatment' to be washed away, neutralised by the bleaching tray under the grill. It had not been used a lot, but in the past it had enabled them to extract highly important information at critical times.

Lumley shot the two operatives furtive glances, a hint of fear in his eyes which he worked hard to cover. His hands were attached to the rings behind the chair via a toughened steel chain link, padlocked in the middle, out of reach of either hand. Given the shoulder injury from the bullet earlier, it was already extremely painful. He'd been tended by some first aiders and the blood flow stemmed, but certainly was not properly cleaned up. No pain relief had been administered. He was shaking from the shock of the gunshot wound.

The first operative was female, blue combat fatigues, dark hair swept back from her eyes, held tightly in a plait at the back of her head and solid black, workman

Progress

like boots. She stood with her hands on her hips and was the first to speak.

"Well, you are going down for a seriously long time for murdering that defenceless little girl and her mother." She started with an aggressive tone and had no desire to be seen as the 'Good Cop' in this exchange. "That shoulder must be painful. You cooperate quickly and we'll make sure it gets seen to properly. Bring you some morphine maybe. If you don't ... it's going to be a long night," she threatened menacingly.

The second operative was a black male with short cropped hair, a mottled complexion and a chiselled chin, that looked like it had taken a few hits over the years. He too was dressed in blue combat gear and solid boots. His sleeves were rolled up and he seemed to have muscles on his muscles, compared to the thin wiry figure tied to the chair in front of them. He stepped round the back of Lumley out of his line of sight, Lumley trying to turn his head to keep him in view.

Cropped hair whispered into Lumley's ear, his hot breath on the side of his head as he pulled the chains backwards, putting pressure on Lumley's arms and making him scream out loud. The damaged, inflamed tissue of his shoulder, got scraped across the shattered bones of his scapula. "See, we need some answers and we need them quickly. Who recruited you to kill the woman and her child?" he asked, releasing the pressure on the chains.

Lumley shook his head. He was determined not to give in so easily. But the pain. He had never experienced anything like it. Gritting his teeth, he looked at the women in front of him, "I don't know what you are talking about," he said.

"Of course you don't. The woman and her four-year-old daughter. The ones you shot dead in cold blood. Assassinated," he paused for the seriousness of the crime to sink in. "The chase at high speed across Mapperley, evading the police, before crashing your van and getting shot in the process. You know nothing about that?"

"No," he fired back. "I thought they wanted me because my van wasn't insured," he blurted quickly, breathing deeply through the pain. "Can't believe the bastards shot me!"

It was a feeble attempt and Plaits sneered. "Seriously? OK Lumley, as far as we're concerned, you, are already dead."

Jack flinched when she said his name out loud. How the hell had they found that out so quickly?

"Fell overboard a few years ago whilst out fishing with the family. Big insurance pay-out followed, clearing the family debts quite conveniently. Where have you been the last few years Jack?"

She stopped in front of him, placed her hand on his injured shoulder and pressed her thumb into the inflamed, exposed flesh.

"Arrrrrghhhhhhh ... STOP! Fucking stop ... please!" His bravado disappeared instantaneously. It seemed to have lasted less than a minute in total.

"We can stop, if you talk." The male operative chipped in. "Who ordered you to kill the woman and the child?" came the repeated question.

"I ... I don't know." Lumley hung his head in shame. More at the fact he was already giving in to his interrogators than to the fact he had just murdered two people, one of them only a child. "I got contacted over Snapchat. I never met them and I don't know who they are."

Progress

"So tell us what you do know. We want to know what they go by? Whether you received instruction from them before? Where did you get the gun?" several questions downloaded to get the ball rolling.

"Someone, they go by the name of Toad, got hold of my details. A few weeks back, I was asked to be on standby around Nottingham for today, in case I was needed like. I came 'ere yesterday, slept in the van overnight. Got a message earlier today my services were required. I didn't kill no woman or no girl though," the latter part of his answer sounded unconvincing, as he dropped his gaze to the floor.

"Seriously? You start telling us who asked you to kill the women and the child and then deny you did it!!"

"They were dead when I got there. Already dead." His eyes flicked up and down, the lie obvious from his facial expression.

The pressure was reapplied to his shoulder again. "Stop messing with us Jack. We got a visual of you from one of the police attending the scene as they ran past you, we found the gun we know was used, recovered from your van. The cases found at the scene will no doubt be matched with that gun shortly. You want try again?"

"Ok, just … please stop. It fucking hurts. I didn't know it was going to be a little girl. I had to … her mother …" Jack looked away. "The woman was first and then I went upstairs to find what I thought would be the husband. This little girl stared at me. She'd seen my face and I realised I'd just killed her mum. I shut my eyes." Again, Lumley looked away from his captives. Plaits wanted to smash him round the head with the baton she had tucked in her fatigues, but she had to make do with clenching and unclenching her fists for now.

"What did the message from Toad say?"

"It just gave me an address, told me two people inside and I was to terminate their contract. Permanently."

"Why? What had they done?"

"I don't know. I'm not to ask questions, just do as I'm asked," his voice getting feeble as he realised he was in serious trouble.

"It's a big leap from faking your own death for an insurance scam to murdering two, defenceless people. Where have you been the last few years Jack and what have you been doing?" Cropped hair dropped his face down to the same level as Jacks and put his hands on his knees.

"About. Odd jobs, you know, a bit of this and that," he winced again from the pain of his shoulder. "Can I get some pain killers now please?"

"Not yet. Is this the first time you've killed Jack?" Plaits was behind him now and the chains made a noise as she took them in her hands. Trying to turn his head to see her, Cropped hair grabbed his chin firmly to prevent him turning.

"No, no ... I've beaten people up before, but never ... killed no one."

"Where did you get the gun Jack?" the chains were pulled just a little to remind him of the power they now wielded over him.

"It was in the van. I picked it up yesterday from out of town. It was in the glove box."

"Who is Toad?" demanded Plaits.

"I dunno. Honest. I never met him. Don't even know if it is a him."

"How much did he pay you for killing them?"

"Ummm, twenty grand," he muttered.

"You are kidding me? Twenty thousand for killing two people. You scumbag" Plaits could restrain her anger no more and she smacked him round the back of his head with her fist. His head snapped forward and it jerked the chains, pulling his shoulder again. Lumley cried out.

Cropped hair continued the questioning. "You communicate via Snapchat. By the phone we recovered at the scene?"

"Yes. The money is in the holdall in the back of the van."

"Did you have any more communications with Toad? Did you tell him the job was complete?"

"No, you got to me before I could."

"Why the fuck would you kill people, for someone you have never met, for twenty grand?" Plaits could feel the anger still mounting, even though she was doing her best to contain it. In her pocket was a taser stun gun which she started to fiddle with, pulling it from her pocket whilst she was still out of sight.

"I need the money," his response was calm this time. Matter of fact. It was like he had agreed to paint your house, not murder two young innocent lives.

"So where have you been the last few years Jack?" asked Plaits. "Answer carefully this time. If I don't like the response you give me, you'll know it," and she grabbed his head, pulling it backwards by his hair and stuck the small metal protrusions from the taser against his throat.

"What the hell are you doing?" The panic was back. With his pulse through the roof and beads of sweat cascading down his forehead, the veins in his neck were visible. He couldn't take any more pain, so he started gushing. "I've been moving around a lot. I've been working in bars and pubs over Europe ... You know, cash in hand stuff. Keeping a low profile."

As he spoke, Plaits sensed he was being honest and moved the taser from his neck.

"Whereabouts have you been? What name have you been living under and when did you get back in the UK?" she enquired as Cropped hair stood back from him.

"Moved across Europe. Some time in Spain and then Italy. Bulgaria and Hungary later. I had a few names, but usually went as Lewis Beake." Lumley was broken now and his adrenaline had faded quickly. Despite the image he tried to portray to others, it was not in his blood to be a hard line criminal. He had learnt to hide behind the barrel of a gun recently, but when it came to physical pain, his threshold was pretty low.

In Hungary, he revealed that he got involved with some petty criminals and soon developed a reputation for breaking and entering. Before long, he became involved with more serious crime. He began dealing drugs for some hardened criminals, who would not think twice about putting a bullet in your head.

MI5 were about to discover he had indeed killed before. Initially in self-defence, when a drug lord thought he had been siphoning off the profits for his own gain. Two heavy weights were sent to terminate him, so Lumley had used a nearby brick to break the skull of the first assailant, then plunged a knife into the heart of the second. The police never investigated properly as it was two drug dealers who had been taken out

Progress

of the community. Infighting was always happening and it helped them with keeping criminality in check, as far as they were concerned. Saved on the paperwork.

Deciding to leave before he ended up dead for real, he heard about a group of eastern Europeans who were getting heavily involved in something to do with Europe and particularly the UK. They were well financed and paid handsomely for the right skill set. Without knowing the details of what he was getting involved in, he started to make his way back to the UK and made contact via the Dark Web *en route*.

Initially his contact had been someone he knew as Sloth2000 and then he was contacted by someone referred to as Toad. Toad as far as he was concerned was the lead. He did not know the real identities of either. All he knew, was that they were infamous on the Dark Web. Hackers he believed, suspecting they were into many things he'd be better off not knowing about.

Over the last two years, he was only contacted twice and so far it earned him fifty thousand in cash and a great reputation. Jack was not clear with his captors on what the first payment had been for, so they had applied pressure to his shoulder wound again. It didn't take long for the real answer to spring forth from the now very dry mouth of Jack Lumley.

"I was to remove a police computer operative. He was something to do with security clearance for recruits into the force. It had to look like an accident so as not raise suspicion. Young Asian guy, I can't remember his name. I managed to force his car off the road one night, he hit a tree and died from head injuries. Made sure it looked like he had been using his mobile at the wheel and he'd lost control of the car."

As he finished his account of the story, he suddenly realised he was responsible for the deaths of at least five other people. He'd never thought about any of them, he didn't care. Five, surely made him a prolific killer? Not a serial killer. He was not doing it for notoriety, or control. He was doing it for cash. That made him a hired hit man.

"What do you know about Bolek Kumiega?" they fired at him, hoping to catch him off guard as he seemed to be talking freely now.

"Who?" he questioned back. "I've never heard of him, or her, whatever kind of name that is. Why?"

"That's not important. Anything else you're hiding?" asked the male operative standing in front of him again.

"No. That's it. I swear. Please can I get some drugs for the pain now?" sighed Jack, his body now limp from the pain, dehydration and loss of blood. Along with his loss of dignity. He had completely capitulated.

Cropped hair stood, clenched his fists and smashed his right one into the jaw of Lumley. The force of the impact snatched his head backwards, his lower lip splitting in two and a fresh stream of blood flicking upwards through the air. Jacks body jerked and he lost consciousness.

"That's for the mother and her daughter. You lowlife shithead!" he called at him as he turned his back and headed out the door.

Plaits and Cropped hair were greeted by the wider team who had watched and monitored everything from carefully hidden cameras in the room. The chair relayed heart rate, sophisticated programmes monitored pupil diameter and body language, informing them if there

Progress

were anomalies in the data. They would know irrefutably if Lumley was not telling the truth. Modern lie detector equipment, but without the suspects knowing they were being monitored. It was far more accurate than the old polygraph systems.

Their handler spoke first. "He told the truth after the initial denials. The story on the computer handler appears to be accurate as well. There were reports in local papers of a young man dying from head injuries after driving without due care and attention. Amazingly, the police actually used the story of one of their own dying, to reinforce the importance of not using your phone whilst driving. That was about eighteen months ago, in February 2022."

Continuing, he said, "Toad is obviously the key to this. Discover who Toad is and we can break the ring. That name came up on a coded message recently. Sloth2000, that's a new one on me. Why do they always have weird names?" he enquired, to a group of shaking heads.

"He doesn't know the mayor, that was definitely true. I'll send the information we've got through to control. We don't have much time. So far, they seem to be one step ahead of us and we've still not recovered the prime minister."

They did not know it yet, but they had just made significant progress in the chase to recover the leader of their country.

Chapter Twenty Four

Download

Night time had well and truly descended. Temperatures were dropping, but the pressure remained high. Number 10, Downing Street had the lights on. The press had been moved back from their usual position on the pavement opposite the front door, under the guise of security measures.

"Given the day's events in Nottingham, and those responsible for the attack yet to be identified, we are taking the precaution of widening the ring of security around those in Government," was the announcement made, as journalists and camera crews were jostled out of position.

At the end of the road, beyond the railings, the army now stood guard, alongside the usual armed police officers. Protected patrol vehicles occupied the road outside. The Foxhound had served the forces well in the desert wars of the last two decades and it looked threatening on the tarmac of London. A show of strength, deterring any would be assailants. Roads were closed, preventing anyone from getting close and the journalists couldn't help but feel a little intimidated as the army started to push them back even further.

Download

Inside Number 10, a rather stressed looking, deputy prime minister, was waiting for an update from the home secretary. Sebastian Horner had never expected to be in this kind of position and it wasn't something he relished. A quiet figure in the EIP, he had been a long-time friend of Barnaby, going back nearly ten years when they both ran successful businesses. Sebastian came from the north of the country and had met Barnaby when they had both gotten involved with the British Chambers of Commerce.

Their story was quite similar, in that new EU legislation seemed to be against them competing fairly in Europe. Sebastian's business developed and sold extremely high-end, powerful vacuum cleaners. Used mostly by industry rather than domestic use, his customers disappeared almost overnight. In 2014, the EU passed a bill to ban what were termed 'Super Vacuum Cleaners'. Anything with a motor above the EU limit of one thousand six hundred watts had to go, in a bid to cut energy usage.

Sebastian's business had not gone under completely, but he had to scale back massively, whilst spending large amounts on remodelling his manufacturing for the domestic market. However, here he was not a market leader. No one had really heard of his products and despite large spending on advertising, his business never recovered to their former glory days. He took his complaint to the British Chambers of Commerce, well before the ban was imposed, asking them to lobby the EU. It was here that he met Barnaby Aitken, who had suffered a similar fate a few years before. Barnaby had failed in his previous endeavour, but was keen to support someone else in a similar situation.

They failed together.

As his business declined, he felt failed by the UK Government and more annoyed at the autocrats in Brussels. To him, many of them seemed to be devoid of anything approaching a normal impression of life and the world in which normal business operated. They had created a bubble for themselves, impenetrable to others, distorting their view of the real world. The world that normal people had to operate in.

After the passing of another ludicrous bill, both businessmen had had enough. Over lunch one day, they discussed how they could really make a difference for British industry. With Labour in disarray, the Tories cutting back to the bone in a bid to reduce the deficit hangover of the financial crisis and everything looking like it was falling apart due to BREXIT, they realised they probably could not rely on anyone in British politics to change things for the better. Although the whole debate had been started by UKIP, their job was done when the referendum result was 'OUT'. Their purpose came to an end. When Nigel Farage resigned, content with the chaos he had initiated, the party drifted from leader to leader over the next eighteen months. None of them stayed in the job very long, as their cause was no longer clear and annoyingly, skeletons kept falling out of closets. The party had imploded. Fallen on their own sword.

The conclusion Sebastian and Barnaby came to, was that they should develop their own political party. One with a focus on England. English industry and people. Divisive politics continued to become very popular over the next few years as infighting and a preoccupation with BREXIT took its toll. The British public lost belief in the two main parties and turned to alternatives to fill the gap. All of that, resulted in Barnaby being appointed PM and he, Sebastian Horner, his deputy.

A loud knock on the heavy set door, brought Sebastian's attention.

"Come in" he spoke quietly and it swung open.

With his hand on the brass door knob, the servant of the house announced the entrance of "the home secretary, Sir", then stood to the side to let Helen Langley past.

"Can I bring you anything Ma'am?" he enquired.

"Coffee, thank you," the short reply, before she turned her attention to Sebastian. He looked like he had aged this day. More grey hairs on his head and definitely more stress lines, she thought to herself. Good.

"Helen, come in," he welcomed her and ushered her to a sofa so they could speak.

"Sebastian. Any news on Barnaby?" she got straight into the important element.

"You know he called in his position?" Helen nodded in response and he continued. "The SAS have been sent details and are on the way there now. Hopefully, we will have him back in our protective custody shortly."

"Thank goodness for that. I've been worried sick about him. It's one thing for all those people in Nottingham to be killed or injured, but quite another for our leader to be targeted in such a horrific way." Helen spoke casually, as she pulled a scarf from around her neck and put her bag on the floor next to her.

Sebastian looked at her quizzically. Did she really just say what he thought she said? He knew she carried an air of superiority about her, but he could not believe she could be so callous about the death and maiming of so many innocent lives. Giving Helen the benefit of doubt, he decided she must be flustered from the day's events.

"Please, Helen take a seat, update me on what has happened over the last few hours." Sebastian sat on a leather arm chair opposite the sofa in the small office. As she started, the door opened and the coffee came in. They waited, both taking it black. It could be a long night.

Over the next twenty minutes, Helen updated him on everything she had regarding the fast moving investigation. From the infiltration of the police by Victor Jansens and Fabian Pichler, through to MI5 and MI6 collaborating. She continued, describing the hit on the mother and her young daughter. The recent acquisition of Jack Lumley, had literally just revealed important information through his interrogation, possibly offering an intriguing insight into why this attack may be happening.

Helen updated him on everything. Everything, except the name Toad, that had now come up twice in the investigation. She wanted to keep that one to herself for now. As a politician it was always good to have a few cards up your sleeve. Never reveal your full hand, even to those in your own party, just in case you got out manoeuvred.

Sebastian had put his coffee down on the table when she relayed the story of the hit on the little girl and her mother. Having recently become a grandparent for the first time, he found that particularly disturbing. Why? Such waste of human life. He rubbed his head with his hand, looking down at the table.

Some would call it a human side, but Helen saw the weakness in him. He should not falter at such minor things, he should stand firm behind his principles and condemn those responsible. In her mind, Sebastian was not the right choice to support Barnaby as his Deputy Prime Minister. That was a role she very much wanted for herself. Helen was about to ensure that it came her way.

"Sebastian, I have to say, you have been fairly impotent today." She looked him up and down, as, for the second time since she arrived, he looked at her quizzically.

"I beg your pardon?" he asked, taken aback by the aggressive nature of her comment.

"Where have you been Sebastian? With all of the events of today, I have seen no leadership from you whatsoever, in the absence of the prime minister."

Her gaze never averted from his. "We need someone to stand at the front of this party, of this country, in a time of crisis and take control. Not someone who hides in the shadow of Number 10, unwilling to take control and confront those responsible." Helen put her cup down on the table and leant towards him.

"I don't think Barnaby would be at all impressed with your performance today Sebastian. It's taken people like me to really move things on. Get things going. Save the day. You know. It will be quite embarrassing for you when he finds out what little you have done to take control, despite the fact that *you* are his deputy."

She pointed her finger at him, demeaning his presence in the very room they were sat.

Sebastian stood up, his temper about to flare. Breathing deeply, he opened his mouth to talk down to her in her seat, "How dare you ..." but as he started to talk, Helen too stood up. In her heels she was above the eye line of Sebastian by a couple of centimetres. It was enough to put him off his train of thought.

"How dare I what, Sebastian? Suggest that you should have taken more of a leadership role today. Dare to ask our deputy prime minister to be a man and take control of the situation. It was I who faced the media. It was I, who ordered the army onto the streets. It was I who closed the airports. What is it you've done Sebastian?"

As she finished her sentence a smile rose at the corner of her mouth, she could tell that she was hitting a nerve or two.

A flushed complexion hit Sebastian's cheeks as he roused himself to respond. "I ... I ... I" he barked back at her. "It's not about you Helen, it's about Barnaby and returning him safely to Number 10. How dare you question what I have been doing today! We are supposed to be working as a team. I expect respect from you, you jumped up little bitch. If it wasn't for Barnaby and I, you wouldn't be here in the first place." His hand was raised and he was pointing at her now, aggression coming to the fore.

"Well, I disagree with you on that statement, Sebastian. What is to happen if Barnaby doesn't make it back safely to Number 10? That would put you in control and I don't think that is right, or good, for the party."

Helen sat back down on the sofa and opened her bag, reaching inside for an envelope. Taking it out, she opened it and placed several photos on the table between the two.

"What's this?" asked Sebastian, looking down at the photos. His head lifted as he realised what they were. "Where did you get these?" he asked, anger rising again, but this time closely followed by fear and self-preservation.

"That's not important Sebastian. What is important is the fact that you ..." her finger tapped on the photo, "are having sex with a ..." she paused for effect, "how shall I say this? Male escort."

Helen tapped the photo again, highlighting a very clear image of Sebastian in the throes of passion. "What would your wife say about this? Or Barnaby? Or the press even?"

Sebastian sat back down in his armchair again. Deflated. Defeated.

"We are supposed to be locating the prime minister and restoring law and order in the country and you pull this out ... NOW! You bitch." It was all he could bring himself to say.

"If Barnaby does not return, you will step aside from the role of deputy PM and allow me to take the leadership of the party. If not, the press will have a field day with this." Helen pushed the photos towards him, reinforcing the point she was making. "Understand?"

Helen stood, sweeping the pictures back into the envelope, a smile returning to her face. It was all about timing in her mind.

Sebastian nodded meekly.

Helen had just killed his political career, whilst accelerating her own.

Chapter Twenty Five

Choices

Barnaby looked at Lee, most of his face obscured by the front seat he was sat behind. Blood completely drained from Lee's face, his body starting to shake, indicating to Barnaby that something bad was happening on the call.

"Don't hurt them ..." he pleaded as a tear welled in the corner of his eye. His fist clenched and then he grabbed the steering wheel in front of him. Desperation had him in its firm grip now, but Barnaby was unclear why. He reached out a reassuring hand to Lee's elbow, but Lee flinched at the touch.

"OK ... OK ... Where do you want me to go?" he asked of the man calling him. Using his own mobile. "Yes ... I don't know, maybe twenty minutes, maybe more ... Yes" his breathing was becoming faster as the anxiety started to build. "I won't," he finished, moving the mobile away from his face to stare at the screen and then held it close to his chest and let out a wail, "NO! No ... Noooooooo." Lee thumped the palm of his hand on the steering wheel and tears started to roll down his cheek.

"What is it Lee?" asked Barnaby, pulling his weight forward to try and see Lee better. Lee, who had been lost in his own little world, spun his head round wiping the tears from his cheeks.

"They got them Sir ... They've got Aidan. They've got Nicky and Dan ... They've got them all. How the hell did ..." he didn't finish his sentence, but started shaking his head.

Barnaby dropped his gaze to his knees and shifted his weight. It was getting uncomfortable in the footwell.

"They know we have Dan's car. They know everything," he gushed. Chocolate bars and crisps, readily consumed just a few minutes earlier, now sat uncomfortably in his stomach. Fat and sugar, mixed with hydrochloric acid. Churning. Repeating.

Barnaby pulled himself out of the footwell to sit on the rear seat, as there was clearly little point in hiding now. Rubbing his legs, he let out a low groan and helped the blood flow back to his feet, his ankle throbbing again as the warmth and supply of oxygen and nutrients, returned to the surrounding tissues.

Fixing Lee in the rear view mirror, Barnaby spoke softly. "I assume they want to exchange me for your family and friend?" he questioned. Lee could not look at him, but nodded his head in response. Taking a deep breath he continued, "Then you must take me to them Lee. I cannot let your family suffer because of me. That is not acceptable."

Lee looked up at the mirror, almost in disbelief at the selfless response of his country's leader. At this, most unexpected offer, Lee shook his head. "No Sir, that's not right. They will kill you. They won't just kill you, they will kill us all" shaking his head again, "Bastards..... My poor boy!"

He looked back at the screen, expecting it to spring back to life. What was he to do? He had an impossible choice to make. Leave his family and friend to be murdered? He couldn't. How could anyone?

The alternative was to deliver the prime minister to them. They had promised to return Aidan, Nicky and Dan, unharmed, in exchange for Barnaby Aitken. He did not believe them. Lee knew that the moment he handed over Barnaby, they would all be exterminated. His stomach tightened and his salivary glands spat forth into his mouth. Grabbing for the handle, he flung open the driver's door, knowing he could not deny this visceral act. His body heaved and the semi-digested contents of his stomach, spewed forth across the tarmac, into the tightening cold of the night.

Feeling light headed, he wiped his mouth with a tissue from his pocket and sat back in the driver's seat. Barnaby patted him on the shoulder again, trying to reassure him that 'under the circumstances' it was a perfectly natural response. Under the circumstances! How do you prepare, or train yourself for circumstances such as these? How do they know how you will react 'in circumstances like these'? Many questions rushed through his confused mind as he tried to figure out what to do. Look at the shameless destruction of life throughout the day. No thought for innocent people being killed. Devoid of normal human emotion, these violent thugs, would not hesitate to put a bullet in the heads of those they sought, and those stupid enough to get in the way.

The amphibian like voice on the end of the phone had left him no doubt. He really was not going to win. Whatever he chose to do, he lost. He felt crushed. His stomach tightened again, but thankfully this time, it was already empty.

"Lee, you have been incredibly brave today. I cannot ask you and your family to sacrifice anything else on my behalf. Where have they told you to meet them?"

"They want us to go to Holme Pierrepont. It's south of Nottingham. A water sports place. Presumably its dark, no cameras. Empty at this time on a Sunday night," he looked up at Barnaby, "Perfect place for an execution Sir." Lees pale face hung low.

Barnaby went to speak again, but Lee stopped him. "Sir, if I take you there, they will kill you. They won't stop there, they will kill us all. You will have given in to terrorism. Terrorism will have won."

Running his hands through his hair, he sat upright as he considered the alternatives he had. "If I don't take you, they can only kill me and my family ..." his voice faltered, "not you."

An impossible choice for anyone to make.

The enormity of the words Lee had just uttered, hit Barnaby Aitken like a spade across his face. Selfless, heroic, beyond reproach. Barnaby was humbled. Humanity had surprised him significantly today. Humanity, in the form of Lee Bevan and his son, Aidan.

Raising his eyes back to meet Lee's, he started, "Lee, I cannot imagine what is going through your mind. To know your family is held to ransom in such a way, is abhorrent. I admire the way you are responding to this ... this threat," he leant forward on the seat to put his hand on the shoulder of his saviour, "but, that decision is not yours to make. I cannot allow your family to perish for this. For me ..." but he was stopped from finishing his point.

"Sir, with respect, my life is crap without my wife and my son around me on a daily basis. That's my fault." Tears rolled down his cheeks freely now. "It would be unbearable, without them both to visit on a weekend. To see them occasionally is the only thing that keeps me going. If I lose that, I have nothing. I have nothing to live for, Sir."

"Lee, you have to take me with you," Barnaby was getting animated now as a thought entered his head. "I have an idea though. Pass me the phone again." Reaching his hand out, Lee hesitated.

"They have the phone number Sir. They can monitor us, listen to our conversations now, see our text messages. They said they would track the phone to make sure I was proceeding as planned to Holme Pierrepont." Pulling his hand back, he gripped the phone tightly. We can't use it, they will know whatever it is you plan."

Barnaby nodded his understanding. "Ok. In that case, do exactly as I tell you."

Barnaby's mind was working overtime now and he started to relay quickly and clearly to Lee what he had in mind.

An impossible choice to make, but they had to make it quickly.

The clock was ticking. Loudly, in both their ears.

Chapter Twenty Six
Family

Chequers, the country retreat for the prime minister and his family, set in the quintessential English countryside, was besieged by armoured vehicles and military personnel. In the village of Ellesborough, Buckinghamshire, the sixteenth century manor house had been the prime ministers country residence since 1921.

Surrounded by dark green, rolling lawns with perfect parallel lines visible, lovingly tended every day. The building rose from the ground, impressive and welcoming. A sweeping gravel driveway wound around the entrance, enormous evergreen trees reaching out across the countryside, enclosing large swathes of the grounds with a protective canopy.

Snipers were positioned around the estate, in trees and ridges, overlooking the surrounding areas. They sported night vision goggles, resting just above their cheeks. They viewed the dog patrols circulating continuously around the perimeter, appearing alien-like, a green phosphorescent light against the dark backdrop. Movement of humans and animals alike were easy to pick out. They turned their attention outwards, to the surrounding countryside, scouring areas of open land. Searchlights erected at the corners of the property, enabling the entire circumference to be illuminated at will throughout the night. Should the need arise.

The staff responsible for the smooth running of the household and ensuring the country's premier family were looked after to the highest standard, were a little disturbed. The normally pristine property had seen numerous security personnel take up residence over the last few hours. The vehicles were in danger of tearing up the quilt like lawn. It was well protected in peaceful times, but in a matter of hours it had become like a military base, locked down on all sides.

The rumbling of the vehicles coming and going were shaking the china crockery that had been set for tea in the drawing room. Several outer rooms of the house were now occupied with other highly trained military personnel, setting up separate secure communications channels to the ones normally used by the prime minister when he was in residence.

Maureen, the prime minister's wife, opened the door from the drawing room to seek out whoever was in charge.

"Any news on my husband yet?" she demanded to know as she reached a tall man sporting a neatly clipped beard. He was adorned with three stripes on the arm of his jacket, a small crown depicted above them.

The Staff Sergeant in charge of the detail at Chequers, now under 'lockdown', turned to respond.

"Ma'm. Mr Aitken has recently been in touch. We have his location on the outskirts of Nottingham. The team on the ground are being sent there now, to locate, rescue and ensure the safe return of your husband Ma'm. We will update you as soon as he is in our care."

Family

"Thank God!" Maureen lifted her hands in the air, putting them together as if to pray. A smile was a long way from returning to her face, but she certainly felt more positive than she had done at any point that day. Turning around, she walked back to the drawing room, pulled the door closed behind her and headed straight for the drinks cabinet. Tea was not strong enough on a night like this.

Mike Lightfoot, her husband's personal secretary, was on his way here, under armed protection. She was expecting him in the next half hour or so and she needed a large gin and tonic to calm her nerves before he arrived. The last thing she wanted Mike to see when he got here, was an hysterical, middle-aged female, bawling at the events of the day. Maureen was normally a calm individual.

With good reason, she had abandoned her typically serene approach today.

Pouring herself a very large gin, there was not much room left in the glass for any tonic. She sipped some from the glass before dropping in a couple of cubes of ice. Turning around, she flopped onto the sofa, suddenly feeling exhausted. It had been a tense day and with adrenaline and emotions running stratospheric, her body needed a rest.

Earlier, she had spoken with both her daughters. Susan, her eldest had been picked up with her husband and taken to a military base not far from their home. Her husband Jack, who was a professional rugby player and more than capable of taking care of himself objected incessantly. They did not want to be dictated to by a group of 'political terrorists'. However, military personnel were not taking 'no' for an answer and politely insisted, until Susan calmed her husband down and suggested it would only be for a short time.

Lisa, the free spirit, had been a little trickier to track down as she was up in the Lake District on a camping and hiking weekend with some friends. With no mobile signal for long periods of time it had been a challenge contacting her. When her mobile finally did blink to life, as she approached civilisation, it wasn't long before a helicopter with armed personnel on board landed outside a country pub and she was ushered inside. Local villagers came out to see what the commotion was, as people started live streaming images of the prime minister's daughter being loaded onto the recently commissioned Wildcat MKII and flown at speed across the rolling hills.

Shocking things, worth recording, seemed to be happening all across the country.

Sinking her head back against the deep cushion of the red velvet sofa, she slaked her thirst with another gulp of her drink. It wasn't often that she thought it was better not to bring children into the world, but the darkness of the day, troubled her greatly. Perhaps it was better that her offspring had not yet born her grandchildren. How do you explain the madness of this world to a small child? How should you protect the innocent? She shook her head in disbelief and her mind turned again to the love of her life.

A noise behind her shook her from her thoughts, the big oak door swung open and Mike Lightfoot was shown in to the drawing room and offered tea by the butler.

"Thanks, that would be great," he acknowledged.

"You can have something stronger if you'd like Mike," offered Maureen, "God knows I need it. I'm sure you do too".

Family

"Very kind Maureen, but I'd better not," he declined and picked up his tea. "I suspect I'll need a very clear head. It may well be a long night yet." He moved towards her and embraced her as she stood, then he sat facing her from the other end of the sofa.

"How are you Maureen?"

"OK, thanks Mike. The staff have been amazing. It's all a bit unbelievable really," she lifted the glass again and finished the last of her aperitif. "I just hope Barnaby is OK, I haven't heard from him since he phoned me. I think that was before they got attacked for the second time." Her chest heaved as she sighed deeply and held the glass to her bosom.

"You know that the SAS have been deployed to pick him up, yes?" he waited for her to nod before continuing. "They will be with him soon. Once they have him safely on board, they will ensure he is taken to a nearby army barracks. It will probably be Kendrew Barracks in Rutland. It's close by, but also out of the spotlight of Nottingham."

Maureen was listening intently to every word he said, following his eyes flick back and forth.

"Once safely on the ground, he'll be checked over by the Medical Staff. Only the best for Barnaby." Mike paused to make sure Maureen was following everything.

"Will he return here after he has the all clear from the medical team?"

"That depends on Barnaby to be honest Maureen. You know what he is like. I suspect he will want to go to the head of the operation and ensure that all military and uniformed officers are deployed correctly. He'll want to ensure every last one of these ... these terrorists, are hunted down and bought to justice. Or killed in the hunt," he added with a nod to Maureen as he lifted the tea cup to his mouth.

Over the next ten minutes, Mike updated Maureen with everything he was aware of through the day. Putting his cup back on the saucer and resting it on the table, he paused. Maureen jumped in quickly with a question. "Any idea yet who is behind this and what it's all about?"

"We have some leads Maureen, but it's certainly not clear at the moment. Not to me anyway. Our very best are working on this tirelessly and they have all the resources they could possibly need."

At that, Maureen looked away, then moved to fill her glass again.

"It's been such a nightmare of a day Maureen. On top of everything that is going on, Helen, I am sure," he turned to look at Maureen to gauge her reaction to what he was about to say, "made a pass at me in her office earlier."

Maureen laughed. It was the first time her mouth had an upward turn to it today. Even in dark times it was possible to see a lighter side of life. "You are kidding me aren't you?" she enquired, but Mike was shaking his head. "But that is ridiculous. No offence, of course Mike ... Well, you are a very handsome man!" A glint had returned to her eye. Maureen put a hand to his shoulder, then leant forward to kiss his now blushing cheek.

"I always thought she was more interested in the females. How wrong I was. She does know you're gay, right?" asked Maureen, but Mike was shaking his head again.

Family

"Given the look she gave me, I really don't think so. To be fair, I was flattered. She is a very attractive women, as women go." Mike replied.

"Well maybe Helen is, what do they call it now, bisexual? Perhaps she thinks you might be too." Maureen found peoples sexuality very intriguing these days. Many seemed to change their mind constantly to suit their needs of the day. Or just to suit whatever, whoever, was available and offering themselves to you at that time. Her mind wandered back to Lisa and she pondered again, whether she preferred women to men. Perhaps she was cut in the same way as Helen? She would have to ask her about it in more detail they next time she saw her. Maureen couldn't quite work out if it made finding a partner easier, or more difficult, these days?

Mike continued, "I just found it odd. The fact that she was even thinking about sex! When the country is in crisis and the prime minister is missing. Not just missing, but he's being hunted by maniacs who are one step ahead of us," as he finished his sentence, he realised Maureen's glint disappeared and she averted her gaze.

"I'm sorry. That was tactless." He put his hand on her knee to comfort her, "We'll have him back safe soon Maureen." Mike stood and moved towards the door. "I should be going Maureen, but please do let me know if there is anything you or your family need. You are all in the safest places now, but you must not look to go anywhere until this is all under control."

Maureen stood and embraced Mike again. "Bring him back Mike. Bring my Big Ben ..." she corrected herself quickly, "Barnaby, back to me safely. Please." She turned her back on him and returned to the sofa, her face away from him.

"We will Maureen. We will. Take care."

Leaving through the door and heading to the front entrance of the expansive Manor House, Mike pulled his coat back on and buttoned the front. As he moved outside towards the waiting car, he wondered how Maureen knew the code name for her husband.

That struck him as very odd.

The prime ministers code name was top secret information, that Barnaby had been forbidden from telling anyone.

Even his own family.

Chapter Twenty Seven

Connections

Food was ordered from just about all the local pizza companies, Chinese takeaways and curry houses that delivered within a mile's radius. Almost every member of staff had been called in, from holiday or weekend leave, to assist. There were hundreds of staff, pouring over screens at their desks, crowded in briefing rooms or pacing the corridors talking into mobile phones. Desperately trying to explain to their families that they may not be back for a few days. They were definitely in for the night and there was not a sign of an English meal anywhere.

Glasses pulled members of M16 into a room with some key personnel of the other establishment, MI5. Crowded round the edges of the room almost everyone with coffee in one hand and some form of nourishment in the other. Eyes were fixed on the screen at the front of the room and the door had been left open, so they did not overheat or get distracted with people coming and going. No welcomes or pleasantries were exchanged between the two groups. They just got down to business. After a brief update on those who had unfortunately lost their lives earlier in the day, they moved on to fresh ground.

"This guy was arrested earlier after being chased across Nottingham. He was seen leaving the scene of a double murder. Young mother and her daughter, single shot to the head, he killed them in cold blood," started Tatoos, pointing at a picture of Jack Lumley on the screen. "They were family, or at least cover, for this man," he paused as the image of the man they knew as Fabian Pichler appeared. "He was shot and killed earlier in the day by Paul Buxton and his team, as they chased after the prime minister and his would-be assassins."

Before he could continue, Irm interjected. "Have we been able to get a hit on his real identity so far?"

"We think so chief. Just trying to run his facial recognition through Interpol. After his image was released to the authorities across Europe, someone at the Federal Ministry of Defence in Austria thought they recognised him." explained Glasses, picking up as part of the usual tag team.

"Ok, do tell," pleaded Irm. "Does it give us more of an idea of what this is about and who is behind it?"

"Bizarrely, the woman who has identified him, at least she thinks she recognises him, used to be his girlfriend a number of years back. She happens to now work for the ministry itself. Chance in a billion maybe!" Glasses sent some more details up to the screen. "We think his real name might be Dietmar Schwarz." He leant back and started pulling his knuckles one by one, a reflex he seemed to have whenever he got slightly excited with a project.

"Schwarz, we suspect now is not actually Austrian, but German. If it is him, his family used to run a very successful automotive company, called 'Reinigen Blau' and were inextricably linked with the failings of VW.

Connections

VW, I am sure you will remember, were accused by an insider, of fixing their emissions figures a number of years back. That led to a mass of claims against VW, sales plummeted and the company very nearly went bust. Well, Schwarz's family seized the moment and positioned themselves at the time as the company to be trusted on emissions. 'Reinigen', for those that are not familiar with German, translates as 'clean'. So, the company name is essentially 'Clean Blue'. Quite emotive and great positioning for an up and coming car company in a crowded market. But, with all the negativity around emissions, it was brilliant marketing!"

"All very interesting, but how the hell does this lead us to a sleeper undercover in our own police force, reaping terrorism on the unsuspecting public of Nottingham?" It was Marcus's turn to question the team and pressure test the hypothesis they were developing.

Someone from Marcus' team who had been linking up with Tatoos and Glasses earlier in the day, to ensure everything was shared across the two agencies, joined the discussions. An older lady, nicknamed Silver by her colleagues, had worked exclusively for MI5 for almost her entire working career. Silver held the respect of her colleagues and was rarely phased by anything. Naturally grey, curly hair hung over the rims of her frameless glasses. Bifocals making her eyes look very large from particular angles.

"Sir, I can answer that one. Dietmar Schwarz was the only son of the owner of the company. He was set to inherit a fortune. However, the UK was the biggest single market for Reinigen, including Germany in that. The drive to be as green as possible, coupled with the tax levels on the old diesel and petrol cars, made it an attractive, hybrid purchase for the customers here." Silver surveyed the room, it was silent as everyone listened intently. Only the sound of the occasional munch, or the lifting of cups to mouths to be heard.

"Fair enough, they have motors everywhere. So what?" replied Marcus.

"Well Sir, since BREXIT was declared, sales already started to decline. But, since the EIP have come to power and imposed further restrictions on our borders, the level of sales in the UK has fallen off a cliff. Schwarz's fortune has almost gone as the business is now in danger of being declared bankrupt. It is possible that they have seen this coming for a while. I don't think anyone is happy at seeing their fortune wiped out, particularly when it was estimated to be in the hundreds of millions of Euros," finished Silver.

"Money, sex and power are the usual culprits when it comes to people doing very extreme things," suggested Marcus. "If people feel they are about to lose control of something, aggression comes to the fore. They will take risks if they are driven by lust, or love, as the grey matter doesn't seem to process things normally."

As he spoke, he realised what he had just said in front of his former lover. He wasn't sure if there was an awkward silence in the room, or he just imagined it, so he ploughed on. "When it comes to power, that is the biggest calling to arms, isn't it? Look at all of the wars over the centuries, it's always about who wants to exert their control over others. Usually men, playing the 'my nuclear button is bigger than your nuclear button' whilst putting the rest of the world at risk of complete annihilation."

"Yes, its 'nearly' always men," added Irm, using her fingers to indicate quotation marks. A light murmuring filled the room. "We definitely need more women in power."

Further titters.

"OK. So this is probably about money and possibly loss of power," suggested Marcus. "Can you show the notes we made earlier in the day?" he nodded towards Glasses, who duly obliged. The list came to the screen, highlighting the industries and countries already identified, linking the terrorists. Alongside it were the names of the hackers also identified:

FARMING	BELGIUM	HaPee as Larry
FISHING	UK	IPFree
EU SUBSIDIES?	AUSTRIA	BOWIE

There were lots of other notes scribbled alongside, but it was the main headlines that stood out. Marcus stood up, trying to assert a little control on the meeting. In his mind, this was clearly M15 territory. Moving towards the screen he started talking again.

"Now, we could add Automotive Industry, alongside that we can add Bulgaria, Hungary and probably Germany. For those that don't know, two of those countries we know Jack Lumley has connections to over the last few years."

He tapped against Bulgaria and Hungary to indicate to the team, then nodded at Silver, instructing her to give another brief update on the information obtained from his interrogation.

Irm, now stood and walked to the back of the room. Mostly to get attention and wrestle some control of the room back from Marcus, but under the disguise of stretching her back and legs.

"Add Sloth2000 and Toad, to the list of hackers then. Anyone come across any of these names?" She asked of her own team members first, when met with shaking heads, she looked at the MI5 contingent.

Silver went on to reveal the apparent 'accidental death', of the police computer operative that Lumley had admitted to.

Standing at opposite ends of the long table, Irm and Marcus eyed each other. Marcus spoke first. "You all know the gravity of this situation?" He was met with nodding heads and looks of determination to uncover the culprits and bring this plot to a close before the night was out.

"Let's work on the assumption for now," his finger tapped on the table, "that this, is a number of highly motivated individuals with connections into all sorts of industries. They are well funded, well connected and seemingly, extremely well equipped, with technological nous, that is quite frankly at a higher level than our own right now. These people feel they are have been hard done by BREXIT and the recent further actions to stem the movement of people and goods across our borders. They have struck at the pinnacle of our democracy and they cannot be allowed to win."

Marcus was speaking with passion now. He knew when he needed to rally the troops. They had been a few steps behind so far and they needed to catch up fast.

Joining forces, an unusual act of unity, Irm picked up from him, "We have to identify those individuals and bring them to justice as soon as possible. We cannot allow any more attacks on our sovereign territory. Whether they are from overseas, or homegrown here in the UK, they will face the courts if we can catch them.

Be assured, you have permission to instruct your contacts working with and for us, they are cleared to use the maximum force necessary, to detain, or remove an imminent threat." Those types of instructions were very rarely given out and most gathered round the room, had certainly not been involved when they had been issued previously.

Marcus had been watching Irm closely. His protege really had reached her potential and he was pleased she led the team at MI6. He finished, "We must work together in the interests of our country, but also with those of the wider European Community. Nothing is to be kept to a single agency. Understand?" he looked directly at Irm, as did her own team for confirmation.

"Understood," she added, before summarising a few actions for the team to focus their efforts on. "I want to know who the hell these hackers are." She pointed at the names on the screens. "Who replaced our dead computer operative and who the hell gave the cover for all the 'sleepers' that seemed to have infiltrated our police force. What are the connections? Finally, I want anything you can find on Toad and any reference to 'The Puppy' from the message we intercepted. There has to be some trail of IP addresses that we can find to lead us to these bastards. They must have slipped up somewhere."

Irm leant against the table on her hands, indicating they were done and the teams should get moving. People stood, notebooks collected and were about to depart.

"One last thing," called out Marcus. "You know the prime minister has been located and the SAS are *enroute* to pick him and hopefully return him safely back to us. Let's make sure he is proud of our response to this atrocity and we can line up those responsible before the night is out." He liked to have the last word.

As the room was emptying, Irm and Marcus exchanged a handshake. It was polite, yet formal. A new footing in their relationship, maybe.

"The phone recovered from Jack Lumley earlier," Irm started, still holding his hand, "You mentioned he used it to connect with Toad." Marcus nodded, Irm didn't miss a thing. "You must be able to use that to find a connection to him, surely?"

Glasses looked up, "Sure can!" he declared ahead of Marcus' response, "Want me take a look for you Sir?"

Marcus released his grip from Irms. "It's Ok, the team are on it, as we speak! I'll let you know when we get something useful," he declared.

As he headed towards the door, Irm was left with a feeling that 'Working together' was directed at her team and was not necessarily applicable to his.

Chapter Twenty Eight
Inside Information

When Toad put the phone down on Lee he smiled. It was not a warm smile. It sent shivers down Nicky's spine and she tried to nuzzle Aidan closer to her side, his head buried in her coat. Aidan's sobbing was incessant now.

The inside of the house was squalid, dirty beyond comprehension. Bowls and cooking utensils covering the sides in the kitchen. Coffee cups on every shelf or window sill. Thick blinds closed over the windows and a small, bare, energy saving light bulb, probably from Germany, threw out some low level yellow light, making the surroundings look cream coloured. Everything had a smell of nicotine and fat about it.

Nicky was cringing, concerned that they might actually have to touch something in this bio-hazard of a place. If they were to get out of here, their clothes and shoes would have to go in the bin. They would never be clean enough for her to wear and she could not bear to see Aidan in the same outfit. It would be too painful. They had to survive first.

"Well, well!" Toad coughed at them, waving Lees freshly charged mobile at them. "It seems your ex-husband is going to play nicely and bring us the prime minister, in return for your freedom."

Habitually, he sucked in the nicotine vapour, holding it for as long as his lungs would allow, before blowing it directly towards his captors. Nicky turned her head away and held her breath. Dan stared at him, hatred in his eyes. The cloth covering his mouth was causing him to gag regularly and he tried to push it off with his tongue. He had counted four heavily armed men so far and this guy in front of them who appeared to be in charge. If he could break free, he would take him out first. Maybe the others would capitulate after their leader had gone.

Toad turned to his hired henchmen and gestured at them, "Put them in the front room, make sure they stay quiet."

Heading back towards the side door, he opened it and headed outside, a cold rush of air coming into the already cool house.

"Move," spoke the man at the back, his black hair held in a ponytail. They were led through by the others and found a small front room, sporting a bay window with a table and single chair within it, the curtains were drawn. In the corner an open door led to the front of the house, a staircase opposite. Two small sofas were arranged against the walls, a small table holding a lamp atop. All three were forced to sit on the sofas. The springs had gone in them a long time ago and they were stained with years of all sorts of liquid spillages. Nicky felt her muscles tense and she was so physically reviled, her salivary glands started to go into overdrive.

Outside, Toad was heading back into his control hub as his phone went again. This was becoming more regular than he had ever anticipated. Their last conversation had gone well, given he now had Mr Bevans family in his possession. He answered without hesitation this time.

Inside Information

"So soon?" he enquired sarcastically. "You've barely given me time to do anything since we last spoke," he started. It was either brave or stupid, he wasn't sure which as the words left his mouth.

"Enough. I realise you are in a better position than you were earlier in the day, but things may not be about to go as you were anticipating," warned the client, a chill to the voice.

"How so? I just spoke with Mr ..." he stopped himself. "The new owner," he continued, "about the puppy. It will be delivered to me shortly and then we can make sure it is exterminated. As planned". Toad was in control and he was smiling broadly now. He was about to become very rich. Wealthy beyond his childhood dreams.

"Unfortunately," the client paused and the usual serene tone was gone, a hint of frustration creeping in. "Our new owner has called in for support. It's possible, they are going to substitute the puppy and give you a ... mongrel in its place."

Toads smile vanished in a heartbeat. "What do you mean?"

"I just heard that the plan agreed to return him to you," a hesitation on the end of the phone as they decided what to say, "is being deviated from. Go to the rendezvous point, but don't take all the bait with you," the caller finished slowly, methodically.

He could feel his hands clenching and releasing. The pressure was building and he really wanted to punch someone now. The fucking cheek of it. He'd make sure that Lee Bevan paid for this if he was not delivered the prime minister as agreed.

"Ok. I'll check on the monitor to see where they are at. Leave it with me. They will not slip the net again."

Terminating the call before the caller had the chance to get under his skin further, he kicked out a pile of trash at the back of the driveway next to the house. "FUUUUUUUCK!" He shouted loudly at the night.

Storming in through the side door of the garage, the whir of computers and monitors greeted him, the heat warming him from the colder, autumnal air. His band of hackers looked up as one, the tapping of key boards paused for just a nano-second.

"Can you lock onto the mobile I called before? I want you to track its journey in real time. Tell me if it stops, where and when. Now we have the car details, see if you can pick it up on traffic cameras. If they so much as spit out the window, I want to know what colour it is and where it ends up." Jabbing his finger at the screens, they could see his rounded face going a deeper shade of puce.

"You got it," Sloth2000 nodded at him, then swung back to his screen and tapped some further commands. In a few short minutes they could see a small green dot moving towards Nottingham. Nothing looked out of the ordinary. Some traffic cameras came to life along the route and as the blue Lexus passed they recorded, zoomed in and played back the footage. Lee could clearly be seen driving the car and he definitely had a passenger sat in the back of the car now, rather than hidden in the footwell. Unfortunately, whatever angle they managed to capture on the car, there was not enough clarity to determine if it was the prime minister.

"Can you track it back and see if he stopped anywhere?" Toad asked.

Inside Information

"Should be able to, but it will take a few minutes. Leave it with me," Sloth replied again.

Heading back to the house, he went to tell his team that there was a slight change of plan. Only the guy would be going with them, to exchange for the prime minister. The wife and son would stay here as a guarantee. Dan shook his head and a muffled "Ooooo. Ats ot fur ..." could be heard coming from behind the cloth.

One of the henchmen punched him in the stomach and Dan doubled over, sucking the cloth further into his mouth. "Leave him alone," shouted Nicky. Toad waved his hands at everyone in the room.

"Calm down everyone and no-one will get hurt. We have had to change our plan, that's all. As soon as we have what we need, you will be released."

Nicky had started to cry again, "Why are you doing this?" She sputtered between her sobs.

"That does not concern you," was the short reply and he turned to return to the garage.

Four of his team members frog marched Dan to the car, moved his hands from behind him, securing them with cable ties again, this time in front of him, so he could sit easily in the seat. The driver pressed the ignition and they headed off into the darkness, leaving the rest of the crew behind them with Lee's petrified wife and son.

"We got something," exclaimed Sloth2000. "About five minutes before we picked them up, they stopped for about two minutes on this road here." He pointed at a map on the screen. "Looking at the satellite shot, it looks like there is a lay by there, but there are no cameras on it."

"Where are the closest ones?" Toad studied the map carefully, looking out for turning points and junctions.

"There are two, one either direction, about three hundred yards away," explained Sloth 2000 and was immediately starting to access the recordings from both.

Over the next few minutes they identified only two cars passing either camera. North of the layby had the blue Lexus coming through only. South though, heading in towards the city centre, gave a little more information. Initially heading north, they spotted a dark, four by four vehicle. Less than five minutes later, the same vehicle came back in the opposite direction, not having reached the camera north of the lay by.

It was following just behind a blue Lexus.

Toad smiled again and looked at Sloth. He was good. He was very good.

Chapter Twenty Nine
Identified

As the prime minister had been picked up by armed police, the message was relayed to the teams in MI5 and MI6. Palpable relief on both sides. A round of applause broke out spontaneously, people stood up from their chairs, clapping and knocking on the table.

Marcus came out from his office, "Ok people. That's the first bit of good news we have had all day. It's not over though. We need answers and we need them fast. Back to work."

"Sir, I think we have something!" Silver called out. She beckoned one of her senior staff members to come over. Gathering her laptop, she pulled up a file. "The phone that we got from Jack Lumley, Sir. He mentioned that this man, Toad, contacted him. Well we have gone through everything and we have been able to extract several numbers from his mobile." She was getting quite excited as she explained herself.

"We've identified most of the numbers, nothing out of the ordinary, pizza houses, taxi numbers and hostels that he has presumably been staying in. There is one however, that is a mobile number, unlisted. Must be a burner phone." Silver nodded at her, and took over the commentary to explain that the last communication between the two was earlier that day, presumably to give the instruction on the hit in Mapperley. They couldn't prove that, yet. It was a leap of faith.

The number had gone off the radar for a while, but it had reappeared recently. They were triangulating, but it looked like an address in Sneinton.

One of Silver's team came running in. "We just had a report of a driverless taxi being diverted whilst *en-route*. It looks like it was manually over ridden by someone hacking the system. We have an address in Sneinton that was the last drop off."

The lady who delivered the message, waved a piece of paper at them, displaying the address. Everyone in the room exchanged quizzical glances. That was more than a coincidence surely?

Simultaneously, over in MI6, Irm was getting an update from Tatoos. The pace of the day was definitely taking its toll on all of them, tiredness waiting to rush in and consume them, should the relentlessness of the operation let up.

"That message we decoded about 'The Puppy'. We decided it was about today's events," they all nodded. "Well, I've been trying to trace the source of it. They have some sophisticated firewalls and decoys set up to protect themselves. These guys are shit hot. However, I've managed to isolate an IP address for the computer that was used to send it." He'd impressed himself with this, so he expected his team to be blown away, but as he looked up, he was met with an icy stare from Irm.

"And?" she enquired. "Who is it? Where are they? Can we locate them and go pick them up?" Tatoos didn't think she was impressed. Maybe she didn't understand just how complicated this was.

Identified

"I'm working on that bit still. It's complicated as they have cloaking devices and alarm triggers. I don't want to alert them to the fact that I am looking, but I have narrowed it down to a locality. Can't give you a specific address just yet, but it looks like it is on line in Sneinton." He stood up and nodded, a smile on his face.

Irm folded her arms, just as Glasses joined them, coming in at speed. "You gotta see this" he said flicking his screen up. "So, the message we had earlier about 'The Puppy', well we've been doing some searching on it and we have a hit, sent about nine months ago." Pointing at it, they read the message together.

We can't use Big Ben.
Need something innocuous.
Refer to The Puppy from now on

Irm looked from Glasses to Tatoos, her eyes widening in realisation. Irm unfolded her arms and leant on the table. From the three of them, only she knew the significance of the message.

That was the 'Top Secret' code name for the prime minister.

"I want to know who those two numbers are sending and receiving that message. Get to it" she instructed as she headed straight over to see her old boss in MI5.

This had to be an insider.

Chapter Thirty

Deception

Holme Pierrepont was pitch black. Lee pulled the Lexus to a stop next to the barrier that had been dropped for the night. A chain wrapped around the red and white pole, secured with a large padlock, was not going to allow them to pass beyond the hotel car park. He was as far away from any other parked cars, visitors to the gym and the hotel as he could be. The last thing they needed was other people getting caught up in this, although he would love to take a horde of people with him. Outnumber them maybe. Except, they seemingly, had lots of weapons at their disposal.

He put his hands on the steering wheel and breathed deeply as his fingers tightened their grip, his knuckles going white. "What am I doing?" he whispered to himself.

"You OK?" the voice behind him spoke. "Do as we discussed and it will all be OK, Lee. You will have your family back soon."

Lee nodded and slowly unlocked the door, pushed it open and stepped out, on to the gravel, crunching underneath his weight. He listened intently, but could hear nothing over the rush of the white water, churning ahead, beyond the hedgerows and the lake. Holme

Deception

Pierrepont, a national water sports centre, where the best canoeists from across the country, the world even, come to test their skill against the artificially created, white water. A channel cut into the ground, weaving through the Nottinghamshire countryside, diverting the wrath of the river Trent, over concrete pyramids, creating rapids, the water turning back on itself. Known as stoppers, crested with white bubbles, tipping people from their inflatable rafts on a daily basis. These obstacles kept thrill seekers entertained for hours, trying to defy the water from upending their boats.

It was surrounded by woodland, meandering walks, taking admirers of nature, past bluebells in the spring and all sorts of wildlife in the summer. On hot clear days, the sweet song of birds could be heard up above, the trill of insects in the grass, bees busy moving from flower to flower, collecting the sweet nectar. It was a beautiful place to while away the days, wandering round the lake. With autumn taking hold, dead leaves were covering the floor now and the woodland was starting to look semi-naked. Families would have been enjoying quality time together, laughing earlier in the day as they played on the wooden climbing frames, chasing each other from tree to tree.

With the parks now closed, the public gone home, it seemed eerie somehow. Lee had been here many times with Aidan over the last couple of years, but now, in the dark and damp he had no desire to be here at all. He would rather be at home, tucked up with Aidan on the sofa, finishing his Sunday dinner and settling down to watch a film together. He had to get his family back.

He moved round the car and opened the door, helping his passenger out.

"We'll have to go on foot from here," he said and pulled the arm with the torn sleeve over his shoulder to offer support. Without talking, they started to move forwards. Lees heart was already racing, but the extra weight he was now burdened with, was putting some strain on his muscle mass.

They moved past the barrier and started towards the edge of the lake, heading for the white water section at the back of the facilities. Both were searching into the distance to see if they could make out any shapes in the darkness ahead of them. They felt exposed out in the open. Anyone who lay ahead in wait, had some easy pickings. Bright lights up ahead standing either side of the white water, helped guide them towards their destination. Gradually, they moved past the lake, the various woodland play parks and other entertainment areas towards the rushing water.

At the edge of the long lagoon, some metal shelving housed a number of heavy duty, plastic canoes. A multitude of colours, they varied in length and the number of seats inside them. Tipped upside down, secured at the end, the last drops of water they had caught in the day, dripping down on to the floor below. Lee steadied himself against one of the racks and caught his breath.

In the distance an owl hooted and he looked up to the trees, holding his breath. Other than the noise of the water, he realised how quiet it was and the sound of their breathing could almost give them away. They used hand signals now to press each other on towards their final destination. Slowly, step by step they went together.

About half way along the lake, they could see the cascading water ahead of them. Just above it, mist was developing at low level, rolling up to the side of the banks, consuming anything it covered. The smell of cold, dirt filled water lifted through the night air to fill their nostrils. Lee shivered.

They had arrived at the point where they had been told to meet. Next to the river, Lee looked all around, but wasn't sure he could make anything out. He felt very uncomfortable. Apart from the spotlights targeted on to the water, the darkness consumed everything. Lee could feel the fear rising again and wasn't sure how many times his adrenaline could surge in this way over a twenty-four hour period, before the 'fight or flight' reflex failed him.

From the other side of the man-made water course, a loud voice shouted. "STOP THERE!" The two men instantly ceased their forward movement. Lee shouted back across the noise of the water "WHERE IS MY FAMILY?" There was no response, but movement across a walkway to his right, above the swirling water, caught his eye.

Coming from the other side of the river, out of the darkness, was his best friend Dan. Hands in front of him, wrapped together with cable ties, he moved gingerly across the footbridge. Dan had fear in his eyes and was shaking his head gently, hoping Lee would be able to make it out in the gloom. Behind him, one of his captors had the muzzle of a gun pushed into his back, providing some motivation to continue forward.

"Where's my wife and son?" called Lee again, a lump forming in his throat as he fought back tears.

"You didn't think we were going to bring them here did you?" shouted back the man on the bridge. He was the heavy sporting the ponytail. He wore a black bomber jacket and jeans, dark boots protecting his feet and he was making it clear that he held Dan at gunpoint.

Lee could feel his stomach tighten again. What did he mean 'We'? Where were the others? He couldn't see anyone. Glancing from side to side, he could feel the panic starting to rise, but he felt a calming hand on his shoulder.

"It's OK. They are in place," came a whisper close to his ear.

"Where are they then?" shouted back Lee.

"We have them, but you have to let me take the PM with me. Once we have what we want, we'll let them go," the man waved his gun towards Lee. "Move out the way, I want to see the prime minister," he demanded. Lee was stood between them, but they were back in the shadows as well now, slightly obscured from his view. He knew if he moved, the gunman would probably pull the trigger. Fighting against everything his mind told him to do, he stood his ground.

"Let Dan go," he nodded towards them, "Dan, you OK?" he asked of his friend as he ensured he was obstructing direct line of sight to their real target.

"You first Mr Bevan, you know we won't hesitate to kill you all if you don't do as you're asked," growled the gunman. He was getting frustrated at the length of this day now. The fact he was in the dark as the night got colder, was irking him somewhat. Use of his services were supposed to be finished with hours ago. They should be on the way out of the country, heading overseas to start a lavish life in the sunshine somewhere. Revelling in the glory of what they had pulled off, along with the large sums of money that he had been promised for tearing the heart of government out of the UK.

"You have until I count to five." he raised the gun and held it to the back of Dan's head, the cold metal pressing against the thin veil of flesh encapsulating his skull.

"One …" he started, as Dan's body started to tremble involuntarily, his legs shaking beyond his control.

Lee moved his arm behind him quickly and held three fingers behind his back. Without hesitation, he removed one then another. As the last finger was clenched back into his fist, the two men rolled down to the right. A shot rang out in the distance, piercing the still night and the rush of the river.

The pony tailed man who had stood behind Dan, holding him captive, fell backwards against the handrail of the footbridge. His legs folded under the instant weight that bore down on them from above.

A sniper's bullet fired from the woodland, ripped through the exposed forehead. It was a perfect target, large and white, shimmering in the small amount of light radiating from the spotlights. Dan, flinched, glanced backwards and saw his captor was dead, the life gone from his eyes, a hole just above his right eye. Instant relief did not stop him sending his elbow catapulting backwards towards the guys chin, knocking the body backwards. Momentum took the gunman over the handrail and into the foaming water below, quickly tossing his corpse around, before being swept away by the force of the currents. His body was taken further down the rapids, back towards the main part of the river Trent.

In the morning, as the sun rose, burning off the mist above the water, the police would find his body floating face down, caught in the reeds at the side of the river. He would later be identified as a known thug for hire from Latvia.

As Dan stood up on the bridge, looking towards the man he had knocked into the river, a second gunshot rang out. Instinctively he ducked down and then started running towards Lee and the prime minister. Lee jumped to his feet, unsure why there was further gunfire. The assailant had been terminated and he was desperate to get to Dan. He was about thirty feet away and as his pace gathered, a flurry of gunfire suddenly erupted on the opposite side of the river. The ground exploded in front of him as several bullets tore up the pathway, chippings erupting and hitting his legs. Lee instinctively dived back to his right, off into the dark again. A large collection of bins appeared in front of him and he moved behind them, offering him some protection. There must have been more of them hiding in the woods the other side. Bugger!

He realised he had left the side of the man he had been helping. However that man was now crouched himself, gun in hand, returning fire across the river. It was not the prime minister.

The man he'd escorted from the car, pretending he needed help to walk, had met them on their journey here from the garage. This was a highly trained police officer, who had willingly replaced the prime minister when Lee had called them to explain what they had been asked to do by Nicky's captors.

After Lee had realised Dans mobile could be monitored by those holding his family, Barnaby had explained his idea to him. Lee had gone back into the garage, asked to use the phone and, after initially being told no, he explained it was to do with the bombing in the Old Market Square earlier in the day, was allowed to call the number he'd been given. Outlining the details to the operative, it had been relayed to the SAS team who were already on way to the garage to recover the prime

Deception

minister. They would soon change their destination, but back up was sent to recover Barnaby Aitken at an agreed location.

Not wanting to arouse suspicion from the terrorists tracking the mobile, they had started their journey back towards Nottingham. Pulling over to a lay by, Barnaby and Lee were met by a small number of heavily armed police officers waiting for them. They decided not to call in the arrival of the PM until they were well and truly sure he was safe on protected land. Instead, they checked him over and positioned themselves with their backs towards them, protecting the immediate vicinity from potential intruders.

The man who was closest to Barnaby in size and stature had removed his own clothing and pulled the prime ministers blood covered, torn suit, over the top of his bullet proof vest. He holstered two hand guns underneath his jacket, along with a can of tear gas which he concealed in his pocket. Pulling Barnaby's tie around his neck, he climbed into the back seat whilst Lee was given final instructions, on what they should do once they arrived at the rendezvous.

Barnaby, already dressed in the clothing discarded by the police officer, came round the car and shook Lee's hand. "I can't thank you and your family enough Lee. I am sorry you got caught up in … whatever this is." He placed a hand on both arms as he looked Lee straight in the eyes. "We'll get them back safe. I prom …" he started, but Lee cut him off.

"Don't do that Sir. You can't keep that promise. Just make sure these guys get those bastards and stop whatever the hell it is they are doing." Reaching up, he grabbed Barnaby Aitkens hand and shook it firmly.

"I'm glad we got you back safe, Sir." He turned and climbed back into the driver's seat of his friends blue Lexus.

Both men in the car had miniature hearing devices placed in their left ears, invisible to anyone more than a few inches away. A microphone hidden on their clothing would pick up any conversation between them, or anyone, within five metres. After checking the devices worked, they continued the journey to Holme Pierrepont. The stop in the lay-by had lasted less than two minutes. That should be short enough not to arouse suspicion, but on that front, they had to hope for some luck.

Lees new accomplice had introduced himself as Miles. With a bone crushing hand shake, he explained how he had been a member of the armed police for the last three years and was trained for 'Exactly this type of event'. Keeping his eyes fixed on the road ahead, Lee openly told Miles that he was not sorry to lose the company of the prime minster. It felt like an enormous weight of responsibility had been taken off his back.

Now, he just had to get his family and his best friend back safely.

Miles continued to explain how there would be the small band of SAS brothers, and sister, with them. They had diverted ahead to conceal themselves in the darkness and shadows of the trees around the water sports facilities, hopefully arriving ahead of the targets. They would stake out the surrounding area, ensure they secured Lee's family and remove the threat as cleanly as possible.

Arriving at the white water facility about ten minutes before Miles and Lee had turned into the car park, the SAS moved silently. They split up, diving into the shadows and skirting round either side of the lake. Using night vision goggles, they scoured the grass and woodland to ensure there was no-one ahead of them, lying in wait. Quickly covering the ground, they took up positions to the east and west of the footbridge, concealed themselves behind trees, or lying flat on the damp ground, minimising their visibility to anyone approaching.

A soft crunch up ahead raised the tension. Looking through the goggles, the female trooper looked to her left. A bright green hue came to life in the darkness. She raised her rifle, ready to engage.

Another crunch. Soft. Deliberate.

A small, muntjac deer raised its head, sniffed the air and crept forward another step, desperately trying not to alert anything to its presence. It twitched its ears left and right, aware of something close by, but uncertain where it was. The trooper stopped holding her breath and the muntjac slipped off into the night.

Speaking softly on the microphone, they told Miles of their positions, explaining that so far, no one was here. They had decided not to send significant numbers of officers into the country park as they did not want to scare off the terrorists, potentially endangering the lives of Lee's family and friend further. They had eyes on the entrance to the car park though, and so far, no one else had entered.

Just as Lee and Miles came round the lagoon into view, the troopers further down from the walkway, spotted movement from the other side of the white water strip. There were five people that they could see, but all looked like fully grown individuals.

"We have movement," the leader relayed softly over the microphone. "Other side of the rapids. No women or children present, that I can see," he continued. "They're splitting up, one heading up, two down river, into the trees. It looks like we are both trying to deceive the other," he concluded.

He had led the troop for two years now and he loved it. He lived for moments like this, but sadly, in his mind, they didn't happen very often. At only five foot six, he had always been picked on at school when he was younger. People considered him an easy target because of his small stature. How wrong they had been. At the age of eleven, his father had insisted he learn Karate, for self-defence. It did not take long for him to work his way through the belts, becoming very adept at incapacitating, unsuspecting playground pricks, who picked on others. Joining the army as soon as he was able to, he became ultra-fit, building on his skill of using his body as a weapon. Whether out on an endurance run, helping others in the team, or refitting his rifle, he practised and practised, giving his all. Never quitting when others were spent, he always gave that little bit extra. Without setting his sights on the SAS specifically, he stood out from the rest of his platoon and was soon being lined up to join the world famous, elite fighting force.

"They must have come from the other side of the river," he whispered again, into his mic. Explaining to the rest of the team that they were splitting up, he kept two of them in his sights as they moved towards the small bridge over the water. "My angle isn't right on them. Looks like the lead one, on the footbridge, is being held at gun point. Anyone got a better line of sight to the bridge?" he asked.

The female trooper responded. "Roger. Gun held behind the lead ones back. I can take him," she cooed, slowing her breathing to ensure she controlled her heart rate.

"Wait until Miles gives the signal," her leader responded. "We have the two to the east."

Another trooper, further upriver, confirmed he had the final member of the group fixed in his sights. As the conversation between Lee and the gunman evolved, all of the SAS troopers silently ensured the safety catches were off on their rifles.

Miles counted down to one, quietly, but quickly, over the mic, the female trooper breathed slowly out and squeezed the trigger. The chamber emptied its contents with such force, the target had no time to react. A perfect shot. She instantaneously moved her attention back to the next target on the opposite side of the river. Rapidly moving to the left, still under cover of the trees, she'd been trained to fire and move, reducing her chance of being pinned down.

The single gunshot had taken Dan's captors completely by surprise, as they were still moving to gain decent positions on those they hunted. Two of them dropped to their knees, firing in the direction of the flash of light. Burst, after burst of bullets, spewed forth from their semi-automatic weapons, bombarding the position recently vacated.

Spinning back to Lee and the person they thought was the prime minister, they both opened fire again, bullets drilling into the ground just in front of Lee, as he sprinted towards the bridge. Watching him dive for cover, they turned their attention to the PM. He was crouched, arm outstretched in front of him, firing a gun towards them.

"What the fu …" one of them started to say, as two bullets tore into his flesh and the life drained from his body, just as he realised it wasn't the prime minister he was firing at. One of the bullets came from Miles' handgun, taken to the abdomen, piercing his large intestine and causing large blood loss. The second arriving at extreme velocity, fired from the high powered rifle off to his left, beyond the bridge. It ripped through his left lung, like a shark tearing flesh from a Napoleon wrasse. Blood gurgled up to his mouth as he gasped for air. He was fighting for a breath he would just not be able to take.

Further down the rapids, two other SAS troopers moved silently and swiftly towards another crossing over the water. Signalling to each to proceed in turn, they covered one another as they ran across the exposed space. They headed to the back of the small island, moving towards the wide crossing of the cold, slower moving, expanse of the dark river. Spreading out as wide as possible for the two of them, they progressed back up towards the ongoing gun fight.

Using the night vision goggles, they scanned the open water. These guys must have come across by boat from Colwick country park, or further upstream, back towards Trent bridge. That meant there could be more of them. Either still in the boat, or on the other side of the river. "Down there, about ten feet from the side of the river bank," one motioned to the other. "It's a rowing boat, single occupant. He is armed and making away from the scene," he relayed over the mic.

Their leader, still exchanging gunfire, replied "Take him out. Do not allow him to escape." Just as he finished his sentence, the second trooper opened fire. The man in the boat slumped forward, dropping the oars into the water with a splash. Quickly, they scanned the opposite side of the river to ensure they weren't about to be attacked by others waiting for the return of their fellow assassins. Detecting no other sign of life, they broke cover, hurrying forward to retrieve the boat and its occupant.

Whilst the female trooper was crawling further upstream and Miles was exchanging gunfire across the rapids, the remaining two members of the troop had worked their way to the start of the white water section. Here, a small bridge, big enough for cars to cross, spanned the tributary, marking the start of the man-made rapids, that spurred off from the river. Sprinting across, they glanced down stream, seeing the zip of gunfire lighting up the darkness, either side of the illuminated course.

One headed for the back, whilst the other maintained contact with the front group. In no time at all, they had located the final assailant of the terror cell. He was just behind his fallen comrade, moving his arms and firing erratically across the water. "Put your hands up and drop your weapon!" bellowed the elite serviceman, giving his target the opportunity to surrender. Catching him completely by surprise, the terrorist, still on his knees, turned towards him firing his weapon, not losing his grip from the handle.

Before the trajectory of bullets could get anywhere near, the training of the serviceman kicked in. A volley of shots fired. None missed the target and he dropped to the ground.

With everything that had just unrolled, not a single one of the SAS had broken a sweat and none of them had a pulse over one hundred and ten. Lee's, it's fair to say, was racing, closer to two hundred than it was one hundred. Shouts of "Clear" echoed round the ground.

Gradually, Lee realised the gunfire had stopped and he heard the message relayed inside his ear. "All targets have been neutralised. Clear."

He peeked round the wooden housing of the bins, which had been peppered with gunshot, splinters sticking out, posts falling apart. Miles, was lying on the ground and looked to be in some pain, but he gestured towards him and shouted it was safe. He had been hit. The kevlar of the bullet proof vest had prevented the projectile ripping his flesh apart. It felt like someone had smashed him with a sledgehammer. It would hurt and bruise horrifically, but he would be ok in a few days' time.

Miles would later be honoured by the prime minister, indebted to him for his loyal service, putting himself directly in the line of fire, to serve his country, in its most desperate hour.

Lee looked back towards the bridge, searching for Dan. Moving towards it, he slowed his pace as he picked out an odd shape on the ground. His hand went to his mouth and held his chin. "No … No … Not Dan." Lee sprinted forward again.

Slumped forwards on the ground, hands still bound in front of him, blood coming from his chest. Dan had been shot in the back.

Lee dropped to his knees and gently turned over his best friend to see his face.

He placed his fingers against Dans neck. A tear welled in his eye and he started to shake.

Lee could not feel a pulse.

Chapter Thirty One
Community Support

Coming past the ice rink in the city centre, the officer driving the four by four checked his mirror again. There was a white transit van that had been behind them for a while. He had made two turns now and the van had done the same. He decided to switch lanes and jumped the red light on the roundabout at the end of Canal Street, heading up the A60.

"You Ok?" enquired the second officer sat in the passenger seat.

Calmly the driver said, "We seem to have picked up a tail," as he indicated towards the rear view mirror. "He jumped the lights with us and has accelerated." All four occupants either turned to look or positioned their mirrors to look backwards. Moving through the gears at speed, he muttered under his breath "How the hell did they pick us up so quickly?"

His passenger immediately got on a secure line and called in their position, vehicle description and the license plate of the van tailing them.

"We need back up. Sir," he said, addressing the prime minister in the rear of the vehicle, "make sure your vest is on and keep your head down." His attendees all unholstered their weapons, just in case.

Turning right across the oncoming traffic he accelerated down Station Street, then turned left at the end, without stopping. An oncoming car from the right screeched to a halt, the driver hit his horn in fright. The van behind turned as well, but did not hold the road as well, smashing the front of the stationary car, sending it spinning into the opposite side of the road. The van wobbled, but regained control after fish tailing a little. Its driver pressed the accelerator hard again. Next to him, the female Russian sniper who had fired at the prime minister earlier in the day, pushed a new magazine full of ammo into her rifle. She dropped the window and leant out trying to get a clear fix on the car ahead. It was the closest they had physically got to the prime minister all day, he was not going to escape this time.

Pulling the trigger, the four by four ahead of them was peppered with dull thuds as the bullets connected with the boot. Its occupants flinched and the driver looked to the front seat passenger. He pulled left on the steering wheel and his companion fired back at the van following them through his open window as they turned into Sheriff's Way. The van driver weaved to avoid the oncoming bullets, throwing the Russian female sidewards, losing her aim.

Barnaby was yet again ducking down inside a car, trying not to be seen. Whilst fear was lingering at the back of his mind, he was not paralysed by fear. His survival instinct was strong. Taking heavy fire, all Barnaby Aitken could think about was, "I didn't come into politics for this kind of shit!"

His driver struck him as incredibly calm. He supposed that this is what they trained endlessly for. The officer on his right hand side was leaning over the top of him in a

Community Support

protective fashion. These guys were all laying their lives on the line. For him.

What an honour, that people were prepared to die for you, in their line of duty. Their calling. Not five years ago, people in power, people in the armed forces, had never heard of Barnaby Aitken, yet here they were, driving at speed under gunfire, to prevent him being killed. It was giving him a new perspective on not just his life, but the lives of the extraordinary people who served the country.

Their vehicle was approaching Wilford Grove in the Meadows and they had opened a little gap to the van trying to hunt them down. Cars were parked on both sides of the road, so the driver was flashing his lights and beeping his horn to warn oncoming vehicles to back off. Given it was a thirty limit, their vehicle hit sixty eight miles an hour as the windscreen suddenly smashed in front of them, a small hole tearing through as a bullet passed through and ripped into the rear seat just above the prime ministers head.

As the screen shattered, the driver pulled to the right to get out the way. The front seat passenger looked down the road and saw another transit van parked sideways across the road, tracer fire from at least two machine guns coming down the middle of the road towards them. On the screen in the front of the vehicle, they could see they were heading past three streets running parallel to each other, but no way out. They would have to come back on to the main road at some point. With the white van chasing them down, they were effectively penned in.

"Where is our back up?" barked the officer occupying the front seat, into his mic. "We are going past Beauvale Road in the Meadows Area and we are under fire. Road block down Wilford Grove, heavy artillery being fired and we are still being chased by the white transit van. Hostiles on board, repeat hostiles on board." He closed his mic, then turned and passed a gun and a spare magazine of ammunition to the prime minister. "Sir, keep this with you. You remember how to change the magazine"

Barnaby nodded, unable to bring himself to speak, dropping the magazine into his pocket. Their vehicle was slowing to make the turn into Glapton Road. The cars on either side of the road were so tightly packed there really was nowhere to escape if someone came towards them. As they accelerated up the road, headlights swung in from the opposite end.

A response came through over the earpiece to the officers, but Barnaby did not hear it. "ETA is five minutes, repeat, five minutes."

"Seriously?" replied the driver, "we'll be lucky if we last that long." He stamped on the brakes and bought the car to a halt as he realised the car ahead had stopped. Its occupants were getting out of the car and they were heavily armed. Looking in his rear view mirror, about to reverse, he saw the white transit van pull into the top of the road behind them, also coming to a halt.

"Get out the car. NOW!" shouted the driver at the occupants, who pulled the brushed chrome handles on the doors simultaneously, sparked into action. They all dropped low out the door to avoid any high gunfire, taking refuge behind the cars parked to the side of the road.

The officer who had been in the front passenger seat, moved backwards to protect the prime minister, pushing him against an old Ford Kuga, two wheels parked on the path. As he did, he lifted his head, to see a white light

Community Support

racing down the street straight towards the vehicle they had just vacated. It reminded him of watching films like *'Platoon'*. Realisation of what was about to happen triggered his neurones into action. He dived back down to take cover, throwing himself over the country's top politician.

It was a rocket propelled grenade. It ripped into the front of their vehicle, causing it to explode. Launching it into the air and a ball of flames licking out on all sides. The heat was so intense it peeled the paint off front doors ten feet away and melted the tyres of cars in the immediate vicinity. The force threw it against the car parked next to it, which the driver had taken refuge behind.

A Mini Cooper crushed the drivers body against the brick front of the housing, then fell to the floor, alight. It was an explosion that woke the entire street. Largely populated by Asians, the terraced houses were also home to students from all across the UK, Europe and further afield.

With ringing in their ears, the prime minister and his protector, managed to scramble to their feet and start moving forward. Training dictated that you should never sit still. That made you an easy target. On the opposite side of the road, the final member of the prime ministers protective squad got to his knees. Checking quickly both ways, he went to sprint over the road to re-join his colleague and fulfil his mission. Lifting his head was the last thing he managed. A round from the female sniper passed through his neck, tearing a hole through muscle, ripping the side off his Adam's apple.

Falling to the floor, his blood left his body. His torso convulsing.

Barnaby had never been so scared in his life. Just as he was starting to think the hunt was coming to an end, a door opened up just in front of him. His protector pulled him up by his bullet proof vest and forced him through the open door.

An old lady closed it behind him. "Quick" she started, an obvious accent from eastern Europe to her voice. "You need to hide." Barnaby almost laughed. Hiding, was the one sure thing, to get him killed.

"Thank you," he responded, patting the lady on the shoulder. The armed officer had moved into the front room and was pulling at a small sofa. "Sir, help me with this." They lifted the piece of furniture and moved it across the front door, then pushed a bookcase on top. It would not stop those chasing, but it may delay them enough to help.

"Is there a way out the back?" asked the officer.

"There is," started the old lady, "but your best chance, is up in the roof." She pointed upwards. Both men looked quizzically at her. "Old terraced houses, the lofts connect" she smiled. "It should give you a chance to ..." she searched for the word, "my English not so good, escape?" She checked with them. "Work your way down the street, past the people who did this to you." Smiling, she showed them the way to the loft hatch.

As Barnaby and the officer lowered the loft hatch back into position behind them, they heard gunfire hitting the front door of the house. They wouldn't know it, but the Polish lady that helped them, died trying to prevent the terrorists getting in. She had followed the news stories in the day, and although she did not agree with the stance, or policy, of the current, or previous, UK governments, she could not abide violence, for one to get their own way. Living in a democracy, she believed you had to listen to the public. When the prime minister had been attacked again, outside her own front door, she was compelled to help him. He had become a vulnerable individual that needed salvation.

Barnaby's other saviour, with a high powered torch, was able to lead the way, through cobwebs and the detritus of people's lives. Manoeuvring past the chimney stack of each house, weaving backwards and forwards, there was a small gap that you could squeeze through without having to break down any boards or breeze blocks. Thankfully they had moved two houses away as those chasing them reached their point of entry. Over the first few houses, their biggest concern was squeaking floorboards, or their weight being too much for the old, infested woodwork to cope with. Standing on the joists as much as they could, they edged their way along, slowly but surely. Barnaby was grimacing against the pain his ankle was giving him, but he had to keep moving.

The occupants from the van and the terror cell at the opposite end of the street, converged on the property in the middle of the street, number forty-three. A hail of bullets that burst through the front door, had killed the Polish immigrant that lived here. Indiscriminate killing. People from all walks of life, race or occupation, it was irrelevant if they got in the way. They had to fulfil their mission. When they tried the door and realised it was blocked from beyond, they turned their weapons on the bay window, next to the front door. Climbing through, they scoured the small house from top to bottom, stepping over the small Polish lady, without regret.

A quick search of the property revealed nothing, so they headed to the rear door, a passageway that led towards the back of the terraced houses. It was like a rabbit warren with broken fences lining the overgrown pathways heading left and right. Only illuminated, by the limited light of the mostly obscured moon, it was very difficult to make out anything. Shadows deceived and they fired their guns randomly into the dark of the alleyways.

Homeowners and renters alike, were pulling back curtains to see what was going on. A group of angry looking men, Asian, European and English, were gathering at the end of the street. Startled by the explosion and the gunfire, they were grabbing make shift weapons, baseball bats, metal poles, anything that came to hand. With bravado and a safety in numbers mentality, they were starting to move towards the car on fire in the middle of the street. Ready to take on those that were causing mayhem. They were no match for the guns they were going to meet, but there was a determined cohesion, to protect their families and friends.

Progressing up the street, several of the gunmen came out of an alleyway, twenty feet in front of the mob. Realising there were between forty and fifty men coming towards them, who had a mix of fear, anger and hatred in their eyes, the terror cell fired a warning shot into the sky. It only stalled the group for a few seconds.

"They can't take us all," someone from the front shouted. "Get them!" another volunteered and gingerly the mob moved forward. It had the desired affect and the terrorists retreated up the street, past the burning wreck toward their white transit van. Climbing in side, they reversed, swung round, crashing into two parked cars, before taking off at speed again.

Barnaby and his accomplice were moving down the row of houses in the opposite direction. Covered in dust, mingled with their perspiration, sticking to their skin, they finally made it to the last house on the street. There was nowhere to go now, but down. Before proceeding, the remaining armed officer tried his mic to control.

"Come in control? Extraction required, repeat, extraction required." No response came. He repeated the call again. Still nothing. "Ok," he spoke to Barnaby, "looks like we have to do this ourselves. When we were in the car they radioed to say they were five minutes away, so they should be around by now. We'll get ourselves outside and try again." He beckoned Barnaby over to their exit point. Barnaby paused and wiped his brow.

Slowly, they lifted the loft hatch and peered into the gloom below.

Hearing nothing, the officer grabbed Barnaby's arms and lowered him down through the gap to the floor below. As his swollen ankle touched the carpet, to bear his weight again, pain shot up his leg and he gritted his teeth, gradually increasing the load on the joint.

The house was quiet, but there were lights on downstairs. Barnaby stood to the side as the officer lowered himself down next to him, removing his gun from his holster. He peered down the corridor, unable to detect any movement. The noise coming from the street outside suggested most of the street, including the occupants of the house, may well be outside, witnessing the attacks in the street.

Slowly, they made their way down the stairs. At the bottom, just a few feet ahead of them, the front door was on the latch, slightly ajar. They could see figures beyond it, waving and pointing up the road. Raising a finger to his lips, the officer gestured towards the back of the house and sent Barnaby ahead of him. Turning towards the back of the house, they crept through a smartly renovated kitchen diner. Sleek cupboards lined the walls, an induction hob built into the wooden work surface. Newly laid, marble effect tiles reflected the low level of light from the front of the house across the floor, highlighting a path to the back door. Slowly, they worked the locks loose, gently opened the door and made their way into the back yard.

Hugging the shadows they moved quickly to the gate on the side of the back yard, again working the bolt loose. Peering out in the gloom, the officer checked the alleyway. Fortunately this one went away from the front of the street, towards the houses on the street parallel, joining exits from several other adjoining houses. It took them right towards the end of the street.

Barnaby's heart was pounding. He moved towards the end of the alleyway, his protector stayed back to ensure no-one was following them. Reaching the end of the alley, he put his back next to the brick wall of the last house in the terraced row. He peered as far up the road as he could without leaving the protection of the shadows.

The street was comparatively quiet to the one they had recently vacated. Everyone must have headed there, driven by intrigue.

It was too quiet. Something didn't feel right.

Just as Barnaby was about to head back the way he had come, a hand reached round the corner of the building, clasping firmly over his mouth.

A voice whispered from around the corner "Don't make a sound!"

Barnaby Aitken could not believe the luck he was having today.

Chapter Thirty Two

Sneinton

Once Sneinton had been identified, every major road in and out of the neighbourhood was blocked with armed check points. They knew they had to move quickly. Word would undoubtedly travel fast as the locals realised they were under lockdown. The army were highly proficient in moving troops to the locality, once they got the nod from both MI5 and MI6. Usually, they would go via the home secretary for approval, but on this occasion, they had no time to lose.

Standing around their armoured vehicle, they were scanning the surroundings. Seeing movements in shadows. Tricks of the light. They were all on high alert. Awaiting their final destination, they were joined by three of the SAS troop that had just been engaged in live fire, on the south side of the river.

"Who's in charge?" enquired the SAS officer. A Royal Marine, hugging his semi-automatic rifle, nodded towards his platoon leader. "How many did you get mate? Hope you took those fuckers out." The question went unanswered. The officer had already gone to seek out the latest intelligence, understand their next mission.

Conversing with another soldier, they were both to the point, brief in their questions and answers, devoid of emotion. It was best to stick to facts. Understand the mission. Route in. Route out. They weren't sure how many hostiles there might be. The SAS officer believed two hostages may also be present. Relaying the story of Lee's wife and son, in case this were the same place that they were being been held. They would have to be cautious.

Quickly, they agreed that the SAS troopers would target the hostiles and the Royal Marines would focus on the safe removal of the hostages. No one was to escape, that was paramount. Front and rear of the property were to be impenetrable to anyone other than the armed forces. State of the art thermal imaging would be used to confirm numbers in the property and if possible, they would place listening devices on the windows or brickwork to get ears inside.

An address was relayed to them, just off Sneinton Dale. Engines sparked to life and four armoured vehicles, were followed by a number of armed police units. Given the events earlier and the late hour, the roads were almost empty. People chose to retreat to the safety of their own home, particularly since night had fallen.

Several of the vehicles drove past the turn off and blocked the next road. Silently, the Royal Marines off loaded, fanning out to take up positions at the end of the street. Others had moved ahead to flank the opposite end of the road. The front and rear of the property had been sealed off.

Lights were on in some of the surrounding dwellings, but many looked as though they had been empty for a while. TVs could be heard blasting from some that were either hard of hearing, or possibly teenager's bedrooms, but mostly the street was quiet.

The officer in charge motioned for the thermal imaging equipment to be moved into position outside of the property in question. It was at the end of the row, next to a small number of run down garages.

The equipment sparked to life and threw out some coloured images against a grey background. The operator indicated there were four people in the house. The clarity was superb. Sharp, contoured lines clearly depicted a woman and child. They were sitting on what he presumed was a settee, in the front room of the house. Next to them towards the window, sitting at a small table and smoking a cigarette was a man, the cold metal of a machine gun outlined over his lap. The fourth body was another man, standing towards the back of the house. He seemed fairly short in stature and as far as the operative could determine was not carrying a weapon. He was pacing backwards and forwards, clearly uneasy about something. Moving the sensor upwards, he determined there was no other heat source in the house.

Two hostages. Two hostiles. The SAS and the Royal Marines all moved into position. The camera operative moved his position slightly and suddenly the garages came into range. It lit the screen up in front of him. The heat signal from the first garage was intense. Burning bright red, making it very difficult to make different shapes out.

He raised his arm to signal to those around him, pointing to the garage. As he did, he spoke quietly, relaying his observation into the earpieces they all wore.

"Wait. Garage to the right hand side of the house" he started, "Major heat signal. Looks like it's their communication hub, computers giving off massive rays."

He cast the scanner around more, then focussed its attention on smaller areas of the small brick building, to try and increase the sensitivity of the readings.

Gradually he built up a clear picture. Three people sat at computer terminals. It looked like each was operating at least two, but possibly more. Fingers tapping keyboards with ferocity. A fourth towards the back of the garage. Possibly armed, difficult to say, but near the side door of their control centre.

One last command was given. "Do not let them destroy the computers."

Everyone was in position. Those inside were oblivious to the organisation that was going on just a few feet away, separated by bricks and mortar. It was decided listening devices were not needed, this had to be it.

It was time to take back control.

Chapter Thirty Three
Professionals

A silent countdown using finger signals only. The professionals who had trained for combat in war zones, acted with instinct and competence, on the streets of Nottingham.

The terrorists, in a small run down suburb of Nottingham, had no idea what was about to hit them.

From the floor outside the garage, a shot was fired on an upward trajectory through the side door of the garage. It hit the unsuspecting watchman in the shoulder, to ensure that if he were holding a weapon, he would not be able to use it. Wailing, he slumped to his knees and dropped the gun he had in his hand. Simultaneously, the door was smashed open and two green berets, burst through following one of the SAS troopers, each with laser sights locked onto a separate computer operator. A small red dot rested on the chest of HaPee as Larry. He stopped tapping his keyboard and looked in horror at the men that had burst in through the door, spinning his gaze to his companion who had been felled.

"HANDS IN THE AIR!" the trooper shouted. "Step back from the computers or we will shoot." The three soldiers continued to move towards the computer operatives. IPFree immediately raised her hands to her head and pushed her chair back from the computer screen with her feet. A red dot was visible just above her heart. No way was she going to die for this.

Sloth 2000 was immediately struck by his tic. It nearly cost him his life. The laser sighting that was trained on him raised quickly to his head, as the soldier started to squeeze the trigger. Sloth twitched again, but also moved back from his screen. All three were quickly pushed face first to the ground, restrained with cable ties, hands secured behind their backs.

A montage of screens and monitors filled several tables, set at different levels. Many displayed scenes from security cameras. Fires were blazing on one, several cars burning and what looked like an angry mob proceeding down the street. Others just had rows of, what appeared to be, random commands. Numbers and letters that made no sense to those not versed in the sorcery that is code.

While the precision attack had been taking place in the garage, all its occupants contained with minimal injury and no loss of life, proceedings in the house, were not quite as straightforward.

A single shot had was fired by a second SAS trooper through the front window from the pavement outside. It had the intention of disarming, or immobilising, the gunman. Just as the trooper had pulled his trigger, the man in the house had stretched upwards, relieving the tension from his weary shoulders. Instead of hitting his shoulder, the bullet killed him instantly. Screams were heard from outside as Nicky and her son Aidan both watched the chest of their captor explode in front of them, blood spraying forth across the floor. His body slumped, putting pressure on his trigger finger, firing half a dozen bullets towards the far wall of the room. That in turn caused the old plaster to splinter back into the dingy room, causing another round of screaming as they thought they were being fired on from a different angle.

Fortunately, neither of the hostages were hit.

The back door had been kicked open and the lead SAS officer burst though as the gunfire was ringing round the lounge. Toad, who had been doing the pacing in the kitchen, was dumbfounded, not knowing which way to look. His chin sagged and he raised his arms in the air as he realised the game was up for him. The forward motion of the accelerating SAS officer, meant he barrelled in to Toad, knocking him to the floor, the breath escaping from his lungs, with the sweet sickly smell of toffee from his vape machine.

To ensure the target stayed down, the SAS officer hit him on the forehead with the butt of his gun. Toad's head cracked sideways, a small split opened up and his body went limp.

Calls of "Clear" rang round the house as the Royal Marines swiftly checked every room. One went to the aid of Nicky and Aidan. Kneeling in front of them and covering the view of the dead gunman, with his own gun pushed behind his back, he spoke gently. "OK Miss. We got you. They are all contained. You're both safe now."

Nicky clutched her son tightly, his head buried in her bosom. They both wept. With fear swept aside, these were tears of relief, but they both still shook from the adrenaline coursing through their bodies.

"Got them!" he called over his mic. If he got close to emotion, he may have felt pride surge through his body, knowing that they had rescued the remaining hostages unharmed. Instead, he stood and nodded in self appreciation.

Following the raid via live video link from cameras on the Royal Marines helmets, Irm and Marcus, stood and clapped, along with their respective teams. It had been displayed on screens, hundreds of miles away from the action, in their own command centre.

The stress and intensity of the day had been exhausting. A few hugged each other, sunk to their chairs in relief. Tears of joy rolled down the occasional cheek.

Together, they had broken the ring. MI5 and MI6. A breakthrough.

Since the car he was travelling in had been attacked in the Meadows area, no-one had heard anything from Barnaby Aitken.

All they needed now, was the safe return of the prime minister.

Chapter Thirty Four
Taken

His heart was racing. Barnaby could feel it thumping in his chest. The hand pressed over his mouth, squeezing his nostrils half shut, making it difficult to breath. The blood vessels on his temples were at the point of bursting, not for the first time this day. Beads of perspiration trickled down the side of his head.

Fear, again, coursed through the body of the prime minister. He braced himself. After everything that had happened today, it shouldn't end like this. In a dark, shit covered, alleyway.

Thoughts of his wife and children flooded his mind. What would they do without him? How would they cope? Would it hurt? Was there anything after death?

Many who faced death had similar thoughts. No one living, would ever know the answers to those questions.

Behind him, further down the alleyway, Barnaby heard his most recent defender come through the gate and head towards him. "He has to see this," he thought to himself, "Please God, let him see the crap I am in!"

Barnaby's head was pulled to the side by the hand clasped over his mouth. A head appeared round the corner of the brickwork, looking directly into his eyes.

The eyes that met his were not full of loathing and hate as he had expected. Instead they were full of relief. Incredulity. There was a soft incandescent glow about them. A familiarity that defied belief. Reassurance sat behind those eyes.

As fear receded in Barnaby's mind, recognition penetrated his frontal cortex. His fear immediately subsided, replaced with relief. He felt the muscles in his body released of their tension.

In front of him stood a man he had known, and trusted, for the last eighteen months. Paul Buxton, the head of his security detail, smiled at him as he put his hands on his shoulders. "I got you Sir. Never thought for a second I was going to lose you ..."

Barnaby smiled, then laughed quietly, pulling Paul to his shoulder. "You took your time. Where the hell have you been?" he joked.

Paul suddenly stood back and pulled his gun up, "Stop right there," he called looking into the shadows. Barnaby realised that Paul would not know who was behind him. "It's Ok Paul, this officer has been helping me ... stay alive." He turned, nodding to the man he had crept through the dust covered, hidden relics, of people lives with.

"This is Paul Buxton, head of my security detail" he finished, patting both men on the shoulder as they lowered their guns and shook hands.

"Let's get out of here quick, Sir. Before they come back for you," suggested Paul. Nobody was going to disagree with that.

An unmarked police car was waiting at the end of the road. "I've got him!" Paul relayed over his mic. The car reversed towards them so it was facing out of the rows of terraced houses and their dead end streets. The doors of the car were opened from the inside. Paul stuck his head out to check the street was clear then beckoned them out towards the car. Stepping out from the alleyway, Barnaby jumped as he suddenly realised that each side had been flanked by two other members of Paul's security team. Smudge and Junior had stuck with Paul through the day and they saw them safely into the car.

Pulling away, the two men stayed behind, weapons drawn to ensure nobody else followed. Reaching Wilford Grove, two armoured vehicles were waiting for them. The car pulled in between the two of them and they proceeded towards Nottingham Forest Football Club.

"Sir, we have a helicopter on the ground and as soon as we can we will have you evacuated to a military medical centre," stated Paul. "I am bloody relieved to have you back."

"How did you find me Paul?" enquired the now exhausted prime minister.

"I have been chasing you all day Mr Aitken," started Paul, turning towards his back seat passenger. "After we lost you on the Old Market Square, we followed the guys chasing you. Managed to nail two of them, but the rest got away. We had no idea at the time if they had you or not." Paul turned and dropped his eyes to his knees, almost ashamed of the fact that the person he had responsibility for protecting, had been put through the trauma of today.

After a short pause, he continued. "They pulled in the mayor for questioning."

"Bolek! No way?" questioned Barnaby, in surprise. "Is he involved?"

"Not sure yet Sir. I don't think so. They beat him up pretty bad and he didn't say a word. Most people cave in under such intense scrutiny."

"They beat him? That's not right Paul," stated Barnaby in disgust.

"At the time Sir, he was the best possible lead. They had to know if he was involved and, if so, what he knew. We had to get you back safely Sir."

"At what cost?" Barnaby sounded angry. He was not going to condone violence, whether it be terrorism, or the police force under his command.

Paul moved the conversation on. "Anyway, after you called in from the service station a while ago, I was tracking your movements and going to join you at the football ground. Your driver called it in that you were under attack. We moved out to come and help, but you were cornered before we made it to you." Paul had a look of guilt about him, like he had failed his boss.

"It's Ok Paul" he rested his hand on Paul's shoulder. Paul continued with his recount of how he had happened upon the prime minister again.

"By the time we turned up, your car had been attacked and we heard a broken message afterwards. There was a mob that had congregated after the explosion, coming from the bottom of the road, heading up towards your car. We saw your attackers come out of the alley way, then back away from the mob, climb into the transit van and head off as we arrived. No sign of you though. From there, we headed up the alleyway to see if they had ki ..." he corrected himself, "got you. But again, nothing. A quick look in the house you went in and we saw a small piece of insulation from the loft on the carpet under the hatch. Easy to miss in the dark when you are chasing someone."

Barnaby nodded in approval. That was why Paul Buxton was his head of security. He never missed a detail. "I put myself in your shoes, or rather those of the officer helping you, at that point. To go back the way you came from was foolhardy as everyone expects that. Logic dictates you are likely to run into trouble. So, if you can, head as far away from the scene as you can undetected." Paul, turned his head back towards Barnaby. "We arrived at the alleyway as you came out from the back gate. Good to have you back Sir!

The officer who had helped Barnaby laughed. "Man, you are good!" He too was relieved to be alive.

"You never gave up on me. Thank you," Barnaby looked out of the window. "How many died today?"

"That's not entirely clear yet Sir." Paul looked away and hung his head. "Too many" he whispered towards the window of the car.

Whilst they were heading to the helicopter, other armed officers and army personnel cordoned off the Meadows. Wilford Grove and all the surrounding streets were on lockdown as they started the recovery of those that had defended the leader of the modern democracy. Fire engines moved down the street to douse the flames of the burning vehicles under heavy armed protection. The mob that had seen the terrorist group back off, stood round congratulating themselves on forcing them back. Recording all sorts of footage that they would later sell on to the media at significant cost. It mattered not to them, that the body of one of the fallen was in fact a father, a husband, a son to others. They could make some fast cash out of their suffering.

Everyone was on high alert for a white transit van. With Her Majesty's Armed Forces striking out everywhere, it would not be long before it was found and the occupants either detained. Or killed.

Pulling up outside the City Ground, the security now around the prime minister was reminiscent of those from the Second World War. Except, there were cameras on every soldier, recording all the details and the equipment they used was far more accurate and lethal.

Barnaby Aitken was transferred, with his head of security to the awaiting helicopter. He shook hands with the police officer that had been his most recent protector, then embraced him. "Thank you," was all he said.

Barnaby Aitken had been rescued. He did not dare think he was now safe, but he certainly felt a lot more confident than he had done since eleven o'clock this morning. Sitting down for the first time, he really noticed the intense pain of his ankle. Sure, it had hurt through the day, but he had to run on it to survive. Adrenaline, he realised, was a powerful analgesic. Now, he needed the aid of pharmaceuticals.

He checked his watch as he got on board the military helicopter. It was eleven o'clock in the evening. Barnaby, knowing he was as protected now as he could ever be, donned his earphones, put his head back against the headrest and shut his eyes.

It was twelve hours since the nightmare had begun.

Chapter Thirty Five

Money, Movement and Madness

Sunday night passed with no other major incidents. Barnaby was flown to the most secure military hospital, tended by some of the finest physicians in the country. Two other military helicopters had joined them on their journey, taking up protective roles, to ensure no further incidents arose. After being treated for his minor injuries, a shower and a few hours' sleep, the prime minister had been taken back, at his command, to Number 10 Downing Street.

It was seven thirty in the morning, the sun was breaking the cold of the night, bringing a fresh perspective to the United Kingdom at the beginning of a new working week. Barnaby was met in his office by the head of MI6, Irm Brown, head of MI5, Marcus Poole, his personal secretary, Mike Lightfoot, his deputy prime minister, Sebastian Horner, and the home secretary, Helen Langley.

Of course, the press had been informed, through a leak somewhere, of the prime minister's safe return. They were there in greater numbers than normal, to try and photograph the historic event. He had been briefed and de-briefed on the day's events. He hung his head low, in mourning for those that had lost their lives, on the previous terrible day.

The death toll of the innocents stood at thirty-one. Thirty-one.

Many had died in the Old Market Square. Some, from the chase towards the Broad Marsh shopping centre. Mother and child of one of the perpetrators, executed in their own home. The armed police that had protected the prime minister, as his vehicle was blown apart in the Meadows. The old Polish lady that helped him escape in the Meadows. Death had come to many innocent lives yesterday. Regardless of their colour, race, age or sex.

Barnaby was relieved to hear that both Lee, his saviour from the earlier part of the day, and his estranged wife and son, were all safe. Without Lee, he knew he would not be alive.

Then, there were the terrorists themselves, that were taken out by the armed forces and the prime ministers own security detail. He would not mourn their loss, but others would.

"Thank God you are back safely Barnaby," said Mike, helping the prime minister to his chair. Barnaby nodded, acknowledging his companion. "Thanks need to go to all those that put their lives on the line Mike. Not God." Barnaby's stern face softened a little as he looked around the room at those before him. The others all extended their relief to him that he was alive and back in command.

"Do we know who is behind these outrageous events?" Barnaby enquired.

Money, Movement and Madness

Marcus and Irm looked at each other, he nodded for her to start.

"Sir, firstly, we are relieved you are back safely. We believe we have the majority of those responsible for these events contained now. They are either lying in a morgue, or in secure units for thorough interrogation," started a confident Irm. "We are still hunting the occupants from the transit van, that shot at you over the river Trent and attacked you in the Meadows area last night."

"So what was this all about? Me closing the borders yesterday?" Asked Barnaby.

"We believe it's bigger than that Sir. This took months of planning and preparation. Whoever is behind it, placed sleepers in our police, and possibly elsewhere, deliberately targeting you at the event yesterday," continued Marcus.

"What we need to know is how the hell did they manage to do that?" Helen quipped angrily across the room. "Our security forces seem to have let you down Sir. Let us all down." Helen locked eyes with Marcus.

"On the contrary Helen," responded Barnaby, "Our security services responded magnificently to the threats we were faced with." Barnaby bought his fingers together at their very tips, thumbs clasped under his chin. "Hackers are remarkably talented people and it is almost impossible to understand what they can do, let alone where they are going to do it. Or indeed, when. Unless we have very good intelligence, we cannot kid ourselves we can stop every possible attack."

Irm and Marcus both nodded their appreciation towards the prime minister. It was unusual to be supported by a politician.

"We should applaud them," he went on, "not deride them."

"With all due respect Sir ..." Helen started.

"Were it not for MI5 and MI6 Helen," he interrupted her, "we would not have captured those responsible inside twelve hours. Please. A little gratitude would not go amiss." Looking at her, he extended his hand, suggesting she applaud them. Helen smiled and looked away.

"Tell me Irm, if it's more than closing the borders, what is the motive for this attack?"

"Well Sir, from those we have been able to question so far, there is a common thread. We have in custody, people from seemingly innocuous backgrounds: farming, fishing, the automotive industry, to name a few. There are some from the UK, others all across Europe. Austria, Belgium, Germany, Poland."

Marcus, unable to stop himself, took over. "The list goes on, Sir. Every single one, feels that BREXIT is to blame for their livelihood being decimated. Movement of people is one part, but it looks like there is a well-connected group determined to make the UK pay for the referendum result. Each of those industries Irm mentioned, is losing out in Europe, because their number one customer does not have a trade deal with the EU. Revenue is cut off. If you are on the other side of the Channel, the UK was such a strong fiscal contributor to the EU, that the subsidies to the farmers they are now paying, has gone down substantially. They are having to bail out their failed economies again, in Greece, Italy and Spain. On top of that, their fisherman can't catch fish in the waters off the coast of Britain anymore."

All the time Marcus spoke, Barnaby listened. "They can't sell their cars or other goods here. Those industries have suffered in the UK too. They can't export in the way they were able to before. They feel they have been robbed of their future. Their inheritance. Their income."

"Ok. But that has been the case for a number of years already. Why now?" Asked Barnaby.

"That, we are not sure of. It could be that it just takes a while for a group with similar feelings of discontentment to connect. They need to work out who it is safe to trust and who not to" went on Marcus.

"Not only that," interjected Irm, "but it would take a while to place sleepers in the way they did and amass the level of arms they seemed to have available to them. That is some underworld, or dark web connections, that you need to make. Plus, it also needs funding. A lot of funding."

"Do you believe we have ... everything under control now?" A perfectly understandable question in the circumstances. The small circle of those around him, privileged and burdened, with the safety and security of the country, exchanged glances.

It was Marcus that answered. "We think so, Sir," he nodded reassuringly. "Having the army on the streets helps. Although alarming to the citizens, it is reassuring at the same time. More importantly, it's a distinct deterrent to any left who may still be trying to get to you" he shot a glance at the prime minister, who met his gaze and gently nodded his appreciation.

The deputy prime minister, who had sat with his head hung low, looked up. "Barnaby, we cannot bow to pressure from those that would terrorise you through these types of atrocious attacks." Glancing sideways at

Helen, his movement was missed by the majority in the room. Not Barnaby though.

"What do you think we should do then, Sebastian?" Barnaby questioned, not looking at him, but instead focussing his attention on Helen. 'What has happened between these two?' he thought to himself.

"Of that, I am not sure. Throughout history though, progress has always been opposed by those that feel they will lose out. People like the *status quo,* unless they believe they can benefit from the change."

Irm picked up again, feeling they were getting lost in ideology, rather than the facts. "What we know, is that someone known as Toad, who we believe is central to this, was apprehended last night in Sneinton. He was in the house where Nicky Bevan and her son, Aidan, were being held hostage. We are trying to establish his real identity, but he is currently being questioned. Pressure is being applied, if you know what I mean" risked Irm, without wanting to suggest there was anything untoward going on.

"We should reinstate capital punishment," suggested Helen, looking rather glum.

"Hmm. Ok. Thanks Irm. To you and your team. I won't forget the effort that has gone in here" Barnaby clapped his hands together in applause. "For you too Marcus, and your team. Sterling job."

Mike stood, moving over to some pots of tea and coffee that had been left at the side of the room. Steam was still rising from the spout of the silverware. He poured several cups of each, offering them round the room. Everyone took one gratefully, not realising how thirsty they were.

The silence, as they sipped, was deafening.

After a reflective few minutes, Barnaby put his coffee cup on the table. "We might have been wrong," he declared.

Those around him, raised their faces towards him, seeking to understand. "What do you mean?" asked Sebastian.

"Immigration" said Barnaby, lifting his hands as if to fend off some pesky grandchildren. His audience looked up, dumbstruck by this revelation.

"Yesterday was a terrible day," started Barnaby. "Many people lost their lives through no fault of their own. They lost it to the actions of those hell bent on maintaining what they had. They died, needlessly. Directly as a result of the actions of this government and those before us. Yes, we were acting out the 'will of the people'" he lifted his fingers to give it inverted speech marks. "Sometimes, you have to stop and ask yourself if you have done the right thing."

Barnaby was leaning forward, his elbows resting on his knees. "Was it worth thirty-one dead bodies? People, like you and me. Just men and women wanting to enjoy life. Make a difference. They died through no fault of their own, but because of the actions of this government, and previous governments. We have their blood on our hands here today."

Barnaby scanned every face before him in turn. His own eyes were full of sorrow and regret. Glances were exchanged around the room. No one quite knew what to make of this revelation. The only one who held his gaze, without shaking her head, was Helen.

"We can't turn back the clock, but ... we should recognise the good people that we have in this country, regardless of where they were born. Yesterday, I witnessed people from the UK and abroad, wanting to help. Wanting to right the wrongs of others. There are some who have made England their home, despite not being born here. They have contributed to society. They aren't sponging off our welfare. They aren't leeches on society. They are ...were ..." he paused, thinking of the small Polish lady, who gave him shelter in her house, leading to his eventual escape, "good people, who wanted to help.

"Everyone who lost their lives trying to help me, is to be given state funerals, if the families will accept that offer. I want Lee and his family looked after. Security if you feel it's necessary, but financially they are not to go without. If they need psychological support, particularly for young Aidan, they get it."

Surveying each of them in turn, he looked round the room. He did not need to check they understood. They knew he meant it. It would be so. He was almost in disbelief at himself, but he had become aware, under the most dangerous of circumstances, that the path he had been walking, was not the right one for him, or for the United Kingdom. Clarity had come from the desperate state he had found himself in. Out of Europe's ridiculous plan for ever escalating central governance, yes, but that did not mean they had to completely isolate themselves, fuelling hatred and bigotry.

It was possible to govern his own country without closing the borders in the way he had. Movement into the country was a sign of prosperity. It had served them well in the past. It could do so again, in the future. They had to look at the issues of the country differently.

Being able to debate and agree your own countries law was the reason he had voted to get out of the

European stranglehold. Sovereignty. His journey over the last twenty-four hours had taught him more than any consultation group could in a decade.

Looking at his team, he raised his head again. "We will hold those responsible for this attack to account. Of that, you have my word. From this point forward though, we will be looking at our policies differently."

Everyone in the room nodded in approval. It would be wrong to disagree with your leader in his own office. Indeed, at the home of the prime minister.

"Let me know what you get from this Toad character. He had to be working for someone," he requested, "I guess I need to go and face the media. Show them my battle wounds," he smiled, gesturing towards his ankle and crutches.

Mike got to his feet and opened the door, a signal for everyone to leave. The meeting was over. They shook hands with Barnaby and left one by one.

"Sebastian," called out Barnaby, "Just a minute please." Sebastian turned around.

At the door, Helen stopped and glanced backwards. Mike shut the door firmly on her.

Chapter Thirty Six

Uncovered

In a room devoid of anything that related to the natural world, Toad rubbed his head, feeling the welt from the hit he'd taken earlier. He'd been man-handled here, a mask over his head to disorient him.

He was pretty sure he was still in the vicinity of Nottingham as they hadn't travelled for long enough to be in London. Handcuffed to an SAS officer until he reached his destination, he had been emptied into a cell with nothing but a metal bench bolted to the floor and a toilet in the corner.

No blankets. No mattress. He wasn't surprised.

After laying down on the metal bench, he closed his eyes. It had been a long day. He had accomplished so much. And yet, he had failed.

It was an audacious attack on the government of the UK. Indeed, on the prime minister himself. They had been so close to a successful mission. A small step to the side by Barnaby Aitken at the last minute had disrupted everything. Margins of error were small, but they had substantial consequences.

Toad understood that. Raising his arm to his mouth, he pretended to inhale from his vape machine, held his breath and smiled. As he dropped his arm, sleep took him.

Uncovered

An ice cold bucket of water roused him from his slumber. Toad was only asleep for a few minutes. Spluttering and springing upwards, he saw a burly man stood before him, shouting in his face. He was dragged out to an adjacent room that was empty except for a ring attached to the ceiling. Toads hands were pulled up to the ring and fastened securely, leaving him standing on tip toes, calves straining to maintain his weight.

"WHO THE FUCK ORDERED THIS?" His interrogator shouted, pushing him back towards the wall. Toad spat cold water out of his mouth, his skin shivered, goose bumps visible.

"Ordered what?" he responded calmly.

"Oh! You're a smart arse are you?" the man responded. "Well I got a treat for a smart arse." He reached behind him. Another man had entered, pushing a trolley. Sporting shoulder length dark wavy hair hanging loose on his shoulders, he stood over a trolley and passed the first man some paddles.

"What the hell are they?" asked Toad, a hint of nervousness in his voice.

"These? These are paddles that will make you tell me what I want to know," he responded pulling them apart. A small machine behind him let out a high pitched squeal. It was charged. Toad instantly realised he was about to be shocked.

"Okay. Okay." He stammered. "I'll tell you what I know." The colour had drained from his face and his courage wilted in the blink of an eye.

Over the next thirty minutes, Toad explained what the attack had been about. It was nothing that the security services hadn't already worked out for themselves.

"So you are Toad. Who are you working for?"

Toad shook his head, "No-one".

"What's your real name?" The questions came faster as fatigue took hold and there was no way they were going to let this bastard sleep.

"I ... I can't remember ..." said Toad with a wide mouthed grin. It was his last chance to come clean with those asking the questions.

A shock went through his body. One hundred volts delivered via the paddles that had been waved in his face earlier. Not quite as powerful as a proper defibrillator, they didn't want to stop his heart, just break his resistance. Toad cried out in pain as his body pulsated, thrashed and dropped towards the floor. His legs could no longer support him. With his hands attached to the ring above, his arms stretched tight as they now held him up. Another bucket of ice cold water bought him back around. His sides felt like they had been crushed in a vice.

"So, Tamas," started the burly man, "Would you like to answer that question again?" There was a smile across his face that unnerved Toad. He called him by a name that had not been used for many a year. In all his time in the underworld as a hacker, he had been known as Toad. Nobody he worked with, knew his real name or where he came from.

Toad felt broken.

"My name is Tamas, yes," he offered, but said no more.

"We know that. You are Tamas, Olivier, Aemon, Dabici. T...O...A...D ... Correct? You are from Hungary are you not?" Mr Burly had a smug look on his face and he grabbed Toads head in his hands, locking his eyes. He couldn't stop himself from carrying on.

"You must be wondering how we know that? Well Mr Dabici, you were arrested fifteen years ago and we have your records now, courtesy of Interpol. Finger prints, which we took when you were arrested, along with a DNA match, prove your identity." The smile got broader on his face. Toad wanted to close his eyelids to the danger before him.

"Wanted by at least five governments for outrageous hacking offences, I don't begin to understand. You are in serious shit Tamas. And no one is coming to help you." He waved the paddles in front of him, to exert his power and authority again. Wavy hair stood firm in the corner, not intervening, but watching every move. He showed no emotion and Toad realised he was not getting out of here soon.

"I was the mastermind," he declared. "We were pissed off at you closing your borders. It wrecked our trade, our future. You didn't just fuck England, you fucked Europe." Toad had calmed down and was talking freely. "There are hundreds of us, all sorts of businesses, who are fed up with politicians interfering in the natural order of our world. You needed to be taught a lesson." Toad dropped his head, the water still dripping from his skin, desperate for sleep.

"We had hope before. You ruined everything. We decided that we could teach you a lesson, so we took direct action." Toad looked at his captors. "In Hungary we always hoped for more. Dreamt of coming to Europe, to England. You shut up shop and it killed the dreams of many. What is wrong with wanting a better life for yourself, your family?"

Burly and wavy hair did not respond to anything that Toad said. They just listened.

"The internet connects people beyond borders. You can't police it, you can't prevent it. You all use it to reach around the world. You all need it." He was struggling to speak, the weight of his body pulling on his arms and across his chest. "No one can function without being connected these days. It's the boundless way of buying goods, selling, watching entertainment, banking. You name it, we can hack it." Toad managed to pull his feet back under him, to take some of the weight off his exhausted body.

"Well, some of us know how to use it secretly. To do good and bad. To change things in our favour. We used it to get close to your Prime Minister."

"One last time, you arsehole. Who was behind this? Who paid for the hired thugs?" Burly waited for the machine to squeal again. He could see fear in the eyes of Toad as he advanced towards him.

Shaking his head, Toad said nothing, closed his eyes and waited for the shock to hit him.

Chapter Thirty Seven

Courage

It felt like an eternity since he had last slept.

Lee sat on his old settee, in the house of his wife. Aidan lay across it, his head on his father's lap, a blanket covering his body as his chest dropped, then lifted slowly again, drawing breath. Beano was being strangled by the little boy's arm. Nicky slept on the sofa opposite, her head on top of her hands. He surveyed the room.

It was reassuring to be back in his old home.

Outside the front door were two armed officers and a further four were located in vehicles up and down the road, watching for anyone trying to approach the house. A road block had been set up at the end to prevent the press from intruding.

After the events at the house in Sneinton, Nicky and Aidan had been taken to the Queens Medical Centre, where they were both checked over for injuries. Nicky had been inundated with people she worked with hugging her and her son. Colleagues weeping in relief that she had escaped from "These callous bast ..." Nicky had to look at Aidan to remind them to mind their language. It felt weird for her to be on the opposite side for a change. It dawned on her that if she had not been caught up in all of this, she probably would have been called in to be part of the emergency response team. Other than shock and fatigue, Nicky and Aidan were otherwise unharmed.

It was at the hospital, that Lee had been reunited with them both.

Dan was transferred from Holme Pierrepont by ambulance at high speed. Lee had insisted on accompanying his friend. On arrival at Accident and Emergency, an already exhausted medical team, who had worked tirelessly through the day, treating those from the bombing on the Old Market Square, attended to the latest casualty.

Despite CPR being quickly administered by the SAS team whilst on the ground at Holme Pierrepont, there was nothing they could do for him.

Dan was pronounced dead shortly afterwards.

Lee wept, tears cascading freely down his cheeks, as he banged the palm of his hand against the door frame at the entrance to the hospital. Photographers who had not been allowed into the hospital and were being contained outside, recognised Lee from the TV footage earlier in the day. They started taking pictures of his personal grief through their long range lenses. Hearing questions being shouted and his name being called, Lee looked up from his solitude. After the day he'd had, he could not cope with this right now. He backed away, taking cover inside the safety of the hospital.

Sitting in a corridor, sipping some tea that an officer had given him, Lee leant on his knees. It had gone midnight and the hospital was quietening down as two policemen approached him. Explaining that his wife and son had been rescued and were unharmed, they took him to the room they occupied. Relief overpowered his grief, as Lee rushed to embrace his family.

Nicky hugged him tight. Aidan was between the two of them, feeling the warmth of both his parents at the same time. For the first time since ... he could not remember. Tears stained all their cheeks. Lee had kissed them both furiously, stroking their hair, holding them close.

"What about Dan?" asked Nicky. Lee could only shake his head, as the tears welled in his eyes again. Not for the first time in the last twenty-four hours, Nicky's legs buckled. Lee caught her, pulling her closer, whispering apologies to her.

At three in the morning, Lee left them in the security of the hospital to go to Dans house and break the impossible news to his wife, Leslie. Accompanied by two armed officers, his hands shaking, he knocked gently on the front door.

Leslie opened it before he had finished knocking. She had been waiting since Dan left with Nicky earlier in the day for any news. Despite calling Dan regularly, she had heard nothing from either of them. Fraught with worry, she had not slept, but watched the news constantly. She knew that there had been further attacks in The Meadows and Holme Pierrepont, but the details of each were sketchy. It had been reported that the police had made arrests. The SAS had been involved and several of those responsible had been killed. However, with everything that had been reported, there was nothing regarding her husband, Dan.

Seeing Lee accompanied by the two officers, Leslie stepped backwards. She was full of hope, but instinct told her that Dan was gone. Leaning his head to one side, Lee locked eyes with Leslie, clenching and unclenching his fists. His eyes moistened again and he shook his head.

"NO!" Leslie screamed at the night, Lee moved to hold her but she punched out at him. "No ... It can't be ... Nooooooo". As he pulled her to him, her body went limp, her chest heaved and the grief came.

Helping her back inside, he took her to the lounge and explained what had happened since Dan had left. Speaking slowly and choosing his words deliberately, his voice was soft and reassuring. "He was so brave Leslie. He didn't need to help, but ... that was Dan."

No matter what Lee said, it would not abate her grief for the only man she had ever loved. It would leave her bereft. A hole, in the heart of her mind, that would not be filled. As painful as the day her mother took her own life.

Lee promised to come back in the morning, once he had taken Aidan and Nicky back home. The police would stay outside until she felt she no longer needed them to.

Lee had insisted he was the one to tell Leslie. He felt responsible for his best friend's death.

It had been so hard for him to do, but he had managed to find the courage that had evaded him so many times in his life before. In fact, he had been finding it regularly, this last day.

The sun was high in the sky as they were woken by the sound of the phone in the hallway. Nicky pushed herself upright from her position opposite, rushed for the phone, sweeping her matted hair back out her face.

Lee looked at the clock on the wall, it was late in the morning. They had only been asleep for a few hours, but enough to take the edge off the exhaustion. Aidan remained asleep, Lee stroked his hair gently, then moved him off his lap so he could stand. He headed to the kitchen and put the kettle on to make coffee.

Courage

He could hear Nicky talking on the phone. Her soft voice sounded different to how he had heard her recently. The anger wasn't there. It was filled with sadness.

As he stirred the coffee, Nicky headed through and he passed her a mug. She put it down on the counter and hugged him. Her head resting on his shoulder. He returned the embrace.

"That was Dad. He's glad you and Aidan are both Ok," she spoke with a lump in her throat. "He saw the news and knew straight away it was you with Aidan. He's … he's been worried sick. Trying to ring me, but I had my phone taken away."

She pushed herself away from him slightly and stroked his hair, gazing into his eyes. "I'm glad you are safe Lee. It would have been unbearable if we had lost you." Lee smiled back at her and stroked her face.

"I'm sorry about Dan. He was so brave coming to help like that." He offered, knowing his words would set her off again. Nicky looked away and lifted the coffee to her lips, then changed the subject.

"Dad says that the prime minister is back in Downing Street. He was attacked again last night in the Meadows, but somehow he got away. They think they have caught most of those responsible." Nicky paused.

"Thank God he made it!" exclaimed Lee. "He has some serious crap to sort out now. God only knows what it was all about, but I suspect he is about to unleash hell."

The phone rang again and Nicky looked at the number. It was withheld. She debated letting it go to answer phone, but pressed to pick up.

"Hello?" she started. "Oh! My goodness. We are so glad you got back safely."

She shot Lee a glance and waved her hand furiously for him to join her.

On the other end, was the prime minister. Their new friend, Barnaby Aitken.

Chapter Thirty Eight
Breadcrumbs

Everything recovered from the house in Sneinton had been sent to the laboratories of the secret services. The best men and women in the country, were set the task of uncovering any clue that lay on the computers and mobile phones of all those that had been arrested, or killed, in the last twenty-four hours.

Marcus was overseeing the work, desperate to uncover the animal responsible for orchestrating the events in Nottingham. "There may not be much on any of these machines," he started, "But whatever there is, it's evidence and it must be found and preserved."

Every laptop was examined with extreme caution. Concern was evident. They may have been set up to self-destruct the hard drives, if anything unexpected was entered, passwords not inputted correctly.

The three hackers they had in custody were not saying a lot. Marcus suspected that in reality they knew very little. He realised that Toad was their master, and yet, he danced to the tune of someone else. Sloth 2000, HaPee as Larry and IPFree were sought by many governments around the world and they finally had identities for all of them. He knew that if they were deported to face justice in other countries, it was highly likely they would end up working for the respective governments, rather than going to jail.

Better to have the enemy within, helping, rather than sat in a prison cell. These were gifted individuals. Hard to find. They were the modern day equivalent of the 'Gold Rush' pioneers. Gradually, Marcus' team worked out how the taxi had been hacked by HaPee to force it to their hide out in Sneinton. They followed the minuscule digital trail that had been left behind.

Everything leaves its presence felt. Nothing is ever totally deleted.

One team was focussed on the mobile phone of Toad. They knew who he was now. They had access and they were tracing all his recent activity. They phones of Lee and his friend Dan, were recovered, linking the call that Lee had taken at the garage forecourt, back to Toad's mobile.

Someone else had called him a number of times in the last twenty-four hours.

There were no text messages from the number and nothing else on the phone to give any hints. It had to be the connection they needed.

"Get me records from the phone company. I want to know if there are any recorded messages from the answerphone." Insisted Marcus in the early hours of the morning.

After their early morning meeting in Number Ten, Marcus joined Irm for some breakfast, at just gone nine. They exchanged pleasantries, but looking at each other they realised how knackered the other one looked. Neither mentioned it. It was a side effect of the job. They would get sleep soon enough. When the job was done.

Marcus scoffed down a sausage sandwich, whilst Irm nibbled on some muesli with yoghurt. Both washed their meal down with coffee. It was likely to be another long day.

Rushing in from the far end of the room, Glasses waved at them frantically. "You got to come and listen to this," he stammered, gasping for breath. He led them back upstairs into a side room. There were two others waiting for them. Tatoos and Silver and both looked very nervous.

Silver started. "The number from Toads phone. It's a burner, we don't know who bought it, but we know it's still in use. We have also managed to rescue a voicemail left on his answerphone from about three months ago." Silver looked down at the table.

"You are not going to believe this ..." she whispered at them as she pressed play on the audio equipment in the room.

"Let me know you got the clearance codes Ok. You should have everything you need now to make this clean. Make sure the Puppy pays for this. Don't fail me."

Everyone in the room was stunned. They all looked at each in astonishment. "You know who that is, right?" stuttered Silver.

Irm and Marcus nodded at the same time. Irm, looked up, "Have you confirmed on voice recognition?" she asked, just to make sure they weren't about to make a big mistake.

Tatoos nodded back, almost ashamed at the fact he had checked.

Marcus knew what he had to do. He took Irm with him.

Chapter Thirty Nine
Downing Street

Having faced the press, Barnaby Aitken settled back into his chair behind his desk and rested his crutches against the wall behind him. Mike helped settle him down and went to the back of the room to ensure there was tea and coffee coming.

Outside, there had been a barrage of questions. Mostly about his welfare and that of those that had helped him through the day.

"Yes, we have those we believe are responsible for the atrocious and callous killings in custody." He sounded resolute. Firm and unbending, yet compassionate for those that had lost their lives. "We should take a minute to remember all those innocent people who lost their lives yesterday. Taken from their families, without warning, when they should have been enjoying a great day out. Please, a minute's silence for all that perished." Barnaby bowed his head, forcing the media to do so with him.

Even the incessant clicks of the cameras stopped for some of it.

As he started again, he thanked all those that had been involved in helping him evade capture and survive. The armed police forces. His own security team. The

Downing Street

SAS and the army, including the Royal Marines. Even members of the public, caught up in a nightmare. "Some," he said, "paid a heavy price for their bravery. Paid with their lives. For that, I am indebted to them and their families, forever. We will continue to keep the armed forces on the streets, until we are sure there is no longer a substantial threat to ours, and your, safety. Rest assured, we will not stop, until all of those responsible are caught and face the full force of the law," he finished, turning back towards the doors of Number Ten and his office.

Opposite him, on the other side of the desk were Helen and Sebastian. They had stood by his side as he confronted the media. They looked like a team to the outside world. They all knew it was very different now the cameras were not present.

"Now Helen, what is this crap about blackmailing Sebastian here?" he looked down his nose at her. Helen didn't flinch. She had been expecting it.

"What Sebastian does in his own private life is up to him," Barnaby continued. I've known for years he is gay. His wife knows he is gay for God's sake, but they stay together for the sake of their family. It is none of your business and it is certainly not the business of the general public. Christ its 2023 and we still get upset about two men having sex?" he barked at her.

Helen looked a little uncomfortable, this was news to her that she had not anticipated. "I was given some information, that was all," she started, not looking at Sebastian. "If you weren't going to come back to us prime minister, we needed to make sure that it was not going to come out in the public eye. It would have been disastrous for this government."

"Bullshit," barked Sebastian. "You set me up and were muscling in to make yourself the leader if Barnaby didn't come back." There was rage in his eyes.

"But he is back, isn't he," smiled Helen, through gritted teeth.

"Yes," spoke Barnaby. "I am back. Helen, you will return all photos to me and delete anything you have from your electronic devices. Do you understand? Otherwise, I will have the IT team come and review everything on your computers to make sure it's gone" Her eyes dropped to the floor, she certainly did not like the sound of being investigated herself. She nodded in acknowledgement. "Ok."

"If anything, I mean anything, is leaked about this, or a picture gets sent to the papers, I will have you kicked out of this party instantly. You want to mess around with crap like that, it will be the last thing you do." Barnaby's tone spoke volumes. He was not to be messed with on this. He had put her in this position of considerable authority and he would not hesitate to remove her from office if she did not comply.

Barnaby breathed deeply. "You have until this evening to get rid of it all. Now, we will hear no more about it. We have to sort these bloody morons out who were trying to kill me. Where have they got to with this Toad fellow?"

After her scolding, Helen sat upright in her chair to return to business. "Not much so far. I believe they have identified him properly. A Hungarian, called Tamas Dabici. Apparently he is not saying much."

Barnaby, rubbed his chin, then called out to his secretary. "Mike can you get us some tea please and get my wife on the phone, I haven't actually spoken to her properly since last night." He turned back towards Helen and Sebastian.

Turning back towards Helen, he continued. "Is this Toad chap the Mastermind? There has to be someone, or some group, who is behind this. Is it a personal vendetta against me, or against our government?"

Sebastian was about to answer him, as the phone on the desk rang, distracting all of them. Mike was putting the tea down on the table and reached over to pick the phone up. "Mike Lightfoot," he answered.

Whoever was on the end of the phone had Mike's attention immediately. Barnaby looked at him quizzically, knowing that something was awry. "Ok," he held the receiver to his chest as the door opened and two armed police officers walked into Barnaby's office.

"What is going on?" Barnaby enquired as he turned to eye the officers bursting into his office.

"It's her, Sir" Mike mumbled, holding out the receiver.

"What my wife? That was good timing. Pass her over Mike," he held out his hand for the phone, but kept a wary eye on the police. Mike shook his head.

He was pointing with the receiver at Helen. He said again, "No Barnaby, not your wife. It's ... her, Sir. The police are here for your Home Secretary. Helen is behind all of this.'

Barnaby and Sebastian got to their feet, Barnaby using a chair for support, as the officers strode over to Helen and pulled her to her feet, moving her arms behind her back. One of them read her rights to her whilst ensuring her wrists were cuffed. "Helen Langley, we are arresting you on suspicion of the attempted murder of Barnaby Aitken and the murders of at least thirty-one other individuals. You do not have to say anything ..." he went on, but Barnaby heard none of it.

He just stood there shaking his head, looking completely bemused, "You must be joking. This is nonsense. Helen, what is going on?" Barnaby demanded to know.

Helen said nothing initially, looking indignantly back at them, swinging her hair back behind her head, weighing up whether anything she said, could incriminate her further. Realising they must have broken Toad, she figured that whatever she said, she was not going to get out of this situation easily. Her ego got the better of her again.

"Your plans are a disaster for this country. You needed to be stopped Barnaby. What better way to do that, than from within your own party," she sneered at him, giving him his first view of the callousness, of the real Helen Langley.

Her plans had unravelled fast over the last twenty-four hours. All because Barnaby Aitken took a few steps to the side, at the precise time the bomb had detonated. Had he been where he should have been, at eleven am that Sunday morning, Barnaby Aitken would be dead, and she, Helen Langley, would be leading the party and the country.

"How could you Helen? So many people ... dead..." tailed off Barnaby, lifting his hand to his cut head, reminding him of his own recent proximity to death. He was in shock at the latest revelation. Someone he had nurtured, in his own party, to be a potential leader of the future, had gone to such extreme circumstances to get there even quicker.

"That was unfortunate," she smiled, "You should have stood on the right spot, where you were supposed to, in front of the microphone. It would have been a lot less traumatic for everyone."

The police officers turned her away from the three dumbstruck men in the room and marched her out to a waiting car.

"Bloody hell!" exclaimed Sebastian as the door shut behind them. "What a complete bitch."

Mike put the phone down and all three sat, shaking their heads in disbelief.

Barnaby wanted to know everything that had been shared on that phone call.

Chapter Forty
De-Brief

Marcus and Irm sat together in the PM's office. Barnaby was still reeling from the fact that his home secretary had been frog marched out of his office in handcuffs, accused of being behind the whole attack on him.

Someone he had supported, developed and trusted. The more he thought about it, the more it filled him with anger. He had to know everything.

"How is Helen possibly involved in this? Please, do tell me you have made a mistake." He already knew from her few comments that there was no mistake.

"Sir, we know this probably sounds mad, but when you hear the evidence, it will make sense to you," responded Marcus, opening a file in front of him. He was going to refer to his notes.

"You know Helen's background, yes? How she made a fortune in real estate back in the late 2000s?"

Barnaby nodded, "Yes of course, so what?"

"Well" Irm continued, "she lost a lot in the last couple of years. House prices were starting to fall with the threat of the borders closing. If people left in their droves like you wanted them to, her rental income would suffer massively. Her business empire was at risk. Simple supply and demand calculation."

De-Brief

"Ok, so she's possibly going to lose some money! That does not drive you to commit murder. A bomb, for God's sake. In the middle of Nottingham!"

"We believe she made a play to get into politics, to seize power, Sir. She has had a meteoric rise through your party and sits as home secretary, a very powerful position as we well know."

"Haven't we all!" barked Barnaby back at her, reflecting on his own rise to lead the UK.

Realising they were potentially not going to be able to explain Helen's motive driving her actions, Marcus moved onto the facts. "Ok, so yesterday our teams uncovered a coded message that referred to the bomb in Nottingham, where it made reference to a 'Puppy'. We weren't clear at first if that was supposed to be you, but later, when scanning for references to 'The Puppy' we de-coded another message." He pushed the note under the nose of Barnaby who read it aloud.

"We can't use Big Ben.
Need something innocuous.
Refer to The Puppy from now on"

Barnaby sat back. "That's me, isn't it?" he sighed, recognising his own code name instantly.

"Indeed Sir. When we discovered that, we knew it was an inside job. We traced the numbers. One was 'Toads' phone and we have that in our possession now. The other is a burner phone that the team managed to locate, just a short while ago. It was in the glove box of Helen's car."

Marcus went on to explain how there had been recent contact between the two phones in the last twenty-four hours. "Immediately after the bomb went off in Nottingham. Not only that, but again later in the day, just after the time that you called in from the service station and the SAS were *en route* to pick you up. Well, about four minutes later, the SAS were diverted to go to Holme Pierrepont to try to recover Nicky, Aidan and Dan."

Barnaby looked up, unsure what was coming next. "Sir, the SAS' priority should have been your safe return and the only person that could authorise a change in mission, was the home secretary. By diverting them away from you, she gave Toad and his group your new details. That's how they managed to find you so quickly, chasing you into the Meadows area. But for the bravery of the old lady letting you in to her house, they would have assassinated you all."

Leaning back, Barnaby raised his hands to his head again, running them through his hair and letting out a large breath. "Well I'll be bug ..." he started, but realised the inappropriateness of his comment and stopped.

"There is more Sir, a lot more." Irm was finding her feet now. "All of the police officers who had been planted in the Nottingham constabulary were given security clearance. We've recovered the laptops from the garage in Sneinton that were used to hack in to the system, giving them the background covers they needed. Including the two you have heard about, Lucas Jacobs and Fabian Pichler. We believe there were ten altogether. We're still checking all the systems though and we have put alerts out to the police up and down the country for the rest of those identified so far, to be detained.

She continued, "The laptop used to approve each of them has been identified by the Media Access Control,

De-Brief

or MAC address. Every device has one. Unique, and therefore traceable. But, for those covers to be laid down, they still need to be given security clearance codes, which are issued by each police force. They can also be accessed by senior figures involved with National Security.

"Each code that was used, has been traced back to the source that accessed them. Guess where they were accessed from?" asked Irm, looking for some involvement from her audience.

"No way! She did it from her own computer?" started Barnaby. "That's unbelievable."

"But perfect cover right. Why wouldn't the home secretary be able to get that information if she needs to?"

Marcus moved another piece of paper over to Barnaby. "We are looking into her bank accounts now as well. It's not clear at the moment, as she has a lot of business accounts we need to dig into, large sums moving around regularly. However, there does seem to be three very significant payments over the last eighteen months, to an offshore account in the Cayman Islands. Looks like it totals about ten million pounds."

Shaking his head in disbelief, Barnaby poured over the figures. "You could buy a small army with that right?" His informers nodded together.

"We have other people identified who could probably all add similar sums of money to the pot." Marcus added, explaining how they had links into many industries from the network across Europe. Tens of millions potentially, invested to pay for hired thugs. Assassins.

Orchestrated across multiple countries with a common purpose. Force the UK to make a U-turn on its current policies.

"But Sir, the final nail in the coffin. Irrefutable evidence. You have to listen this." Marcus pulled a small recording device from his pocket and pressed play.

"Let me know you got the clearance codes OK. You should have everything you need now to make this clean. Make sure the Puppy pays for this. Don't fail me."

All of them exchanged glances. Barnaby put his head in his hands again. It was the distinctive female voice of his home secretary, Helen Langley.

Not only was she rich, but it was obvious to them all now, that money was not enough on its own. She craved power too. Helen had gone to extreme lengths, to try and get her the most powerful job in British politics. Presumably with him out of the way, she would have then set about reversing the stance of the English Independence Party policies.

A saviour, coming to the fore, in England's hour of need.

Barnaby stood and extended his hand to each of them, a grave look on his face. "Well done. Great work. You did it. You found those responsible and they will be severely punished for what they have done."

The meeting was over.

It was time for Barnaby to right some wrongs.

Chapter Forty One
Open for Business

Barnaby Aitken leant on the podium, preventing his weight resting on his still painful ankle. Next to him were the team that had helped to resolve the situation. They were stony faced and the mood was naturally sombre.

The press briefing was packed with reporters. Digital recording devices were held aloft, numerous cameras recording the historic event, relaying it live around the world. The flash of bulbs, from photographers seeking the perfect picture.

Barnaby surveyed the room as he opened his speech. He raised his hands to indicate he would like them to stop asking questions just now.

"Ladies and gentlemen, it's a relief to be back with you here today. Please can I ask you to save your questions until the end?" The press took their seats, notepads and Dictaphones at the ready, about to burst into life, with every word that came out of the prime minster's mouth.

"There have been many innocent people, who have lost their lives in the last thirty-six hours. Families broken. Loved ones gone. Every single one of those lives, was taken through no fault of their own. Please, let us bow our heads and take a minute's silence to remember those in Nottingham, who died yesterday."

The room fell silent and as one, they hung their heads. Watching on the TV were Nicky and Lee. They clasped hands.

"Yesterday, our country was attacked. An assault on democracy. An appalling assault on the way we live our lives here, in England. Many of you may think this has come about as a result of me closing our borders on Saturday." Barnaby shook his head, he was speaking with purpose now. "That is not the case. This was an attack that had been months in the planning. A sophisticated assault on our own police forces. A disillusioned attack, by some of the world's most notorious hackers, hiding behind keyboards, reaping havoc, often from other continents. Supported by hired henchmen and women, determined to fight for a cause they believed in. Their target was not just me, but the government of this country. If it had been staged by a sovereign nation, it would be declared an act of war." His solemn words resonated through the room. That had been obvious to many of them, but others were taken by surprise.

"Thankfully, our security services have worked tirelessly since the start of this atrocious, appalling attack. They have worked diligently, through the night, to break the ring of those responsible. We believe we have the majority behind this attack now in custody. They will face the consequences for their despicable acts of inhumanity." An experienced reporter went to thrust his microphone forward to start asking questions, but Barnaby had not finished and a menacing stare deterred him.

Open for Business

"It would seem that those responsible for this are from all across Europe, including here in the UK. As you know, many have not been happy about the UK leaving the European Union for a long time now, both amongst the public and across various parliaments. They have gone to extreme lengths to block decisions, hold negotiations up, or try to charge even more money for our exit. Well, it seems some were prepared to take that discontent further, using lethal force to make their point. To try and make us perform a U-turn" Barnaby paused and took a deep breath. He knew what he was about to say, would be a metaphorical bombshell. Right here in this room.

"Unbelievably, it seems that the group of terrorists that were behind this, were headed by one of our very own …" The audience were hanging on every word. You could have heard a pin drop, on a deep, shag pile carpet. "Helen Langley, the home secretary, was arrested this morning on suspicion of murder and acts of terrorism."

Barnaby looked up, blank faces staring back at him in disbelief. Did they hear that right? Did he say the home secretary? Helen fucking Langley? What the hell?????? Cameras recorded. Chins dropped. People stood and machine gunned Barnaby with all sorts of noise.

He soldiered on, ignoring the hubbub, questions fired at him from across the room, reporters clambering to be heard. They fell silent again as he continued. "At this stage, I cannot say any more about who is responsible, or why, but you will of course be kept up to date on proceedings as we move forward."

"As you know, I have been a harsh critic of our previous inability to lockdown our borders and control our immigration. The English Independence Party wanted to stop people coming here. We are over-crowded and our infrastructure cannot cope with the demands placed upon it. Our government cannot afford to pay for the ever growing demands, with the current taxation system we have. We ... I," he corrected himself, "have often seen those from overseas, as malingerers. Those unwilling to work, coming here for a free ride." Keeping his eyes firmly on his script now, he continued.

"The tragic events of the last thirty-six hours have opened my eyes. I have been helped, and welcomed, by many, who had no good reason to do so. Indeed, some of those not only saved my life, but lost their own."

Barnaby raised his head and looked purposefully at the cameras in turn.

"It has become abundantly clear to me, that those who come, do so because they want a better life for their families. Our country prospers because of their contribution. They come because our economy is strong. That is a good sign to send to Europe. That we have not just survived outside of the EU, but we are thriving. We have problems funding our services, but the English Independence Party will look for other ways of paying for our NHS, our schools and enabling affordable housing for families. We can be out of the political grip of Europe, but we should not isolate ourselves from the modern world."

Reporters were aghast. This was a very different tone to the Barnaby that had risen to power over the last few years. A tone they had never expected to hear.

Open for Business

"Lastly," Barnaby pushed himself up, to stand tall, out of respect. "There are many people I must thank for their considerable efforts, this last day. Our security services, MI5 and MI6, working cohesively together, to crack this terrorist ring. The governments across Europe and their intelligence services, who responded swiftly to our requests for help, enabling those responsible to be identified. Our armed policer officers and the emergency services in Nottingham who helped those seriously injured in the attacks around the city itself. The SAS deployed to the streets, along with the army who helped lockdown those streets. Those that gave their lives in helping others escape this atrocity," he moved a hand to his eye, wiping away a tear as it made its way slowly down his cheek. "Particularly, those in the Meadows area, helping me to escape certain death, from those intent on seeing me killed." Barnaby would later pay a visit to those in Glapton Road, who as a mob, had forced the attackers to give up the chase, enabling his rescue.

"Words cannot portray my gratitude to a little boy, Aidan Bevan, his mother, Nicky and his father, Lee." Nicky squeezed Lee's hand, full of pride as they were mentioned by name. "They were caught up in the events that unfolded on the Old Market Square yesterday morning. They helped me escape my attackers on several occasions, as we were pursued across Nottingham. The bravery, and generosity, demonstrated by that remarkable family, is one I may never bear witness to again. Thank you.

"My final thanks are to another remarkable young man, who left the safety of his home to come and help his friends. He did not have to get involved, but he sadly lost his life, caught in cross fire whilst trying to save others, including myself. We mourn the loss of Dan Black and our deepest condolences to his wife, Leslie, their family and friends."

Barnaby dropped his head again to pay his respects. He lifted the speech, folded it neatly and tucked it into his jacket pocket as the barrage of reporter's questions was unleashed.

Sat at the kitchen table, parents with their arms round her shoulders, Leslie wailed on hearing Dans name. Her heart was broken.

England too, was broken. With some determination, it would heal.

Chapter Forty Two
New Beginnings

Over the next two weeks, many more arrests were made across England and beyond its shores. An extensive network, stretching across continental Europe, had been cracked. Many, who would have been considered as law abiding citizens, upstanding members of their local communities, were taken into custody. Links were being established across all walks of life, to this new terrorist network within the EU.

A new threat had emerged without detection. So focussed were the security services on the threat of Muslim extremism, the malcontent of the supposedly 'normal', had passed under the radar. The press nick-named them the "EU-LOGISTS".

World leaders condemned the actions of those responsible. New promises of working closely together were made around the globe. They had to defeat such acts of aggression, from those seeking to strike fear at the heart of normal society. Outwardly, many of those leaders voiced their concern and incredulity, that someone with such hatred had been able to take a seat at the highest level of a democratic country. Those same leaders immediately had security checks run on all of their own party members and those of the opposition. Just in case, they too, had been infiltrated.

Many governments reached out a hand to help. They were particularly attentive, when it came to taking responsibility for the hackers that had been apprehended. It would be better to have them extradited to their country of origin, to face justice at home wouldn't it? Authorities in the UK declined the requests, knowing full well that they would probably be put to use for government purposes, possibly even targeting the UK again in the future.

England's borders were gradually reopened. There were delays, due to added security at the airports, but at least people were allowed to return to some semblance of normality.

In the three days following the attack in Nottingham, the rest of those who had been planning the attack were identified and detained. They had been able to peck away at the trail of breadcrumbs, uncovering another five sleepers within the police force, who had chased the prime minister out of the Old Market Square.

Barnaby paid a personal visit to apologise to Bolek Kumiega for the beating he had taken at the hands of his interrogators. Bolek had no connections to the events that unravelled in Nottingham. Unbelievably, he showed understanding for why he had been treated with such aggression. Putting himself in the shoes of the officers, he realised they were under intense pressure to find, and return, the prime minister safely. His compassionate tone was to grieve for those lost, not to complain at his own treatment. Although he decided not to press charges, the two officers were fired from their jobs.

The police got a clear message that brutality would not be tolerated. Everyone who lived in the UK,

New Beginnings

regardless of their nationality, race, sex, or colour, were to be treated with respect.

The transit van from the attack in the Meadows, was located, burnt out on some waste ground on the outskirts of Nottingham. It did not take long to discover CCTV revealing a pick up car and its occupants. Armed officers burst into a property in the swanky, Park area at four in the morning on the Wednesday. Inside, sleeping, was a female Russian with an array of sniper rifles, along with three accomplices. Surprise and exhaustion had prevented any resistance from them.

Over the course of the next six months, new bridges would be built between the UK and its old companions across Europe. Fear drove these new relationships. *"Lest we forget"* was being used with increasing regularity, to refer back to the EU-LOGY attack in Nottingham.

No longer could the UK turn its back on Europe. Europe could not afford to ostracise the UK. They had to find a more positive footing for a new type of relationship. Free movement of people. Simple, tariff free trade. A new bond, forged with hope, that would drive prosperity for all, going forward.

In a desperate bid to understand why this had happened, Lee started to question the purpose of terrorism. It was supposed to fill the public with fear. Stop them from doing things they wanted to do. Living a normal life. Although people were fearful, it never worked. Life goes on. People work to earn a living. To afford to live. To pay for necessities, food and clothes. Oil and gas continue to burn. The wheels of industry continue to turn. They normalise again very quickly.

Watching the news over the next few days, something profound struck him. Terrorism was rife across the modern world. Not acts of brutality. No explosions or bombs. Media outlets peddling terrorism on a daily basis. Every front page headline is a catastrophe waiting to happen: NHS failings; On-line fraud, robbing you of your pensions; Identity theft; Cost of housing; Failing economies; Russia about to declare World War III; Ebola wiping out half of Western Africa ... and the headlines go on. None of them reporting positive news.

Fear spread through the modern world.

Latent terrorism, infecting our daily lives. Driven by the media and the government to keep the public living in a state of fear. Agendas controlled by the rich and powerful. We consume it constantly, with absolute belief.

Yet, life goes on.

Despite a fresh start with Nicky, Lee was finding it hard to smile. He led the speeches at Dan's funeral and Leslie insisted that he be part of the pallbearers that carry Dan's coffin. It was a state funeral, at the prime ministers request. Leslie was so honoured, she wanted the world to know her Dan. To see how selfless he had been. How courageous.

Barnaby delivered an upbeat speech and spoke of a hero. A man prepared to lay his life on the line for others. Caught up on the fringes of a nightmare. Without hesitation, he went to help his friends. He would not be forgotten. A national hero.

Standing beside her best friend, Nicky with one arm wrapped around her shoulder, the other holding onto Lee's hand tightly through the service. Aidan stood in front of them, his father's hand holding his shoulder in reassurance. He didn't really know what was going on, but the wave of black suits and dresses before him, made him feel distinctly uncomfortable. Seeing his 'Auntie' Leslie crying so openly, disturbed him.

He knew Dan was gone, but Aidan could not understand the procession before him. In losing Dan, bizarrely, he had regained his Dad. "Thank you Uncle Dan. Thank you!" he thought to himself.

In his hand, he held on tightly to Beano.

As they moved away from the graveside, Nicky was hugging Leslie tightly. The tears had been flowing. Short on conversation, Leslie wanted to move away from the crowd.

After shaking hands with the prime minster, they watched him and his security team climb back into the waiting limousines. Slowly they pulled out of the cemetery. Leslie lifted her head high and shouted at the sky. "Not fair GOD! Not bloody fair!" her tears returned to her already blood shot eyes. Next to her, Nicky was not really listening, but gazing across the small road.

Stood just behind, where the prime ministers car had been, was a tall lady. She had shoulder length, mousey brown hair and a black duffel type coat wrapped about her, keeping the ever cooling days of autumn at bay. "Who's that?" asked Leslie, wiping her face with the back of her hand. "There are so many people here I don't know or recognise."

Nicky was staring across the road towards the woman, lost in thought. "I'm not sure" she began, before stepping forward, letting Leslie's hand go, "but I think it's my Mum!"

A few days after returning home, Lee and Nicky's mobile phones were returned to them. Both had been recovered from the house in Sneinton. As evidence, they had to have the recent, relevant information, downloaded correctly. Springing to life as they charged them up, notifications pinged a merry tune. Lee picked his mobile up and squinted at it curiously. He'd almost forgotten what they looked like. He hardly ever got any these days.

Red dots with numbers in them, indicated he had one hundred and twelve unread Facebook notifications, thirty-six text messages and loads of e-mails he had yet to open. He looked again, curiosity on his face. As he started working his way through them, he realised it was people who had not been in touch with him since he split with Nicky. Former, so-called friends, who had ditched him, the minute they thought he had cheated on his wife.

The same people, now desperate to empathise with him on the recent events. People desperate to rekindle the connections, to the now 'famous and courageous', Lee Bevan.

A few months ago, Lee would have craved this attention. This recognition.

Without hesitation, he deleted them all. He'd realised, all he needed, was the attention of his wife and son.

Everyone one else could wait.

*"Intelligence is the ability
to adapt to change"*

Professor Stephen Hawking

Dedications

Over the last four or five years, I have literally dreamt about writing a book. A recurring dream sparked an idea. I just had to build a story around it.

My long-suffering wife and three children have listened. They have been patient and supportive. They had no idea if I would ever finish this project, but they knew it was my dream to write. I'm curious to see if anyone else will read it, but I feel better in myself for having completed it.

So, thank you, Zoe, Connor, Hazel and Zara, for understanding. For looking like you were interested, even if you weren't. For that alone, I love you.

Thanks to my sister-in-law, Anne, who read my first few chapters, and from Australia, sent me encouragement to finish the story I had started. With uncertainty in my bones, I asked some close friends to read a little and let me know what they thought. Amazingly, they all seemed to quite like it, but maybe they were being polite. Kim, Dan, Charlie and Bob, thanks for your positive contributions and enthusiasm to continue. Alex, as a communications expert with experience in 'government' I appreciate the positivity.

It would have been easy to let this go. It was a lot more enjoyable to finish it.

Finally, to my Mother-in-Law, who we lost too soon. We love and miss you Jean.